THE WATCHERS' CLUB

THE WATCHERS' CLUB

A Novel of Innocence and Guilt

G. Kim Blank

SANTA FE

Sunstone books may be purchased for educational, business, or sales promotional use.
For information please write: Special Markets Department, Sunstone Press,
P.O. Box 2321, Santa Fe, New Mexico 87504-2321.
Printed on acid-free paper
∞
eBook 978-1-61139-716-1

Library of Congress Cataloging-in-Publication Data
On File

WWW.SUNSTONEPRESS.COM
SUNSTONE PRESS / POST OFFICE BOX 2321 / SANTA FE, NM 87504-2321 /USA
(505) 988-4418

In memory of dear Mom, for keeping all that stuff

AUTHOR'S PREFACE

One third of this novel is true; one third is not true; and one third is somewhere in-between.

The story behind and within *The Watchers' Club* has been brewing for a long while—too long, in fact. What should you know? That a few names have been tweaked as you enter the rural community of "Eastfield" and to a time many decades ago? In truth, it's only a slight name change from the real neighborhood that spawned the story. What you will find? Mainly, a motley crew of roving Eastfield kids, doing things that, they hope, might never get back to their parents. Their mission is to meet up at places within a landscape that offers protection from too many eyes. What they are not quite aware of: that it is possible—in fact, likely—for them to make disquieting discoveries on such outings, as you will see. But one October night, on one mission, it turns out there are too many eyes. Caught in the act, as they say. Yet not all eyes see.

A moral? Well, in the end, it is in the nature of these young creatures to get up to no good, though this story does not go as far as *The Lord of the Flies*, when, left to their own devices, a group of boys descend into brutal tribalism.

So, who is caught in the act out there among the tall evergreens? The victims? The gang of kids? The community? Or are we, the readers, somehow complicit?

Still, even back in our real world, things can go very wrong at any time, and they can go wrong without looking for or deserving trouble. Like the narrator in *The Watchers' Club* says, it can all come down to being at the wrong place at the wrong time.

—G.K.B

THE OLD BOX

Dear old mom, bless her heart, kept almost every scrap of paper and bit of paraphernalia from my early years: ribbons from sports days, report cards, class photos, team photos, school concert programs, snowflake Christmas cards, and Boy Scout merit badges earned during the one year I spent trying (in vain, it seems) to "Be Prepared." In all, about dozen years' worth of growing-up concentrated in an old cardboard box that, at one moment, in the middle of my adult life, she passed onto me. "Put it all together, in a scrapbook or something," she said. "For your children. For your story."

I took the box, but let it sit for a few years, undisturbed and gathering forgetfulness.

But then, one quiet night, with the kids in bed, and with the TV in the background driveling on about the latest version of covid or some climate crisis, I began to go through the box, not knowing exactly what I was looking for. Maybe mom's recent passing urged my attempt to put things in order. But why—and for what? My own passing? Well, that's what you begin to think about when you raid your past.

As I layered the kitchen table, there, among the bits and bobs and trivial kudos, one item held me still: a large envelope that contained a yellowed newspaper clipping and an old class photo. The clipping pushed me back and then drew me in:

Two dead found in Eastfield. Foul play suspected

SILVERFORD—The Silverford Sheriff's office reports the discovery of the bodies of two persons in the Eastfield area. No other details have been released. Unofficial sources suggest foul play may have been involved. The names have not been released, pending positive identification and notification of next of kin.

A full investigation has been launched in cooperation with the Coroner's Office.

The TV fades, and a rooted memory surfaces: a bunch of us kids yelling out stupid insults into the clear, cool night...then running full speed, tearing through the bushes and around the fir trees, tripping, falling, laughing...and gathering in the dark to celebrate our quest.

It turns out I hadn't forgotten at all. Not at all.

1
JACOB

Boys will be boys

That's what adults sometimes say when they can't figure out why young males of the species act cruel, violent, or stupid—or when they just plain get up to no good.

Out there in the bushes, backyards, and woods of Eastfield, we were definitely boys being boys, especially as we closed in on full-blown adolescence. What we did with bugs and baby birds and the occasional small animal was one thing. We were investigating nature's limitations and endless variety. What we did to each other was now and then borderline. But how we acted toward one particular kid who lived up the road was quite another. And then there's the leap to what happened and—well, sometimes the unimaginable can be reduced to a cliché: the wrong place at the wrong time.

Boy, was it ever.

That particular kid was Jacob Slough. That wrong place was Lovers' Lane. And that wrong time was one October Saturday night.

Though we let Jacob hang around our small gang, we sometimes turned on him, maybe to show off, maybe just to have a laugh at his expense. Much of the time we acted as if he wasn't there. We weren't yet ready to let guilt temper our actions. After all, we knew Jacob Slough would never squeal or turn on us, no matter what we did. We knew he would never repeat what he heard. And we thought he would never do anything about what he saw, though that turned out to be deadly wrong.

When Jacob wore his god-help-me smile, when cruel words or objects were directed toward him, or when we acted like he wasn't there, we didn't look too deeply into his large, dark eyes. We didn't know what kinds of windows those eyes were. Or mirrors. In fact, we sometimes looked at him without really seeing him, and he certainly didn't often look us in the eye. Was he scared? Uncertain? Just thinking?

And when we split up in the evenings to make our various ways home, we didn't dwell much on his life inside his small, brown, run-down house. We didn't ask about what he was going to do, or if he had a favorite baseball team, comic book hero, or radio station. Heck, we didn't even know if he listened to the radio or even had one. We didn't say, "See ya tomorrow." Jacob Slough's life was not a mystery we needed to solve.

That would change.

EASTFIELD

The Slough family lived toward to the top of Eastfield Road, a few properties up from where I lived.

Most people in the Eastfield area owned at least a couple of acres of bush and forest, with stretches of old pasture here and there that cut across the narrow, mainly undeveloped properties off Eastfield Road. But a couple of residents, like the cranky Mr. Bryer, also just up the road from us, were determined to see Eastfield change. With his sparkling green and white house, with the ongoing fencing and clearing of his land, with the planting of lawns and hedges, and the building of a gazebo, Mr. Norman G. Bryer felt Eastfield deserved like-minded citizens.

"Too many bumkins 'round here. They otta clean up or clear out. The lot of them. Riff-raff. Can't trust them. Mark my words."

Who Mr. Bryer had in mind was more or less clear, but we wondered why, if he disliked Eastfield so much, he didn't pack up and leave. We kids wouldn't have missed him, his little wife, or their yappy dog that used to bang its head against their living room window when anyone walked by. "That mutt is as dumb as a bag of hammers," noted Arnold, one of my friends.

Mr. Bryer's darker views spread further than the local scene. If he had his way, that mysterious Cold War that existed somewhere beyond Eastfield's seemingly rural peace could have done with a little warming up. "Should'a finished off the commies when we had the chance. Things are backwards. Germans starting to make the best cars. Everything else is from Japan. China, too. Mark my words—they'll take over one day. Get 'em before they get us. While we got the edge in the A-bomb department."

Standing there as a fidgety twelve-year-old boy with my dad, I was vaguely intrigued. The image of a glowing, growing mushroom of atomic fire fueled visions of how it might create mutants and mega-beasts. At least "Duck-and-Cover" drills at school had made us feel somewhat prepared for The Bomb.

SLOUGHS

Eastfield, then, was an odd mix. A few youngish families who enjoyed the space and inexpensive "fixer-up" properties. Self-sufficient types for whom front yards were parking lots for unfixable vehicles and old farming contraptions. A couple of old-timers and eccentrics hid away in run-down old farmhouses. Deserted places in permanent disrepair, like the old house down the road from ours, once owned by the now dead Mrs. Raskolnikov— who, when we were younger, we wanted to believe was a witch. She could, after all, tell the future. And she did. Twice. Bad things, too.

Those Eastfield residents who bothered to care were divided over amalgamation with Silverford City, which was only a few miles away and beginning to show signs of growth. A new, big pulp mill called Sawmac had an immediate impact on the district's fortunes, and when the wind was right, you could get a sulfurous whiff of the prosperity that poured out of the huge mill, twenty-four hours a day, seven days a week, three shifts a day, there perched on the inlet. When someone farted, we even had a joke: "Was that you, mac, or Sawmac?" My older brother, Simon, had a line that, thankfully, we weren't old enough to get: "My girlfriend asked me to kiss her where it stinks—so I took her to Sawmac."

Adults endlessly debated amalgamation and growth: water, roads, sewage, streetlights, traffic, taxes, jobs. Boring boring boring. The future was not real enough that it needed addressing—so long, that is, as we kids remained free to roam.

One thing about Eastfield: there was plenty of room to get into trouble, most of it out of the sight of adult eyes, where they couldn't watch.

As for the house that Jacob Slough and his family lived in, it was one of those places Mr. Bryer definitely did not approve of. A small, dark, grungy house in the damp shadows of some towering evergreens. An uneven roof covered in spreading lumps of moss. No lawn, no landscaping. A tattered wire mesh fence across the front yard framed junk scattered all over their yard—an old tub here, a broken ring-washer there, small piles of wood everywhere—with a rusted metal gate, whose function seemed to keep things neither in nor out.

A few times I stood just inside the Slough house, waiting for mom to pass on the monthly community newsletter that she helped write and distribute. I got a peek. A few magazine images of Jesus were tacked onto the walls—except, here and there, some small, delicate sketches of birds, flowers, and little animals. Everything else I could see—the floors, a little furniture—seem a lusterless, uneven pale yellow.

Something else about the Slough house: it smelled like cat pee, though they didn't have cats. What they did have, and where the smell came from, were dozens of rabbits out back of their place in small makeshift pens. Jacob's job was to take care of the rabbits until they were ready for his dad to slaughter them. At one time, the pelts were sold to Mrs. Raskolnikov, that old witch-lady down the road, who tanned the leather and made various items—slippers, gloves, hats, and stoles. Since her death, no one wanted the skins, and they piled up and were occasionally burned. The smell from that fire was recognizable around lower Eastfield. "Old Man Slough barbequing bunnies again" was how we kids put it.

The rabbit meat was sold to a man from town who once every few weeks pulled up to the Slough place in a red and black van. He didn't speak much English. In one of those conversations that parents think kids aren't paying much attention to, dad once said to mom, "The guy takes advantage of the Sloughs. Underpays. He's a piece of work, he is."

Mr. Slagmann was the meat buyer's name, and on the side of his black and red van, in chipped, yellow letters, was written, "SLAGMANN'S BUTCHER. Mr. Zoran Slagmann, Proprietor. Silverford. You Can't Beat Our Meat." Simon used to have a laugh at that one, too, though, as usual, we didn't know what he found so funny.

We also knew of Mr. Slagmann through the stellar accomplishments of his seventeen-year-old son, David, who, as a junior at Silverford District Senior Secondary School, was one grade behind Simon. He was the only grade eleven kid to make the high school's basketball team starting lineup, and was still, by far, the best player. My brother made the team—not as a starter—and with my parents I watched some of the school's home games. With his flashing, light blonde hair and obvious superior athleticism and intensity, David Slagmann was hard to miss—and the cheerleaders did indeed often cheer him on. He'll probably get some big deal college scholarship, so everyone thought. Now that he was a senior, and even more the star, there was always something about him in the newspaper. At basketball games, Mr. Slagmann, wildly protective of his son's prospects, would suddenly stand up and shout things in some language or other at the referee if his son was charged with a foul or got fouled. He also randomly yelled if his son wasn't playing well, which wasn't, thankfully, very often.

How the Sloughs made money beyond selling rabbit meat to Mr. Slagmann was uncertain, although the father, Caleb Slough—short, barrel-chested, suspendered, heavy eyebrows—delivered commercial flyers once a week, and he had something to do with the Silverford City chapter of the Salvation Army. In fact, he seldom appeared without his green Salvation Army hat perched high and back on his huge, square head. Every dog in the Eastfield barked like mad at him as he made his rounds. Probably the smell of butchered rabbits he carried around, but the dogs seemed more scared of him than he of them.

I once asked my mom, who was tolerant of just about everything, about why the Sloughs were so "weird." She did not like the question. She could only come up with a diverting answer: "Well, they're very...well, dedicated to some things. You don't go judging people, you hear?"

Dad casually added: "They take sin real seriously." Mom gave dad a look.

We kids were wary of Mr. Slough. Apparently, he had no problem using his heavy leather belt to deal with family issues. We also heard that he had once broken a table in half with one slam of his fist, but this story may have made its way around Eastfield on the powerful imagination of kids who relish tales that combine power and fear. We had, though, with our own eyes, witnessed from afar how he dispatched his rabbits with his bare hands, or maybe sometimes using a club—and that he could do so with deadly, quick ease. This was more than enough to keep the wheels on any terrible tale about the brutal Mr. Caleb Slough, the stocky, large-headed Salvation Army bunny slayer.

BLACK AND WHITE

The shoebox my mother had kept for me had more to pause over. The grades 6-8 school photograph from Eastfield Elementary and Middle School. There's Jacob Slough. Back row, far left, shoulders hunched. His skin a little darker (or dirtier) than most of us, an uneven bowl cut, his face strangely narrow, his bottom lip large and drooping, mouth slightly open. A large, bony frame. There he is in black and white, in overalls and that ever-present plaid shirt—staring out somewhere past the camera. You can't tell if he's wearing gumboots, which he did most days, rain or shine, summer or winter. In fact, that's what we usually called him when we were in our little gang: "Gumboot." Gumboot Slough.

The rest of us in the photo are a motley crew—fat and skinny, short and tall, blonde and dark, clean and scruffy. There's Mrs. Easterbrook, our enthusiastic but frustrated teacher, just showing pregnancy, smiling as best she can, probably wondering how she will make it through one more year, with three grades crammed into one class.

The gang is scattered throughout the photo.

Arnold Rheinhurst—front center, holding the chalkboard naming our class and year—is the only kid with a bow tie and white shirt for the occasion. The smartest kid, a little warped, smirking with confidence, his hair combed back. Arnold shaped our views and lead us into action while namedropping movies and the books he read. In some ways, Arnold was like Daniel Caine, the older kid I shadowed for one hot summer when I was six and Daniel was twelve. He was behind a grim, shocking incident that Eastfield had done its best to forget about—and it happened right across the road from my house. But Danny Caine, unlike Arnold, didn't pick on other kids. Danny's energy was directed to a painfully eloquent understanding of nature, and it turned out his only hate was for his father, a commercial fisherman with a secret. That's another story.

The class photo. Middle row, toward the right—Julian Weissman. Wiry, curly dark hair, often excitable and sometimes uncertain, the fastest runner in our school. He knew the stats of every professional baseball player. Just plain goofy, but he was my best friend. He was funny because he was always trying to be funny, and he usually wasn't. He was easy to be with.

There's Billy Luckhert—hidden away in the middle row, just left of center. Freckled, clumsy, nervous, constantly plagued with the hiccups, who simply followed the flow of whatever it was we did. Despite being under Arnold's spell and desperately seeking Arnold's approval, Billy often drove Arnold nuts. Every second sentence he uttered seemed to start with, "Sure, I guess." One other thing: he smelled like soup.

"You smell like soup, Billy," I once said as a few of us horsed around in a camping tent we set up on a summer day, playing army camp or something.

"No I don't."

Julian nodded and Arnold piped in, "Yes, you do, Billy. You smell like soup. All the time. You're a soup boy."

"I don't smell like anything."

Arnold added, "Everything smells like something, and you smell like soup."

This should have been the last word. Arnold specialized in last words. Billy, unwisely, attempted to trump the charge with a question.

"Yeah, so Arnold, so what do you smell like?"

Hmm. This was a better-than-average comeback, especially for Billy. Arnold, though, was weasel quick: "Me? I smell like a soup-smeller." Ha! That Arnold!

Finally, in the photograph, top right, beside the teacher—there's Teddy Sullivan, by far the biggest but, thankfully, not the meanest kid in the class, smiling back broadly, testosterone flowing through his thick arms and legs years before the rest of us had much of a clue about what was lurking in our glands. Academically, he operated at a pretty careless level. His passion was cars—tearing them apart and putting them back together. We weren't sure, but we thought he was supposed to be in grade ten. His parents, who ran a garage that looked more like a junk pile, didn't seem too interested in or worried about what Teddy was up to. He even smoked. My parents weren't thrilled that I sometimes hung out with him, so usually his name was kept out of earshot.

Only Jacob Slough was as strong as Teddy, maybe even stronger, though we had never seen Jacob use that strength to defend himself or attack anyone. And because Jacob always slouched over and hunched his shoulders, he looked much smaller than he was. Only his Popeye forearms betrayed his power. In our myth-making, we decided that if there were a fight between Teddy and Jacob, Jacob would win, because he wouldn't know well enough to quit.

What held us all together was this landscape called Eastfield. What suddenly disturbed our world was an unthinkable event that clearly took place among us—but, less clearly, by whom—and why.

It wasn't just poverty that made the Slough family unusual—in fact, many of the families in the Eastfield area were poor. In snatches of conversations around our house, mom referred to the Sloughs as "a simple family." This meant something different than the Sloughs being plain or ordinary folk, and the description may have emerged to satisfy what they lacked. Such subtle equivocation was not part of Arnold Rheinhurst's repertoire. The Sloughs, he said, were a "bunch of dummies." Arnold confined Jacob to a movie or book reference we didn't know, though we somehow understood it: "A regular Lennie Small," he said. Arnold didn't say it to tease or insult. He said it as a cold, unalterable fact, and sometimes right to Jacob: "Gumboot, you dumb bunny."

Yes, he probably was, and they probably were.

Mrs. Slough, tiny and round, aproned and always with a kerchief on her head when out-of-doors, seemed to have an eternal smile. But sometimes late at night, haunting Eastfield Road, you could hear her call out for her boy to come home: "JA-cob! Ja-COB!" Where he was, what he was up to, while the rest of us were preparing for bedtime and reluctantly cleaning behind our ears, was a mystery. We would go our own ways before going home, and he would just be kind of left there. He would, it seemed, eventually wander home.

Jacob also had a brother and a sister. The brother was maybe ten years younger than Jacob. He always seemed to be rooting around the Slough property with a stick in his hand. A perpetually runny nose, ragged overalls. His real name is forgotten now, but Arnold came up with one that stuck: Piggyboy. On the way to or from school, we would sometimes spot him in his front yard rooting around. One of us would say, "Hey Piggy Piggyboy. Sou-ee! Sou-ee!" The snot-nosed kid would turn toward us and kind of snort, and we'd have a good laugh while snorting back at him.

Esther was Jacob's older sister. She was sixteen or seventeen years old and a few inches taller than both her mother and father. Her face was round and friendly like her mother's, and her reddish-brown hair was kept very long. Like the rest of her family, she was something on the slow side, but not as slow as Jacob. But what was noticeable about her—what everyone noted—was impossible not to note: her chest size. She didn't need to dress in any particular way to promote her shape—her ample hips and slender waist as well—but it was clear guys sometimes looked at her in a lurking, letchy way, and women with embarrassment or scorn. Rumors that circulated slightly above our level of understanding claimed she was "easy"—usually from some of the older boys who were obsessed with the whole make-out scene. Esther Slough was also known for having a fine singing voice, which we often heard at church or school events. She could belt out the national anthem like no one else around these parts.

Mom would say: "What a voice that girl has!" Dad would respond, "Great lungs." Then mom would elbow him—pretty hard, too.

Teddy Sullivan had his own dreamy comment about Esther: "Bet she's got the biggest bazoomies in the whole world!"

"For sure," we would all say, though the rest of us did not quite get this or what was so interesting. Teddy seemed to know why, and that was good enough for us.

"Melons," he would add.

"Yeah," we would say. "Definitely melons."

We never thought what Jacob Slough might be thinking when he heard such talk about his big sister, or if it meant anything to him. But it was said, and he must have heard it.

BEETLES

Jacob Slough did some of the regular schoolwork, though he couldn't really keep up. To hear him read aloud in class, even in the late elementary grades, was painful. Teachers patiently pushed and pulled him along, correcting him every few seconds, though attention was not given to all of his errors. Who cared if he always pronounced "through" as "ther-rug"? We fell into fidgeting or watching the clock when it was Jacob's turn to read.

What Jacob could do, however, was draw—better, in fact, that any of us. Often we got him to sketch hot rods with gory drivers, but if he had his choice and was left to his daydreams, he would endlessly draw fanciful figures and animals, floating here and there on his work pages and book covers.

"What you drawing, Jacob?"

"Fairies and giants. Pussy cats and birdies," he'd answer, without looking up, and often biting his tongue on the side of his mouth. He never seemed to have a new pencil. They were all short, blunt, chewed on, and without an eraser at the end. But he made no mistakes when drawing.

Beyond his drawing, then, Jacob was almost a ghost at school—except maybe twice. On one occasion, we were supposed to put together a collection of things from nature as a science project. Each day a different kid would bring in a collection to "share" with us, and then talk about it. For a couple of weeks we had your regular collections of leaves, rocks, bark, grasses, flowers, feathers, and bottle caps paraded before us. Mostly boring, though one kid did have a collection of nails.

When Jacob's presentation day came around, we weren't sure what to expect. Maybe nothing. So when we gathered around the table at the back of the classroom where Jacob placed a large rectangle of discolored cardboard, we were surprised. What he had were dozens and dozens of insects pinned to the cardboard. Some of us weren't too keen because, first of all, it was an insect collection, and second, the bugs were dead.

Mrs. Easterbrook, awkwardly dazzled, asked Jacob the question she asked all of us when we presented our project: "So, Jacob, can you tell us all about what you have here, what you've collected?"

We waited, looking between Jacob and the bugs.

Jacob bit his fat, lower lip. Mrs. Easterbrook would surely come to his rescue. Finally, though, Jacob gave us his talk. It was, no doubt, the shortest talk in the history of science projects, but what he said made the collection all the more impressive.

"Beetles," he said. "Beetle bugs."

Beetles. Yes, beetles! Big and small, long legs with short antennae, long antennae with short legs. Some flat, some round, some long, some square. Some gray, some a little spotted, some black, some with flashes of metallic color. Some with distinct heads, others with a one-piece body. All covered in armor. All of them beetles. Amazing!

Some of us closed in, pointing and murmuring. Everyone, that is, except Arnold, who never had much time for anyone else's accomplishments, let alone Jacob's.

After a few minutes, Mrs. Easterbrook was ready for us to move on to regular class work, in this case an evil designed to destroy the souls of most elementary students: long division.

"Well," said Mrs. Easterbrook, "before we get back to work, do any of you have a question you would like to ask Jacob...about his big beetle collection? The only thing I know about beetles is that there are more kinds of them than any other species of anything in the whole world."

Most of us knew better than to ask for further information from

Jacob, but one of the braver girls piped up. "There's a lady bug there. Why is it with beetles?"

Good question.

We waited. Had Jacob even heard the question? Mrs. Easterbrook let the question sit in the air. Jacob finally unbuttoned his lip and answered pretty much to the point: "They're lady beetles."

Imagine that: Jacob Slough had the best science project in the class!

The other time Jacob made an impression at school was grade three/four. It was "Pet Week," which meant, on our assigned day, we could bring a pet if we had one, and then talk about it a little. Naturally, dogs, guinea pigs, and cats dominated, though one girl brought a colorful bird that entertained us by squawking and crapping uncontrollably. As for Jacob, on his day he brought a black and white rabbit in a stinky, old wooden box. The girls cooed their favorite word: "cute."

Miss Hubert, our teacher at the time, prodded Jacob along when it came time for him to say a few words.

"So, tell us, Jacob, what's the name of your rabbit?"

After a few long moments Jacob finally told us: "Goliath."

"Hmm. 'Goliath.' That's a, um, nice name."

A few of us snickered. We expected something more along the lines of "Flopsy" or "Snowball." Goliath?

Miss Hubert, a little surprisingly, pursued it. "Is 'Goliath' a special name? Did you get the name from somewhere or someone?"

Jacob lifted his head a little: "The Bible book."

"Oh, I see," she said.

Then, to the surprise of all of us, Jacob actually volunteered something: "David killed Goliath."

"Yes," Miss Hubert said. "That's right. In the Bible story."

Then, surprising us even more, Jacob added firmly, "Smote him."

Miss Hubert was almost buoyed by Jacob's unexpected though wayward participation. She pushed on in a different direction: "So, Jacob, what do you feed your rabbit? Goliath, I mean?"

This didn't get a response. Miss Hubert tried another question.

"And how long have you had him, Jacob?"

Jacob didn't exactly answer the question, but his response served the purpose: "Seen him borned."

"Oh. That must have been very interesting. And where do you keep him? Do you have a special place for Goliath?"

"With the rest."

"'The rest?"

"Rest of the rabbits."

"Oh, you have more rabbits, Jacob?" Again, Miss Hubert was pleased with Jacob's willingness to string a few words together. He kept going as she smiled at him:

"My fodder grows 'em."

We all giggled a bit, but were shushed by Miss Hubert before she went on. She was surely buoyed by Jacob's sudden eloquence, awkward though it was. "Oh, he does? Well, that's nice. Then he sells them? As pets, to others?"

"Nope. Yep."

More giggles.

"What does your father do, then?"

"Sells 'em."

"But you said he doesn't sell them." Miss Hubert was a little confused.

Jacob Slough, now looking down and then to his hands, made it clear. "He kills 'em. Then sells 'em. To the butcher man with the truck. The Slagmann man."

The answer stilled most of the class. A couple of the girls who were stroking the rabbit stepped back and looked at Miss Hubert, as if for help. Miss Hubert didn't ask a further question, probably because she didn't really want to hear about Goliath's possible fate.

After an awkward moment that seemed to steal the air from the room, poor Miss Hubert could only say, "Well, well thank you, Jacob."

2
CHEESE

At the time it seemed like a good idea.

On some Friday and Saturday nights toward the end of summer, our little gang—Arnold, Teddy, Billy, Julian, and myself, with Jacob almost always trailing somewhere behind in the darkness—began making little treks with the hope of sneaking up on couples who were parked and making out, even though what exactly what might be going was unclear to some of us. These couples, usually teenagers it seemed, would drive to the relative privacy of one particular place—the dead end of an old mining road among the bushes and trees. Our plan was to make them victims of our stealth, though in truth they were the victims of our immaturity. We would disturb the apparently frolicking couples—shout out something stupid, and then run off. That was it. We had been modestly successful on a couple of these trips, but sometimes there was no one there. Arnold explained (though we had no idea how he might know) that the real "heavy-duty" parking took place much later at night, whatever that might mean.

The unsurprising name of this place was Lovers' Lane.

To manage our spying escapades, most of us needed to stay out a little later than we were usually allowed, which often meant giving our parents the on-the-run I'll-be-at-so-and-so's-house-is-that-okay-thanks-bye-I-won't-be-too-late speech. For this to work, you had to be out the door before your parents had a chance to think too deeply about an answer or come up with a curfew. If you caught one of your parents at the right moment—talking on the telephone or otherwise distracted—what you said about where you were going and who you were going to be with was a profitable blur.

Teddy, of course, didn't need this get-away strategy. His parents didn't dole out curfews or make too many rules. Jacob, too, probably didn't need such tactics. He likely wandered away, unnoticed. At the end of the evening, when we broke up to head to our homes, it wasn't clear where exactly Jacob went, and given the calling of his mother up and down the road late some nights, it seemed he didn't always return right away. I pictured him sleeping in a pen with all those rabbits that he took care of before his father did them in. Arnold once said that he bet Jacob howled at the moon.

Our plan in heading to Lovers' Lane usually began by meeting up along Eastfield Road, but not in front of one of the properties of the more vigilant parents or neighbors. If any of us had candies or a chocolate bar or potato chips, ritual dictated sharing the wealth. Arnold was the most reluctant—"You know, I'm not Santa Claus"—and on the other end there was Billy, who was often embarrassingly generous: "Hey, yeah, sure, I guess. Have it all. It's okay." If anyone had anything cool that had not been seen before, like a lighter or a new pocketknife, it was passed around for inspection and hoped-for approval. These were the obligations of our coming-together in the growing darkness: to confirm we were one unit with shared resources.

Using a path known as The Trail, which ran through the acreage of my family's property all the way up to some of Eastfield's deserted back roads, we would make our way to Lovers' Lane. If Jacob was around, he followed well behind the last person. We quietly circumvented my house in order to avoid my immediate backyard and any possible parental intervention.

Once on The Trail and in single file, talk was kept to a minimum. We knew the way well, but since we were on my property, I was allowed to lead. The only interruption was usually a swinging branch that swiped the person behind, or a fart, which often solicited the usual flurry of whispered quips, charges, and counter-charges:

"Okay, who cut the cheese?"

"Not me."

"Man, that stinks!"

"Come on, who laid that reeker?"

"Smells like soup. Must be Billy."

"Not me!"

"Yeah, a souper pooper."

"Whoever smelt it, dealt it."

"Whoever supplies it, denies it."

"Hey Gumboot, was that you back there that let one rip?"

Jacob, somewhere behind, never answered, but we all giggled.

After about ten minutes of walking through fairly wooded area with one or two open spots, The Trail broke up and my property ended. Here we would fall into stealth mode. Talk was reduced. Arnold took over with hand signals or quiet conferences. We had all seen those army films where soldiers crouched and trotted along, finding the next bit of cover, surveying their next move, calling up the ranks, then moving on again. We liked to think we were on some kind of covert mission, when what we were really up to was plain mischief.

Like I said, at the time, these missions to Lovers' Lane seemed like a good idea.

MEETING

We usually gave our little gang special names if we carried out particular regular activities. During the summer, we had been, at various overlapping times, The Snake Catchers' Club and The Tree Fort Club. Such formality made us feel exclusive and helped define purpose. It also promoted rules.

When, in the last weeks of summer holidays, we got into the habit of spying on the couples parked at Lovers' Lane on Friday or Saturday nights, we called ourselves The Watchers' Club. Billy suggested calling ourselves The Lovers' Lane Club. Arnold pointed out that this sounded too much like The Lois Lane Club, which, despite the high esteem most of us had for Superman, was just not right. The relationship between Lois and Superman was, for us, an awkward and unnecessary diversion in the storylines of the Man of Steel. Surprising, though, the most memorable but odd comment came from Teddy: "If Superman banged Lois—wham, bang, splat!" This was not altogether clear, except for Teddy.

§

September slid into early October, and the cool, autumn darkness had begun to cut into the summer evenings. Arrangements had been made to get together for an evening or two of Watchers' Club shenanigans. We had been on a quick mission the night before, Friday, but no one was parked at Lovers' Lane. We would try again Saturday night.

We agreed to gather around eight o'clock about a hundred yards up from my house. I had been out on the road playing baseball with Julian under the only streetlight along the middle section of Eastfield Road. After tossing our mitts and the ball onto my back porch, we made our way to the meeting place. Teddy was already waiting, looking like he'd been there forever.

"Hey," he greeted us.

Teddy was impressive leaning against the telephone pole. He was putting out a cigarette with his heel as we wandered up. He was developing something of a hard-rock teenager look.

"Hey Teddy," we answered.

"Who else is coming?"

"Everybody said they'd be here. Time is it, anyway?"

We were waiting on Billy and Arnold. Jacob would probably tag along if he happened to be around. No one invited him, but likewise no one told him to get lost. Somehow he always seemed to know what we were up to. He would slide out of the shadows to join us, but usually from a little distance.

I answered Teddy: "Maybe wait a little longer. Better when there's more of us."

The night brought us together, but inactivity made us socially awkward. We were more comfortable doing things. We hadn't yet learned to banter about the weather, like our parents did when they needed to fill the void. We did, however, have baseball to talk about, and Julian was completely obsessed with the Los Angeles Dodgers and the World Series that was just under way. He was capable of coming up with at least half a dozen boring declarations in a few seconds.

"Hey, the Dodgers are the best team ever, and if they don't win this year, I'll eat snot for a week."

I felt I should at least argue with Julian. "You already do. They're not that great, you know."

"Yeah. Just wait."

"No, you wait."

"Wanna bet?"

"I don't bet with suckers. I buy 'em at the store."

"Yeah?"

"Yeah."

The arrival of Arnold and Billy from two different directions at more or less the same time saved us from more useless sallies.

Arnold summarized us with his usual scorn: "What you bunch of geniuses standing around for?"

Just as usual, when we snapped to some kind of attention, he christened the event for historical purposes: "Watchers' Club, it's the first Saturday night of October, a night to remember. Move out!"

THE FLASHLIGHT

Just before we started out on our trek to Lovers' Lane, Billy stopped us. "Oh, hey—look what I got."

Billy produced a flashlight from within his bulky jacket (his mom always saw to it that he was overdressed).

"Let's see." Billy handed it to Arnold, who scrutinized it: "Super heavy duty. Stainless steel. Waterproofed. Like the police and firemen use," he said. "The army—they paint these dark green. Takes four 'D' batteries."

We liked what we were hearing. We liked equipment.

Arnold continued: "Bigger, more powerful than your regular flashlight. Long range capability. Perfect for hunting down mole people."

This sounded pretty good.

"Watch."

Arnold aimed it to the ground and, after fiddling with the switch, turned it on. The lower halves of our bodies were instantly exposed in almost blinding powder-white light, which made the surrounding night a little more absolute and creepy, and, ever so slightly, we moved together within that perfect circle of light. The light clicked off, but not without a bit of fuss.

"The switch is stiff or something." Arnold added. "Maybe not worn in."

Arnold passed the flashlight to Teddy. "Nice piece of hardware." He swung it a few times, like it was a club. "Carry a good wallop, too."

He passed it Julian: "Bet it doesn't weigh as much as Roger Maris' bat. He uses a thirty-three-ounce bat, you know. The best ever."

We didn't know, and we didn't care.

When it was my turn, I had to admit that the weight impressed me, too. "Weighs a ton."

"No kidding," said Julian. "It's probably like the lights they use for night games at Dodger Stadium, except those ones are way, way stronger, and they have thousands of them, you know."

Again, no one bothered to follow up this dumb comment, so I asked Billy where he got it.

"My dad keeps it in the basement. He's in the volunteer fire department. Keeps it with his special boots and hat and stuff. They gave it to him, I think."

Temporarily pilfering one of his father's important items was impressive, if not a little out of character for Billy. He earned a few brownie points for his contribution to the evening's expedition.

Billy now had the hiccups and stopped talking. He held his breath for as long as he could with the hope of getting rid of them. He hoped we wouldn't notice.

Then Arnold had an idea: "Know what? We could use this tonight. On a couple. In their car. Get us a quick, instant flash of what's going on. Like a flashbulb. Scare the begeezus right out of them, whoever."

We silently agreed. Could be interesting.

I tried to add a little color: "Smile, you're on Candid Camera!"

Arnold turned to Billy. "I'll use the flashlight."

If you didn't know Arnold, you wouldn't be able to tell if this was a request or an order. We knew Arnold, and we knew it was the latter.

"Sure, I guess," gasped Billy, still working on his hiccups. Arnold took the flashlight and had one more comment before we departed: "The flashlight smells like soup."

We didn't know if he was joking, but it was kind of funny.

And off we went into Saturday night to Lovers' Lane, armed with mischief, a vague plan, and one heavy-duty flashlight that may or may not have smelled a little like soup.

SHHH

We set off down Eastfield Road. Our plan, as usual, was to cut up through The Trail, which meant passing through the far reaches of my property. Make as little commotion as possible.

Just as we were about to cut through to The Trail by going over a low fence near where my dad had grown some fruit trees, we heard a noise somewhere a behind us. We didn't expect anything, but because we were aiming to be up to what our parents called "no good," and because it was already dark, we were more edgy than usual. At the same time, we also knew better than to act suspiciously if we came across any adults, though it was not likely.

Before any of us could pinpoint what startled us, Arnold whipped the flashlight around and turned it on after a few clicks. A split second in advance of the light hitting its target, Arnold said, "It's just Gumboot—or Boo Radley."

Boo who? Arnold carried all these references around that we didn't always get. Jacob was some yards behind the rest of us. The light flashed across his face for a second, and then to his feet. As usual, he was wearing gumboots and his beaten-up plaid shirt. We were left with a ghostly snapshot of his helplessly surprised grimace, like he was there for a moment, then gone.

"Geez, Jacob, do you have to sneak up on us like that?" said Billy, whose hiccups now seemed to have been scared out of him.

"Shhh. For Christmas sakes, Billy, keep it down!" ordered Arnold.

Jacob remained in the shadows, waiting for us to move on so that he could follow at a distance.

"He was there all the time, you dolts," said Arnold. "If you care to notice, not that its worth noticing."

Arnold returned to business. "Let's go. Must be getting on past nine. Keep it down." As usual, we let him lead us forth into temptation.

Just as we entered the bottom of The Trail, Billy asked Arnold, "Can I carry the flashlight while we're going through The Trail? I'll give it back when we get to the top."

You could tell Arnold didn't want to give it up. The issue at this point was not clumsiness, though Billy was notoriously all thumbs. Last year in class he managed to drop a large pickle jar full of tadpoles, right at the very moment the teacher said, "Now Billy, be careful with that!" Neither was the issue about ownership, for if anyone had the right to carry it based on property rights, of course it was Billy. The issue was control.

Arnold thought for a moment. "Okay. Here. I'll need it when we get to the top of The Trail. The Billy club. Get it? And don't turn it on."

With this punful letting-in, Arnold could appear both generous and in charge. And appearances, of course, were everything. Even in the dark.

THE TRAIL

Since I knew The Trail so well—it had been my stomping ground for as long as I could remember—I led the way through a couple of acres of evergreens, bush, and salal, which was part of my family's long strip of property.

The Trail was fairly easy to follow, though at a couple of dark turns beneath the fir trees you had to watch your step on the knuckled roots that randomly surfaced. Except for a few low, drifting clouds that every now and then dulled the light from the quarter moon, the night was clear.

The Old Orchard was about halfway to our destination. No one said anything, except Billy, who at one point stumbled over Teddy's heels— "Oops. Sorry Teddy."

Arnold spoke back to him. "Keep it down, you klutz. We don't need to send a telegram to let 'em know we're coming, you know. You're like Godzilla back there!"

"Sorry."

"Cripes, keep it down!"

"Sorry."

"Quiet!"

Arnold could barely stand such exchanges.

We slowed. I moved steadily but carefully forward. Stealth was part of the excitement. We still had some ways to go. There might not be anyone parked at Lovers' Lane, especially given that it was still not that late. Our best bet would be teenagers in their parents' cars.

When it came time for Arnold to direct, we knelt down behind some bushes. We were now beyond where my property ended, and where the top of The Trail opened out. Jacob lingered some yards behind. Arnold spoke in low tones: "Billy, pass me the flashlight."

Billy gave it to him, but weakly added: "Maybe I can be the one to shine it?"

"Maybe," Arnold answered.

Arnold went on: "We'll go over to the bluff end of Lovers' Lane. More cover for the approach. Stay together, unless we get chased, then scatter. Every man for himself. Meet up at the Old Orchard down The Trail. And keep it down 'til I give a signal. Got it?"

We did. The bit about scattering and "every man for himself" got us jacked.

What happened the other few times is that we retreated helter-skelter after getting—or believing we got—the attention of the parkers. Arnold's style was to almost saunter away, casual and arrogant. Julian was away in a flash, leaving all of us in his wake. Billy would trip and fall down all over the place, getting caught up in bushes, hiccupping all the way. Teddy, like a bulldozer, would simply crash straight through anything in his way. I tried to be strategic and pick my way around the trees and stumps. As for Jacob—well, we never saw how he left the scene, though he eventually showed up in the shadows of our meeting place at the orchard.

In our retreat, we would shout out perfectly juvenile things like, "Hey, getting any feels, buddy!" or "Zipper stuck?" Teddy always shouted the same thing: "Squeeze her melons for me, man! Honk honk!" Like I said: Teddy was into cars.

A few weeks before some guy we disturbed yelled back at us, "You little bastards! Wait 'til I get a hold of you!" He may have even chucked an empty beer bottle or something in our general direction. This was just the response we wanted and what we needed to make us shout even more idiotic things as we disappeared into the night. We figured no one would likely bother to follow us, since chasing a bunch of dumb-ass kids in the dark through some bushes was hardly worth the while.

Eventually we would each make our way to the top of The Trail before heading down to the Old Orchard to glorify our daring operation, and to re-live what we had seen. Or thought that we had seen.

Moving Out

An old, dirt road led to Lovers' Lane. The parking area was really nothing much more than a clearing at the end of the road, and surrounded with bush and a fair number of evergreens. Besides the parkers, the area was sometimes used by persons who wanted to dump old stoves, sofas, hot water tanks, carpets, tires, and the like. My dad hated these people, and one day he hoped to catch a dumper and report him.

When we were within about fifty yards of where the old road came to an end, we came to a dead stop and knelt down behind some cover. It had rained a few times during last week, so the ground noise was softened. We weren't quite in a position to see if there was anyone parked or not. We would circle around first to get a better vantage point.

"Julian," Arnold whispered while we gathered around. "Scout ahead. See if anything, anyone, is there."

Julian lived for such reconnaissance. He dashed off. The rest of us waited, uneasy but excited in our silence.

Teddy said he felt like a smoke.

Arnold advised him matter-of-factly. "Not a good idea. The light might be detected."

Though Teddy did not like being told what to do by anyone, like a good soldier he deferred to Arnold.

For no particular reason Arnold turned away from the direction Julian had headed in and added in a low, spooky voice, "Gummmbooooot? You-who there? Shouldn't you be home taking care of your rabbits before daddykins hands them over to the bunny burger man?" Arnold turned back, knowing there would be no response from Jacob.

Billy giggled, "Bunny burgers."

Billy felt he had to keep on Arnold's good side, and he often echoed Arnold's jabs at Jacob. Funny thing was, Jacob's presence in our gang was probably more important for Billy than anyone else, for without Jacob, Billy would have to assume the role of low boy in our gang.

I could just make out Jacob's outline ten or so yards behind. He likely didn't even hear Arnold's taunt. Like us, he was kneeling.

We waited.

Then, out of nowhere, Julian was back. He was breathing fast. We tightened around him.

Arnold: "So?"

"A car up there, for sure...almost about the end of the road...top of that bit of slope up there." He took a breath. "Didn't get real close, so I couldn't really see the car. But there's a car there."

"How d'ya know?" asked Arnold.

"They're really going at it or something," Julian added. We looked at him, uncertain. "You know, noise coming from them," he added. "Muffled, kind of, but you could just hear 'em."

Julian caught his breath once more, as we waited for more. He became specific enough to get us a little eager: "Noise like, you know, they were doing stuff—or something, I think."

Teddy added his enthusiasm to the imagined scene: "Maybe he's trying to take off her over-the-shoulder-boulder-holder and he got it stuck around her neck and it choked her."

Billy felt he had to giggle. Arnold shushed him.

"Let's get going, then," Arnold said. "Before they leave. Catch them in the act. Red-handed."

Teddy couldn't help himself. "Beep beep," he said quietly, making a squeezing gesture with his hands in front of himself.

Teddy: boobs on his mind twenty-four hours a day.

Arnold quietly issued us forward again: "Watchers' Club, move out. And keep it down."

APPROACH

We slid forward with Arnold and Julian leading the way. Arnold issued his final orders. "Julian—with me. To the left. Billy—stay with us. You two fan out beside us. To the right. Flank out, stay down."

We nodded.

Every five or ten yards we stopped behind some cover—a tree, some thick bushes, uneven ground. When everyone was steady and the ground ahead of us surveyed, we moved a little further. We spread out as we moved forward. Jacob, I could just make out, was on his own, some yards further off to Teddy's right.

Soon we were within about twenty or so yards of where the car was supposed to be. We still couldn't see it, mainly because we were on lower ground, and there was heavy bush and some low-branched evergreens between. We would need to get up the side of the small incline before it would come into view. We might be able to get pretty close. The angle we were coming in on would probably be side-on to the car, since our approach was parallel to the road.

We could just hear a little of what Julian reported: sporadic noise rising from the direction of the road. Definitely stuff going on. A female pitch could definitely be heard in muffled snatches. Then for seconds no sound at all. The silence made us listen even more closely. It seemed safer to move in when the noise started up.

Teddy whispered, "Let's get closer. Bet they're going at it."

Lined out, we began to go up the little rise, bit by bit. Arnold and his group were only a few yards away from us, on our left, as we closed in. When we got to the top of the rise, we would only be about ten or so yards away from the car. Maybe less. We would be able to glance over to at least see what was there, but we would have to get on the same level and behind some bushes to get a good look.

We crouched and closed in. For a couple of seconds, the sounds from the car seemed frantic—movement, not voices—before they again died down to nothing. The noise gave us a chance to get our heads within a foot or two of the top of the small rise. We froze and waited, hugging the side of the little hill. We didn't peek over the top yet. We would wait for Arnold. If nothing more came from the car, we might have to do our yelling and carrying on from where we were. We knew that Arnold would prefer to get a little closer, maybe a few yards beyond the rise behind some bushes. That would take us about six or seven yards from the car. The thrill would be how close we might get before starting our commotion. Only once before had we got right up to some bushes beside a car, and that was scary. Most of the time we kept our distance, especially if it was a clear night and we might get spotted. But even though it was quite bright this particular evening, with some moonlight sifting through the low clouds, we felt willing to push our luck.

We froze. Once more movement from within, but there was also a momentary sharp-sounding voice. Female. Arnold signaled that we move up a couple of more feet so that we would be able to at least get the car in view. We followed his lead and poked our heads over the top. The vehicle came into view from the passenger side, though a few bushes and some smaller fir trees stood between the vehicle and us. Teddy and I were furthest toward the front end of the car, and Jacob was another five yards or so further along beyond Teddy. Arnold was beside me, to my left. Then Billy and Julian spread out a little beside him.

Arnold suddenly ducked back down the hill a couple of yards, and we moved sideways so that we could be closer to him and while we confirmed our strategy. Billy was almost too excited. He whispered so that we could barely hear him: "That's old man Slagmann's butcher truck. What would that crank-ass be doing out here?"

Arnold answered immediately. "Not the old man, you idiot. It will be his kid, David or whatever his name is, making out with some hot cheerleader from the high school, I bet."

"Oh, yeah," Billy murmured.

Arnold was thinking.

"We'll get closer," he whispered, speaking quickly. "Here's the deal. Julian—take the flashlight. Sneak around to the front of the truck, ten yards away in front of it. Aim the flashlight right into the front seat, so we'll be able to see inside. Turn it on right away when you see us stand up behind those bushes and trees just up ahead. You should be able to see us stand up." He pointed up, a little in front of us. "Keep the light on for just a second, 'cause you can be sure it will be you, if anyone, he will come for. Got it?"

"Yeah," Julian whispered, anxious as usual to show his stealth. "Ten yards in front. Wait for you to stand. Shine the flashlight in the truck for a second. Then vamoose. Meet up at the Old Orchard."

Arnold nodded and gave the flashlight to Julian. Billy, surprisingly, objected. "But you said—you said I might be able to use it, the flashlight, maybe."

Just then a strange, muted noise, almost a moan, came from the car. We were a little startled, but more excited and hurried.

Arnold answered in a low, intense voice, "No time for this!"

Julian, who now held the flashlight, wasn't sure what to do. "Okay," hissed Arnold. "Give the stupid thing to Billy. Get going. Quietly. Don't screw up, Billy boy. Sneak about ten yards in front of the van."

Billy could hardly believe he got his way. None of us could believe he got his way.

"Aye-aye," and off Billy went, as best he could, into the darkness, around and out front of where the van was parked.

"Shouldn't take him long," Arnold whispered. "Time to close in for the kill. Move up, fan out. Run silent, run deep." Arnold could tell we didn't quite know what he meant by his last words, so he dismissively helped us out: "It's a movie, you idiots—subs stealthing up to destroy ships." None of us said anything. "Geezus," he muttered, and following his lead with everything seeming to speed up, we spread out and crept to the lip of the small hill again, and fully poised to stand up and move the few yards to the low bushes that would separate us from our prey.

Slagmann's truck would be in almost full side view, passenger side closest to us. With the light from the flashlight intruding into the front seat, we might get a glance of what was going on inside. Catch 'em in the act of who-knows-what! The flashlight was taking The Watchers' Club to a new level.

Once more I looked across our line: on my left, Arnold, vigilant, and Julian, more tuned into Arnold than the van. On my right, Teddy, chomping at the bit. And then Jacob, further off to the right in the dark, who, given how the truck was parked, might have a better view being more in front of the van, rather than beside it. If all went well, we'd have something to talk about, for sure. A grand moment!

Now. Now was the time.

Following Arnold, we all stood up from behind the bush so that we could see the vehicle, sideways, in front of us. The flashlight was supposed to go on—now! It didn't. Trust Billy! There was just enough light for us to see some of the yellow lettering on the side of the car: "SLAGMANN'S BUTCHER. You Can't Beat Our Meat."

After a few long seconds the flashlight finally did its duty. The white light first hit the truck's hood for a split white second before it briefly found and lit up the dark interior of the truck. For just a moment we had a perfect, frozen, ghostly view of van's cab. Then the light dropped away, but not off. What?

But in that side-on snapshot I could see David Slagmann's profiled face, flushed and surprised, squint toward the source of the light around the front of the van. Blinded. I could also see what appeared to be the back of someone's head pressed against the lower part of the passenger window. That was about all we saw before the direction of the light went elsewhere.

What the heck was Billy doing?

The sudden darkness gave us the moment to make our rambunctious exit as we crashed and tore away through the bushes and trees, retreating roughly the way we came. Teddy, as usual, called out something about squeezing melons. Arnold yelled, "Nice one, Fagman!" Julian came up with some nonsensical remark about cutting up all the meat, and I used my regular line: "Can't get her panties off, eh…?" Nothing usually came from Jacob, but as we all beat our noisy, haphazard retreat, he may have said something, a word—

But we were off and running! Every man for himself!

I didn't hear anyone coming after us—not that it was expected. Maybe the sound of a car door in the distance behind us, and then a flash of light flicked past us. The flashlight? Or, more likely, David Slagmann and his girlfriend leaving Lovers' Lane in the butcher's van, and it was the light from headlights spraying the landscape as the truck turned around. Good riddance to pretty boy David Slagmann and his dumb girlfriend! Ha!

Together and apart, we ran into the darkness, tripping, falling, and laughing, and—at least for this moment—with guiltless, innocent fear.

Mission accomplished!

At the Old Orchard we would meet to glorify this, our most successful Watchers' Club outing.

And, as it turned out, our last.

Speedy Julian was already at the Old Orchard when I got there. "Cool, huh," he greeted me. "With the flashlight and all! Slagboy probably crapped his pants!"

I was a little out of breath, but managed a good one: "If he had them on."

We laughed and sat on the ground at the base of one of the old, wizened apple trees and waited for the others to show up. It seemed darker here than up by Lovers' Lane.

I couldn't resist asking Julian, "What did you say—yell, I mean—when we were running away."

"Dunno. Something like, 'Hey, cutting up all the meat,' or something like that. Should have said something roasting beef or something?"

I laughed a little because it was so stupid. "What's that supposed to mean, anyway? 'Cutting up all the meat'? 'Roasting beef'?"

"I dunno. Just came out. You know. The truck belonging to old man Slagmann, being a butcher and all that. What was I supposed to say? 'How's the meat business going'?"

"Yeah, that would be good."

"Huh?"

"You're weird, man."

"That really hurts, panty boy."

The mutual teasing was well taken, especially with our spirits so high. Julian now tried to one-up me with a knock-knock joke while we waited for the others.

"Knock, knock."

But I resisted. "Julian, oh geez. Knock-knock jokes. They're for kids."

"Come on. Don't be a sophead. Knock, knock."

"Okay. Who's there?"

"Boo?"

"Boo who?"

"Cry baby!" Julian gave me an elbow in the arm and said it again, trying to mock me. "Cry baby...boohoo. Get it?"

I shook my head, and thankfully Teddy arrived. He sat down beside us and took out a smoke.

"That was weird, man," Teddy said right away. "What'd Billy do? Why didn't he turn the stupid flashlight off after he aimed it, instead of aiming it up, or wherever? The guy's a klutz, I'm telling you. A klutz, with a capital C."

Julian answered. "Well, you know Billy."

At that moment Billy in fact arrived, breathing heavily. We didn't say anything to him. He seemed to be shaking or something, or, more likely, just trying to keep his hiccups in. He sat down and kept his head low. Teddy lit up the cigarette. We watched the tip glow in the night air. It made us feel older and experienced—and dangerous.

Arnold arrived a minute or so behind Billy, like he strolled back.

I broke the conversation with the obvious: "That was David Slagmann, all right. You see the look on his face? When the light hit him? He spooked, huh!"

Teddy nodded a "Uh-uh, yeah," but there was a sneer in his voice.

Arnold added, "Yeah, it was him. Parked in daddy-o's meat paddy wagon."

Billy still hadn't moved or said anything. He pulled his knees up into his chest and tucked his chin down. He was still breathing pretty hard.

Teddy asked, "Wonder who Slagmann junior boy was with?"

"Couldn't really tell," I added. "But I—"

"Yeah," interrupted Julian. "Probably that cheerleader from high school. Sounds like they were having quite the time, all grunty and stuff."

Arnold added, "Yeah, they were at it, all right. David Slagmann. Pretty boy. His dad would kill him if he knew what he was up to in his butcher jalopy."

Julian couldn't resist the meat theme. "I bet he was saying to her, 'Hey, how do you like my wiener? Got any buns?'"

This was so stupid that it was funny.

Normally by this time Billy, the most insecure of us all, would have been ranting and raving about what we'd done. Glorifying his part. Instead, he rocked back and forth a little, his chin still tucked into his knees.

Arnold finally addressed him directly and spoke to the obvious. "So, Billy boy, why'd it take you so long to get the flashlight on after we stood up?"

Billy hesitated, them mumbled, "What?...Oh. The switch. It—it stuck. For a bit."

Arnold continued his inquisition. "And what was with the light shining across the trees? What was that about?"

Billy again didn't answer right away.

"Yeah, what?" Julian piped in.

Billy looked up and said, "Huh?"

Arnold asked him again: "The light. What's the deal with that? You aimed it across the opening after you shined it in the truck."

Billy kept his head in his knees. "I—I left it there."

"What? You left what there?" Teddy questioned.

Billy didn't answer right away, but we heard him right. "The... flashlight. The switch—jammed or something."

"So?" questioned Teddy. We waited again.

"So I—I just—just left, dropped it. And ran."

"What'd you do that for?" Teddy asked. "You lost your marbles? Your old man will have your nuts in a vice if he thinks you took it—and then lost it!"

"When I—I couldn't—" Billy stopped talking and lifted his head a little: "Did you...see—?"

Teddy interrupted: "Yeah, we all saw, all right."

Arnold, measuring this exchange between Billy and Teddy, went back to the flashlight. "You just left it there? Switched on? Shining across into the clearing, or the trees, or somewhere?"

Billy seemed to have nothing more to say. Arnold added, "Not good, Billyboy."

That much we all knew.

We sat for a few more moments to watch Teddy smoke his cigarette. We could just make out him blow a few smoke rings up into the night sky, and they seemed to fall apart and blend into the darkness at the same time. All of us, except Teddy, knew we had better head back to our homes before our parents got too suspicious. In fact, I knew I was going to be late if we didn't get going right away. Curfews were a thing. With the switched-on flashlight on the ground, there suddenly seemed little momentum to further glorify our outing.

Except for Billy, we all stood up.

"So, Billy," Julian asked, "You going back and get it, or what?"

We all looked at Billy, though we couldn't really see his face. I, for one, figured that David Slagmann and his girlfriend would be gone by the time Billy made his way back to Lovers' Lane. But then again, with the flashlight there, still shining, David Slagmann maybe took it. But at least Billy should try to get it. His dad would probably notice that it was gone in a jiffy, and that would be some story.

"No," he said. "No."

"Why?" I asked.

Billy still sat there, acting weird. "Did you see—? What he was doing...?" Billy's words petered out and fell into a few hiccups.

What was he on about? We all saw David Slagmann's face. Billy, positioned more or less in front of the car, would have been able to see into the cab, straight on. But so what?

Teddy didn't have much patience, and he said to Billy, "Yeah, we all got what the Slagmann kid was doing."

This only made Billy look up at us, and we all looked at him, waiting for more, if there was more. What was with him? He looked down again. Teddy blew a smoke ring in Billy's direction, and it fell over him like a noose and then melted into the darkness.

Billy's bumbling and now his mumblings had to be left behind for now.

Arnold ended the discussion: "Suit yourself. It's your nuts, not mine. I gotta go—now." He took a step forward. "Watchers' Club, move out."

We walked off in silence and continued down The Trail. Billy got up and was the last in our single file. He walked like a zombie and fell behind a bit.

After a minute or two Arnold stopped. "No Gumboot."

"What?" Julian asked.

"Gumboot—not here."

We looked back, beyond Billy. Arnold was right—Jacob was nowhere to be seen. This didn't count for much, but it was unusual for him not to eventually be found tagging along somewhere behind. Mind you, Jacob also had the habit of fading in and out of scenes, unseen.

Teddy, having a tease at Billy, added, "Maybe he stayed behind to get your flashlight for you, Billy. Save your ass."

This was harsh, and Teddy couldn't resist piling on another comment: "Maybe Gumboot wants to shine it up his own butt to see if anyone's home."

Except for Billy, we all snickered.

Thinking out loud, and not really asking a question or saying anything important, I said, "I thought I heard him say something when we were all yelling stuff out and taking off."

This sat for a few seconds. Arnold, trying to sound like he didn't care, followed up: "Like what?"

"Don't know, something like 'horror' or something."

"Yeah, I heard him say something, too," added Teddy, who was closest to Jacob. "The weirdo. I thought maybe he said, 'horse'."

A couple of us sort of laughed—"horse"? Huh? But what did it matter what Jacob said, or if he said anything?

Homeward bound and picking up speed, we let our exploits fade away into the evening air, not knowing they would return.

SLEEP, PERCHANCE

At home. Through the back door and into the kitchen, quietly. A light on in the living room. Dad was probably reading the newspaper. The guy could spend a whole evening with The Silverford City Daily Free Press, which was strange since he said there was never anything in it worth reading.

Even if it was quite late, I felt like a bowl of cereal or something, but I thought I better not chance a pit stop. Harder to hit a moving target. And I might have been a bit late. Mom was likely down the hall in the sewing room, which, ever since we got a piano from the auction, doubled as the music room. There was a rollout couch in there as well, so it was also the spare bedroom, though mom liked to call it "the guest room." All those names for one room gave the illusion that our house was bigger than it really was.

Of course all my stealth was not worth the effort. No matter how quietly I made my way into the house, mom knew the moment I was home. I swear she had radar.

"That you, dear?"

As if she didn't know. "Yeah."

"What time is it? A bit late, maybe? Who were you with?"

I had to come up with something, or further questions—or worse yet, repeated questions—might follow me.

"Oh, just out with Julian and Billy. Hanging around, playing ball—talking out on the road, up by the street light."

I didn't mention being with Arnold or Teddy, since she didn't care for them all that much—not that she ever said so, but I knew.

"Well, start getting ready for bed. Don't forget to wash up."

"Yeah, okay."

I ran the hot water full tilt in the sink while looking into the mirror to see if any zits were on their way. According to my older brother, Simon, they were coming soon. Now that he was attending the new community college on the other side of Silverford, his attitude toward me was, at the same time, more worldly and smug. He smiled when he forewarned me, as if cursing me with them. "Just wait," he said, "you'll get them." Looking closely into the mirror through the steam condensing on the mirror, I had a flash of David Slagmann's profile when that bright, white light hit him, and I didn't like that either.

Back in my bedroom, which had one window that faced Eastfield Road, I might be able to squeeze an extra hour out of the day. A late night. My most recent private-time activity was finding new radio stations on a big, old wooden radio dad picked up from grandma, who didn't use it anymore. I hunkered into bed with an old issue of *Mad Magazine*.

Some minutes later, dad came in to say good night. He mentioned something about helping him clean up the basement tomorrow. Mom followed shortly. She stopped to pick up my pants and shirt, which, of course, I had dropped in the middle of the floor.

"Young man," she said, "hang these up." She then hung them up for me. I dropped the magazine on the floor, and she turned off the radio. She had quit kissing me at night, though she sat on the side of the bed for a moment or two before exiting. I think she was always sizing me up, looking for clues, or something.

She switched off the light. "Goodnight," she said. "Don't let the bedbugs bite."

"G'night," I said. She closed the door but left a little gap for the hallway light to come in.

In bed, I pulled up the covers and turned toward the window facing Eastfield Road. There was usually little or no night traffic. The darkness would occasionally be punctuated by the bark of dog, which set off other dogs. I pulled up the cover more and rehearsed the evening's events: the butcher truck under the moon and the flashlight's glare on David Slagmann's frozen face...our get-away through the bushes...Jacob saying something... boo who and Boo Radley...Billy leaving the flashlight...Teddy's smoke rings disappearing into the darkness...It was pretty cool, our Watchers' Club, but as sleep slowly but unstoppably rolled over me, in the distance a woman's voice called out from the dark, "JA-cob, Ja-COB!"

3
MISSING IN ACTION

Sunday morning. Woke up, turned on the old radio, and returned to bed, pulling the covers up over my head to shut out the day. The music drifted in and out of reception. I had begun to enjoy sleeping in on the weekends.

When I woke up for the second time, there was only one thing: breakfast. Maybe pancakes. Being Sunday, chances were good for a big, unhurried breakfast. I vaguely remembered that dad wanted some help to tidy up the basement or something. I ran through possible excuses.

Mom sat with a cup of coffee at one end of the kitchen table. Dad was at the other end, thumbing through a hunting catalogue.

Both looked up when I came in.

"Would you like some breakfast?"

"Pancakes?"

I sat down at the table while she turned on the stove and put the pan on. She'd already made the batter. Dad was still looking at me. "Sleep well?"

"Yeah, okay."

Mom joined us at the table, so I was more or less sitting between them. Surrounded. They were acting a little strange, not relaxed—not quite staring at me. But there was something.

And then it began. And, in truth, it never stopped. Not even now.

Dad leaned slightly toward me. "Mrs. Slough came around this morning, not too long ago. Looking for Jacob."

This didn't seem too strange, since she always seemed to be looking for Jacob. Even last night...falling in and out of sunken dreams with her calling for him...*JA-cob, Ja-COB.*

"Why'd she come here? Jacob's always somewhere around."

What was the problem? Jacob wandered out somewhere this morning and wasn't around when Mrs. Slough needed him for something. Wasn't even lunch yet. What was the big deal?

"No, you don't understand."

"What?" I asked. Mom and dad continued looking at me, odd-like.

Dad continued. "Last night. Jacob didn't come home last night. Why she's looking for him. That's why she came around this morning."

Dad sat back and pushed the catalogue aside. The page was opened to pictures of hunting rifles held by smiling hunters in camouflage clothes.

Last night, I thought. Last night…It began to float back. David Slagmann in his old man's meat van up at Lovers' Lane making out with some girl. The look on his face. The flashlight—Billy leaving his dad's metal flashlight there. And Jacob? Yes, Jacob somewhere there behind us. Then beside us when we crept up on the truck. And then . . . What? Jacob didn't go home after that?

Mom began. She asked what she had to ask: "Did you see Jacob last night? Were you with him at all?"

The frying pan gave off a little smoke, even though no batter had been poured in.

"It's burning, mom." I didn't want to get to my answer yet. Maybe her question would go away if I let it alone.

She went to the stove and poured in the cream-colored batter.

Dad repeated mom's question: "Were you with him at all? Last night."

"Yeah, I think we saw him."

I knew this would never do, but it was the best I could come up with. Mom was at the stove, ready to flip the pancake.

Dad continued. "You 'think' you saw him?"

"Well, you know how he hangs around, kind of coming and going, you know."

"Where?" he asked.

I thought a bit, but I didn't want it to look like I was thinking at all.

"Oh, under the light up the road. We were just hanging around. Throwing a ball with Julian. Talking and stuff."

Again, my gut told me to be vague. The Watchers' Club outing to Lovers' Lane was not even to be hinted about.

Mom set the pancake in front of me. It almost filled the plate. It didn't seem to be cooked as much as usual, which wasn't like mom. I put on a slab of butter and poured the syrup while mom went to the fridge to get some milk. She poured me a glass and asked, "Who else was there? Anyone else besides you and Julian?"

By this time my mouth was stuffed with a large chunk of pancake, which bought more time. Mom turned off the stove, removed the pan, and once more sat at the table with her coffee.

"Huh?" I managed to get out.

Mom continued: "Who else was around, who might have seen Jacob, besides you and Julian?"

"Oh. Yeah. Arnold Rheinhurst came by, with Billy Luckhert for a while. Oh. And Teddy Sullivan, too, I think. He came by, too, for a while."

Dad once more leaned forward a little. "Did they see Jacob? Were they with him, or did they go with him anywhere?"

"Not sure," I said, wolfing the pancake. "Don't think so."

Maybe if I hurried up I could get away without too much more fuss. Jacob not coming home last night. He didn't join us after we ran away from Lovers' Lane to meet up at the Old Orchard. I tried to just let it go, like it was nothing: "Maybe he just slept outside somewhere last night, or something. Or got lost. You know Jacob."

"What time did you see him, about?" dad asked.

"Maybe . . . maybe, I don't know, at about eight, or a little later."

"And?"

"And then, he was around, and then, like, he wasn't. Went off somewhere, I suppose."

"By himself?"

"Yep. I think so."

Mom and dad exchanged a glance, which I wasn't supposed to notice. Could they tell I was hiding something, or were they signaling? I ate faster still. Somewhere in the back of my mind was the worry that this conversation might be going on, in various ways, in the kitchens of some of the other kids. Not good. We might all say different things.

I tried to sound helpful, but I needed to find out: "Where else did Mrs. Slough look? She talk to anyone else?"

"We don't know," mom answered. "She's doesn't know who else he might have been with, besides maybe you. She knows you are kind of a—well—a friend, a neighbor."

Mom paused. She knew I would never refer to Jacob as a "friend." "Mrs. Slough knows our family better than most others, I'd say. She hasn't called the sheriff's office yet, but she'll have to if he doesn't show up in the next little while."

The sheriff's office? What? I better get out and warn the others, if I could. If it wasn't too late. Maybe Jacob fell asleep somewhere and hasn't woken up yet. That would be the best. There were times when he wandered to school an hour late as if nothing was unusual. Anything could distract Jacob Slough. Maybe he got lost, but not likely. He knew Eastfield as well as anybody, since he spent much of his time just wandering aimlessly around, exploring the ditches, ponds, woods, old pastures, and side roads.

It didn't seem like my parents had anything else to say, but it was clear I had to leave them with something. "I'll tell—ask—some of the kids—if I see them. Maybe go out and see if they're around." I threw back the last slug of milk and stood up.

Mom commented, "That would be nice. Let us know, right away, if you hear anything. Right away, you hear?"

Mom was serious and worried. Dad was harder to read. He gave me the once-over as if assessing my performance. He was usually quiet on domestic or neighborhood business.

I felt a bit better as I took my plate to the sink—maybe even a sense of minor triumph. I had avoided giving up information, and it may be that none of the other kids knew about Jacob's disappearance or had been asked about it. We had to get our story straight. An itch in my stomach registered the lie I told them about last night—and what I did not tell them. How could I have said that I was with him, especially given what we were up to at Lovers' Lane in the name of The Watchers' Club?

I was about to disappear down the hallway into my bedroom for a quick change and exit, but dad stopped me: "Esther Slough. She's missing too. She didn't come home last night, either. Did you see her at all—last night?"

I had to turn around and look back into the kitchen. Mom was back at the table with her coffee. Dad looked at me straight. Mom seemed almost afraid to. Esther Slough? Not home, too? What was going on—brother and sister gone?

I came up with something I hoped sounded reassuring, and at least something fully true: "Esther? No, for sure, didn't see her. Maybe they went somewhere together, on a trip or something."

As soon as I said this I realized it sounded stupid. But it was all I had. At least there was a reason, for the time being, to avoid helping with the basement.

"Maybe," mom said. "Let's hope so."

PUDDLES

Within moments I was out on Eastfield Road on my bike. It was already moving on toward noon, but the light was heavy and dark, hinting of cooler weather to come. The clouds, spent and low, hung above with, it seemed, nowhere to go.

It must have rained hard during the night, though the downpour hadn't slid into my sleep the way Mrs. Slough's calling out for Jacob had. Brown, muddy puddles, some of them quite large and disguising potholes, formed along the road. I drove through as many as I could on my way to Julian's house, raising my feet off the pedals at the right splashy moments.

It was a good five-minute full-out ride to the very bottom of Eastfield Road to where Julian lived. I didn't get why my mom hoped that Esther and Jacob took off on a trip together.

Let's hope so, she said. It took me a while, but I did come up a question I had to ask myself as I flew through another puddle: Instead of what?

An answer didn't come. Jacob and Esther's whereabouts were, for the moment, less important than keeping the lid on last night's secret escapades of The Watchers' Club.

GARAGE TALK

I pulled into the driveway of Julian's property and ran to the back door. His mom said he was out in the garage. Everyone called it the garage, but his father had walled up the garage opening and turned it into an all-purpose rumpus room, with an old couch, a couple of chairs, some shelves, a dart board, piles of comic books, board games, and scrubby old dining room table. It was rough, but a good place to have a bit of privacy. It was our favorite place. Our big hope was that Julian's dad might one day put an old TV out there.

Julian was at one of the chairs, going through his massive collection of baseball cards. There was a big game today, so he was likely more obsessed than usual, playing the game in his head.

He didn't even greet me, except to ask, "Who you think hit the most doubles last year?"

I flopped down on the couch. "Mantle."

"Wrong. Frank Robinson. Fifty-one."

"Who?" I barely heard of him. I was not a baseball nut, unlike Julian.

"Okay, one more. Who had the most home runs?"

"Gotta be Mantle," I trotted out confidently.

"Nope. Willy Mays. Forty-nine."

Julian continued to go through his cards.

I cut in: "Remember last night?"

"Yeah." Julian looked up, "Kind of freaky, huh. But cool, too. The Slagmann kid in the van or truck or whatever it is. Wonder if Billy's dad found out about his missing flashlight yet? Billy will in big trouble, eh."

"No kidding," I said. "Maybe he went back this morning to find it and take it back home."

"That's what I'd do."

We both thought on this for moment.

"Billy was acting weird last night, I mean after we met up," I noted.

"Yeah. He looked spooked."

I nodded. "But guess what?"

"What?" asked Julian.

"Jacob Slough's mom came around our house this morning—looking for Jacob."

"So?"

"So—so he didn't come home last night after we were up at Lovers' Lane."

Julian kept going through his cards.

I repeated: "He didn't come home last night. After he was with us. Remember? Even Arnold noticed he wasn't there—on the way back, coming down The Trail. Jacob wasn't there. You know how he's around behind us, somewhere—but always there."

"Yeah. Oh, yeah," Julian said, obviously trying to rehearse last night in his mind's eye. "Yeah," Julian said. "He was there when we were out by Slagmann's van. Out past where you and Teddy were, I think—when we were creeping up on it. That's when I saw him last, I think."

That was about when I'd seen him last, too.

Julian continued, trying to remember: "Then we took off a bit after— after Billy dropped the flashlight, I mean. We all took off, right?" He put down his baseball cards.

I continued, "Mrs. Slough came 'round this morning, to my place, looking for him. My parents wanted to know if I saw him last night. They grilled me," I said, "like I was cheese."

"You said you didn't—didn't see him?"

"No—I said I did. I said I did see him."

"You did? Really?"

"Yeah. I said we saw him last night. Hanging around. But not with us."

"What? You didn't say anything about going over to Lovers' Lane, did you?"

"Yeah—I told them everything. I even told them what you yelled out about cutting up the meat."

Julian's eyebrows almost hit the ceiling.

I relieved him of his panic. "Of course I didn't tell them! Think I'm nuts? My parents would have a hairy hemorrhage if they knew I was sneaking around up there, spying on people making out."

Julian calmed, but I had to make sure he got it: "So, that will be your story too—right?"

He nodded, "Yeah, that will be my story, too, if my parents ask me, or anyone else. We saw him, but he was just hanging around, on the road. Nothing about Lovers' Lane."

We sat on this for a few moments before Julian tried to figure things out: "Jacob didn't come home. Where you think he went?"

"Don't know," I said. "You know Jacob. He could probably wander around all night and not even notice it was night."

"Yeah, for sure. The kid's got something missing between the ears, right?" I could tell Julian was a little happy to remind himself of this—and me, too. It made Jacob's disappearance easier to put aside.

"But here's the creepy thing," I added.

"What?"

"Esther—you know, his sister—she didn't come home last night either."

Julian shrugged. I asked him what my parents asked me, though I was sure I knew the answer: "You see her anywhere last night?"

"Nope. For sure."

"I said I thought that maybe they went somewhere together. You know, on a trip or something."

Julian had an idea. "Hey, maybe they took off, ran away, on account of their dad. I would, too. I mean the guy's a—a psycho. Look what he does to those rabbits—with his bare hands! Snap, crackle, pop." Julian momentarily relished the idea, though it didn't help with what we were trying to figure out. He added, "Maybe they joined the circus."

I ignored Julian's wisecrack. "My mom said that Mrs. Slough might call the sheriff's office if they don't show up soon."

"What? The sheriff?"

"Yeah, the sheriff."

"Geez."

Julian packed all his cards away. We sat.

"What do we do?" he asked. "Tell the others?"

I was still thinking about last night. What happened. What we saw. Where Jacob went.

"Billy," I said. "Gotta see Billy before he spills the beans. He was acting dozy last night. Remember?"

"Yeah. And the others—Arnold and Teddy?"

"They won't have been talked to yet. They're both a bit more out of the way."

"Yeah. See Billy. Pronto Tonto." Then Julian added, "You know, there's a ball game this afternoon."

"Like I care."

In a flash we were on our bikes and off to Billy's house. It was, in a way, good. We had a goal: get to Billy before anyone else. Protect The Watchers' Club and its best-ever mission.

Is Billy Home?

Billy lived a bit further down Eastfield Road and just off a bit on a short side road. Riding our bikes like mad, it didn't take us more than a few minutes to get there. We skidded to a halt and let our bikes fall where they may.

We knocked at Billy's back door. We hoped his mom might answer. Facing Mr. Luckhert might shake our confidence. Someone approached the door. Julian whispered, "Is it his mom or dad?" Mrs. Luckhert opened the door.

"Hi," I said.

"Hi boys."

"Is Billy home? Can he come out to play?"

"No. Afraid not," she answered.

"Oh," I said. "Know where he is?"

"What? No—I mean he's home, but he can't come out right now."

"Oh," both Julian and I said at about the same time, vaguely nodding, although we weren't quite sure what this meant. I had a picture of his dad reaming him out about the flashlight. No doubt Mr. Luckhert was capable of getting information out of Billy—if, that is, he thought there was information to get. We both stood there for a moment too long.

We said "Oh" again, with a little more concern, as if we understood. We were about to leave with our worries when Mrs. Luckhert gave us a little more information.

"He's not feeling very well, I'm afraid. He came home last night—a little later than usual—not very well. A little feverish—a cold coming on, or a touch of the flu, maybe."

We gave her an aw-too-bad nod of understanding. She added, "He hasn't been out of bed yet. He should probably rest all of today, and hopefully he'll be better for school tomorrow."

Julian spoke up, though what he said went nowhere fast: "Yeah, we saw him, Billy, I mean, last night, when we were all playing along the road, most of the time, talking and stuff—along, up the road, doing nothing, really, you know. Maybe it was kind of cold then, so maybe he's got a cold."

"Oh," she said.

I thought it best to pull Julian away before he volunteered any more fractured accounts of last night.

"Bye," I said.

She gave us a hint of a smile in return. "Bye now. I'll tell him you came by."

As she was about to close the door, we could see Mr. Luckhert coming up the stairs from the basement. He caught a glance of us as the door closed.

We walked quickly to our bikes.

"Why'd you say all that stuff about last night? You made it sound, kind of—like it was something!"

"No, I didn't," he answered. "She said he came home later, so I thought I better just mention it. Like, you know, it was no big deal about last night or anything."

"Yeah—well, she looked at you like you were a fruitcake. That's all I know."

"No, she didn't."

Well, maybe she hadn't, but Julian did babble on for no reason.

We had an unspoken credo: Never volunteer information to parents or teachers. Be hurried, be vague, or be quiet.

We picked up our bikes and saddled up, and as we made our way down the driveway, we could see Billy's parents having a conversation in their front room. For a second, it looked to me as if he was holding his hands apart about the length of a certain flashlight. But maybe not.

RESOLVE

We cycled back toward Julian's place—a slight uphill climb. What we did last night was not the worst thing, for sure, but it was easily enough to land us—or at least me, Billy, and Julian—in some hot water. And Arnold, too, though he'd likely talk his way out of it. And now it was worse: I had not told the whole truth to my parents when they asked me straight out about what I had been doing and when I last saw Jacob. His strange disappearance made the situation more confusing. Maybe, I thought, he was back by now, with his sister, and the whole thing would just go away.

Julian was mulling away, too. "What should we do? Tell Arnold and Teddy? At least Arnold?"

"Yeah, we should," I said. "Go by his house."

This plan offered some resolve. We quickened our pace.

Going up to Arnold's along Eastfield Road, past my house, would take us by where we had met up last night, where Billy first showed us his dad's flashlight, and where Arnold gave it a good once-over, and Teddy, being Teddy, said it would be a good club. It would also take us past Jacob's house, further up. Maybe we'd get a sign about whether he had come home. He's got to be home by now.

SUNGLASSES

Eastfield Road rose, with a few ups and downs, from bottom to top, in more or less a straight line. A mile or two of a bumpy, dirt road, with a good size ditch running beside it. Because of the slight ups and downs, you couldn't see the top of Eastfield Road where it ran into a main road.

By the time we cycled to up to where I lived, we could see a few cars gathered way up by the Slough place. Julian and I looked at each other. A little closer and we could see who they belonged to. "The sheriff's cars," Julian murmured. "Geez."

"Maybe bringing Jacob back, I bet."

"Yeah," Julian agreed, but his confirmation, like my theory of why the sheriff was there in the first place, held more hope than certainty.

We slowed down even more. Two cars, one on each side of the road, faced us. On our right, one guy, talking on his radio, leaned up against his running car. On the left, in the front of the Slough yard, talking to Mrs. Slough, were two other officers, both wearing the official khaki pants and the dark brown leather jacket of the District Sheriff's Office. The shorter guy, wearing a kind of cowboy hat, took notes and did all the talking. The bigger guy with wire-rimmed, reflecting sunglasses, gazed steadily ahead. When we were about even with them, the big guy turned slightly and took a long look in our direction. Mrs. Slough continued to talk and the shorter guy kept taking notes. Julian and I immediately sped up and didn't look back until we were a good hundred yards further up the road and at partially out of view.

Julian skidded to a stop. I got off my bike, too. We walked beside each other.

"What's all that about, ya think?" Julian said.

"Don't know."

"Does that mean Jacob is back—they're just bringing him back, maybe? I didn't see him, did you? Or his sister."

"Don't know," I said. We walked on. "They could be in the house, you know."

"Maybe with Old Man Slough—ready to get a major belting, I bet."

"Could be."

Julian began to ramble: "But maybe they were just asking questions... about where Jacob was last night, what time he got home, like, who was with...where he was last night."

"You already said that," I interrupted.

"Yeah," said Julian, who wasn't listening. "Huh? What'd I say?"

"Nothing. Never mind. Did you see the way the big guy looked at us when we went by?"

"Yeah," said Julian again, only this time he was listening. "He took one long look, that's for sure."

"He's the Silverford sheriff, I think."

"Geez," was about all Julian could come up with again, and we retreated into silence.

"Come on," I said. "Find Arnold. Let's go past the schoolyard before we go to his place. He likes to hang around there."

Arnold, who could lead us into temptation and who always seemed to have an answer. Arnold, who found order in chaos. Arnold, who could muster confidence and control. Arnold, who never seemed to get into trouble despite his skill for starting trouble. Arnold, who could talk his way out of handcuffs. Yes, Arnold was needed now.

Light rain began to fall, and we hopped on our bikes and sped toward Eastfield Elementary and Middle School.

Toy Soldiers

Arnold was indeed at the back of the school in one of the covered areas where the girls often skipped rope during lunch hour and recess. The rest of the schoolyard was deserted. Arnold liked to play around the school, even on weekends. We knew he had to be more restrained around his house. Here he was safe to do what he wanted.

Arnold was kneeling on the cement, his back to us. He heard us coming across the school field on our bikes, turned, and seeing it was us, went back to whatever he was up to.

We put our bikes down and jogged over to him.

"Hey, Arnold," we both said.

"Hey," he replied, without looking up.

We knelt down to see what he was doing. Spread out before him was a fat, white candle which was lit. Matches, tweezers, some small scissors, a little bottle of red model paint with a brush in it, and a pile of green and brown toy soldiers—the cheap, molded kind that all of us had, though we were all on the verge of being too old to play with them.

"What ya doing?" asked Julian, obviously intrigued.

"Making after-battle carnage. Mutating GIs in the aftermath of atomic war."

Arnold's imaginative mode was beyond most of us, though in some ways it was younger. Maybe it was all those movies he was always talking about, where atomic fallout turned regular people or animals into giants and mutants. Or maybe it was comic books he devoured, like WEIRD WAR and SERGEANT SLAUGHTER.

"Observe," he said.

He took one of the green plastic soldiers who was carrying a machine gun. He held the machine gun part of the soldier over the candles flame until it began to smoke and bubble. The plastic was soft enough that Arnold could now pull the machine gun away from the body with the tweezers, leaving two misshapen, stunted arms, which he quickly shaped with scissors. He inspected the soldier closely and then set him down. The plastic hardened quickly. He took up the tiny brush, already covered in thick red paint, and touched up the ends of the stunted arms. The paint immediately transformed the green plastic into bleeding flesh, and it made the soldier look gory. Arnold summarized the scene: "Hands blown off by an alien ray-gun." We nodded approval. He stood the soldier to one side with other soldiers who seemed to have undergone various brutal accidents or mutations.

Arnold next selected a brown soldier who held a walkie-talkie to his ear. He held the front of the soldier over the flame until it was softened and wrinkled. Taking it off the flame, he laid it down and quickly sprinkled some sandy dirt over the melted areas. The dirt stuck to it, and, with the flat face of the scissors, Arnold squashed the dirt into the softened plastic so it looked embedded in the soldier, rather than coating it. Arnold: "Hit by radiation." We should have guessed.

Arnold picked up a third soldier identical to the first one. Again he removed the machine gun with the flame. But now he re-heated the stunted arms, making them sticky-hot, and then, going into his pocket, pulled out a thin, shiny, silver screw that he put into the soldier's arms, pressing it so that it stuck. He blew on the soldier's arms to speed up the hardening process, and then tested to make sure the screw would stay in place. He dabbled a bit of red paint on the head of the screw. Arnold's story: "After the atomic war, most weapons will be useless. Soldiers will have to use things like metal clubs to bash the heads of their enemies. This fellow has already made an impression on the skull of something with his metal club."

Arnold's wonderfully gruesome transformation of his army men held us, and for a few moments we forgot about last night. Future warfare was far more interesting.

Arnold considered his work finished. "So, what's with you two numbskulls?"

Julian could hardly wait to give Arnold the lowdown: "Jacob didn't come home last night. His mom was looking for him this morning. The sheriff and some of his guys are at the Slough place, right now. They were in the front of their place, talking. And his sister didn't come home either, last night. They've, like, disappeared! Gone!"

Arnold stood up and looked at me. I confirmed Julian's potted account: "Yeah. Mrs. Slough came around to my house early this morning, asking my parents if I was with Jacob last night, or seen him. I told them we saw him hanging around Eastfield Road. I didn't say anything about going up to Lovers' Lane—or that Gumboot was with us then. I'd be in crap if my parents knew what I was up to."

Arnold, no doubt unconcerned with my problem, was thinking. "He was with us when we snuck up on David Slagmann and whoever was in the meatmobile with him—"

"Yeah," he was there," I interrupted. "Over beside and past Teddy and me."

Julian added, "Yeah. Didn't see him after Billy dropped the flashlight."

Arnold picked up and carried forward the story: "And he's not there when we meet up at the Old Orchard, or when we leave and go down The Trail, right? Remember? When we stopped. He wasn't behind Billy. No Gumboot."

We walked around under the sheltered area in quiet, kicking a few rocks. The rain began to fall more heavily.

"So," Arnold said, thinking out loud, "that means he took off after we did our yelling at David Slagmann, and he didn't go home after that."

Arnold thought a bit more. "He must have met up with his sister somewhere. Too much coincidence that, like, on one night they would both not go home." He looked out into the light rain. "Where was she, I wonder? And so they haven't come home—"

"Well," I said, "we're not sure of that, really."

"What d'ya mean?"

"Well, they could be back by now. We couldn't tell when we went by the Slough place—I mean, if Gumboot was there or not. Or his sister. The sheriff's guys might have been there bringing them home, or just asking questions and stuff."

"So what's the big deal, then?" Arnold lightened, now out of deep thought. "Gumboot and his sister don't show up last night. Maybe they slept with the rabbits in one of the rabbit pens in his back yard—ha! Maybe Old Man Slough got them mixed up with the rabbits and took hold of their necks or thumped them with his bunny club. Snap and bonk!"

We didn't quite share Arnold's exuberance. He added another possibility: "Or, maybe they're not back—maybe they've gone for good. But where could a couple of goofs go? What's it matter?"

What did it matter? Were Julian and I just worrying about nothing? Arnold almost flattened our worries.

"Well," I began slowly, "I told my parents that I—we—didn't see Gumboot except earlier last night, hanging around the road. And they wanted to know what time that was and if anybody else saw him. I didn't say anything about going to Lovers' Lane and all that—I'd be grounded if they knew I was up at Lovers' Lane, sneaking up on parked cars." I even made myself a little nervous just talking about it.

Julian added, "And then that lost flashlight stuff with Billy, because if he gets caught about that, he'll have to come up with a story, or the truth, about where we were, and maybe about Gumboot being there. Billy will just blab it all out if he gets scared. He'll fink on us, all of us, maybe, if he gets forced. If he gets asked about the flashlight. We'll be up shit creek without a paddle!"

Arnold put together the pieces with a plan. "So, we need to get to Billy—tell him. We just go see him, to find out if he's said anything. Or if he went and got the flashlight this morning, then—"

Julian interrupted: "We went to Billy's. He wasn't allowed to come out. His mom said he was sick or something. Came home sick last night, she said."

We knew Arnold would not want The Watchers' Club's activities to get back to his parents either. In fact, his parents were probably stronger on the discipline front that even Julian's or my parents—it was just that he seldom got caught at anything.

"Okay. What we do," said Arnold, pacing a little. "We go to Billy's house. You guys stay hidden. It might look suspicious if you show up again." We nodded. "I go to the door. Tell her I have to talk to Billy for a second— about school or something. Mrs. Luckhert will let me in. Suck-hole to her a bit. When I see him, I'll find out if he went and got the flashlight and returned it. Or if he's said anything about last night. If he hasn't gone back to get it, then we go back to get it. If he has, there's no trouble. We're in the clear."

We nodded confirmation and Arnold continued: "Remember: Gumboot, when he finally gets back, or if he's back, isn't going to say anything about last night. When they ask him where he was, he'll just say, 'Duh, I dunno'."

Julian laughed, probably because he felt better.

"How do we get the flashlight to Billy if we find it at Lovers' Lane?" I asked.

Arnold answered, "We'll think about that later. First things first."

He had a point. He always did.

Arnold collected his soldier stuff and put it into a cloth zipper bag.

"Let's go," he said. "Back to my house, get my bike and drop this stuff off." He held up the bag: "The dregs of battle."

A LITTLE SMOKE

We three came flying down Eastfield Road on our bikes, full speed. The rain had let up a bit. We slowed down when we got close to the Slough place. The sheriff's cars had gone.

Arnold ordered, "Let's walk by. See what we can see."

We dismounted about forty or fifty yards before the Slough house, but on the other side of the road. We didn't want to look suspicious by rattling to a stop right in front of their place.

"Take a look," said Arnold, "but don't make it obvious. See if you can spot Gumboot, or his sister. Or anything."

From the angle of our approach, we could catch glimpses into the Slough backyard through the scattered evergreens surrounding their property. I thought I could, for a second, see someone out behind the rabbit pens, but because of the short bulk of the figure, it looked like Mr. Slough.

The front yard was still. Arnold crossed the road so that he was on the side closest to the Slough house. Julian and I kept on the left-hand side of the road, the side with the ditch. The only activity we could make out was a little white smoke coming out of their chimney.

When were further down the road, we cut over to Arnold.

"See anything—anything?" asked Julian. We kept walking.

"Nothing," Arnold said. "It was dead."

"I think I saw someone in the backyard," I said. "Out by the rabbit hutches or whatever they are. Pretty sure it was Mr. Slough, though."

"Should we go back and check it out?" said Julian.

"No—not a good idea," answered Arnold. "Too suspicious if we get seen. We don't want anything to do with all this, remember." Arnold turned to me: "You're pretty sure it was Old Man Slough, then?"

I returned to the picture in my mind. "Yeah, well—sort of sure."

"Okay. Let's get down to Billy's. You guys stop way before we get there. I go in on my own. Keep out of sight."

We continued down Eastfield Road, Arnold leading the way.

HORSE-EES

Julian and I pulled up short of the Luckhert house. We put our bikes by the side of the road and moved up behind the cover of some bush so that we could see the side of the house. Arnold continued into their driveway on his bike. He leaned his bike against the back stairs and went to the door and knocked. He looked back in our general direction for a second, probably to make sure we were hidden. The door opened. Mrs. Luckhert. The two of them stood there for what seemed to be a long time talking and gesturing. She finally let Arnold in and the door closed.

"I knew he'd get in to see Billy," Julian said. "I knew it. Arnold can talk his way out of a vault."

"Huh? Wouldn't you want to talk your way into a vault? Arnold wants to get in, not out."

"But it would be harder to get out of a vault than get in, duh."

"Not if it's locked. But Arnold had to get in."

"You got serious problems, man."

"Yeah. I got you."

We could carry on like this for hours.

Another minute passed while we watched for Arnold. I noted it was lunchtime, and I would have to be getting home soon.

"Same here," Julian said. "I'm starved. I could eat a house."

"A 'house'? You mean 'horse'? So hungry you could eat a horse."

"What? Who'd wanna eat a horse? Horse-ees are nice."

"You're so weird."

"I know you are, but what am I?"

"If there was a Weird Store, you'd be for sale there."

The sound of a door closing silenced our banter. Arnold joined us in a couple of seconds.

Julian rattled questions: "What'd Billy say? Did he get the flashlight? Did his dad notice?"

Arnold surprised us with his answer to Julian's hyper questions: "We're idiots."

"Huh?" said Julian.

"Of course he didn't get it! He wouldn't have gone back last night. It was too late. And remember how shaky he was acting on the way back? Probably thinking about what his dad was going to do to his nuts. And this morning he was sick, so he wouldn't have been able to get out to get it."

"So what'd he say?" I asked. We started walking down the road pushing our bikes.

"To make sure, I asked him, like, about if he got the flashlight. He said 'no'."

"Nothing else?" asked Julian.

"No, but as soon as he said he didn't get it, I told him we would go back to Lovers' Lane and find it. Get it back to him before his dad noticed."

"Yeah—we can do that," added Julian, who was raring to go.

Arnold added a little more: "Billy looked kind of lousy, and he started to say something—something, I think, about David Slagmann, in the van—but then his mom came in, and he stopped. She said I had better go so that he can rest."

"So we go get it, right? The flashlight," added Julian.

"Yep," said Arnold. "Sooner the better."

Once more, Arnold's sense of purpose and resolve bolstered our reserves, which were beginning to wan as hunger passed over us.

I noted as much: "But we should hurry. I gotta be back for lunch."

"Me too," said Julian. "I'm so hungry I could eat a—" Julian stopped and pulled a face—"a horse-ee!"

I couldn't resist: "He says he likes horse-ees. He says they're nice."

Arnold looked at us. "You guys are both a waste of space." Julian and I exchanged faces.

Because we didn't need cover, we took the side-road route to Lovers' Lane and to the clearing where David Slagmann had parked. Unlikely anyone would be around. Wouldn't take more than ten minutes or so to get there.

Arnold gave us hope as we mounted our trusty bikes: "The flashlight should be easy to find. We know pretty well where Billy was when he dropped it—the klutz."

"Yeah, the klutz," Julian confirmed.

And, once more, we were off.

Lower Eastfield's back roads were old, bumpy, and narrow. Some almost overgrown in places. They were not used much since mining activities had left the area years ago, leaving behind a few slag piles among the bushes, trees, and stumps.

We knew these back roads well, especially since the beginning of this last summer when we took advantage of the freedom our bicycles offered. Saddled to our Raleighs and Schwinns, areas once beyond our reach were now our easy domain.

We raced down to the end of Eastfield Road, and then took a side road to the right that circled back behind where most of the properties along the north side of Eastfield Road ended, including my own. This was a hard five-minute ride before we turned off into another, even smaller side road—this one without any name—leading to the clearing we called Lovers' Lane.

We could hardly wait to get there. The silver flashlight should be easy to find. We hadn't worked out how we would smuggle it back into Billy's basement once we had it, but Arnold would think of something.

The last bit the dirt road before we got to the clearing was straight for about fifty or sixty yards. But when we rounded the right-hand corner that would take us to this last straightstretch, what we saw ahead of us, right where we were last night, brought us to a jaw-dropping stop. Julian spoke the only words for those strained seconds while we stared down the road: "What is—!"

There, unmistakably, was Slagmann's meat truck, parked, it seemed, just about where it was last night. No question about it being Slagmann's vehicle. It was easy recognizable, even from fifty or more yards. You couldn't make out the exact letters painted on the back of the truck from where we were, but the yellow patterning of the writing with the red and black background was as clear as our confusion. SLAGMANN'S. BUTCHER.

"What is it doing...?" Julian asked.

What was also clear was that the driver's door was open. No one could be seen.

We froze until Arnold gave orders: "Let's get outta here!"

Arnold and I hopped on our bikes and made an abrupt turn. Julian still gawked. "Weissman, you idiot, clear out, before someone sees us!"

Julian snapped out of it and turned, and in no time at all he passed us as we made our getaway. We didn't stop until we were back to the safety of the bottom of Eastfield Road.

MAYBE

We got off our bikes and walked for a while up the road. We crossed over to the ditch side, since there was more room. It took a minute or two to catch our wind.

Julian, openly confused, and not one to gather his thoughts, babbled about what he saw: "What was the Slagmann truck doing there? You think that he—I mean David Slagmann—came back looking for, like what, the flashlight, or something else? Maybe looking for us—to pound us, if we came back? For bugging him when he was making out, or something? I didn't see him, or anybody—"

"No," I said. "No one. The door was open, though. The driver's door."

Julian caught up to Arnold, who was walking his bike a little ahead of us.

"So what's he doing back there at Lovers' Lane?" Julian asked.

"Don't know," said Arnold, who never liked not-knowing. "Maybe— maybe looking for us." Arnold had to think about this: "But why would he think we'd even be there—in the middle of the day? Why would he think the idiots—us—who snuck up last night, might go back and hang around the next day?"

He was right. Didn't make a lot of sense.

"Or," Arnold added, "is there some other reason he's there?"

"Well"—I spoke up from behind—"we did—go back, I mean. Like, we returned, just now, to get the flashlight. Maybe he has the flashlight. Maybe he thinks we'll come back to get it. It's a valuable flashlight, sort of. Maybe he picked up the flashlight last night, after Billy dropped it. Now he comes back, brings it back. Waiting for us."

Arnold wasn't so sure—"It's just a flashlight, not bait"—and he questioned all the possibilities: "But what would the chance be that we would come there when, right at that very same time, David would be waiting—right there in the open? Same place. We'd see him. He's not going to stick around waiting for whoever was there last night. Why care about catching a bunch of kids who didn't do that much?"

Julian offered something. "Maybe he left something there. Came back to get it."

Julian was forcing himself to believe that David Slagmann was not after us.

I tried another idea: "Maybe he came back with his girlfriend. To make out again."

"Yeah," said Julian, beginning to loosen up. "They were going at it last night. Round two—ding ding! Or maybe whoever he was with left her underwear there." Julian snorted a little at his own comment.

Arnold dismissed all of this: "You don't make out with the door wide open. Also, Sunday, lunch-time, broad daylight, is not make-out time."

This was tough.

We continued to walk up Eastfield Road, pushing out bikes. The ditch beside us was running fairly heavily.

We were almost up to Billy's house. We were all a little tired and hungry. As we plodded along, a car came down Eastfield Road toward us, slowly. It didn't take too long to dawn on us that it was one of the sheriff's cars. Questions about David Slagmann evaporated.

When the car was about even with us, it stopped. Two people were inside. The passenger was the big sheriff. The passenger side window rolled down and the deputy called out to us from the driver's seat: "You boys from around here, right?"

We stopped and nodded our yesses.

"You know the Slough kids?"

We nodded again.

"You boys seen them around? The older two? The boy and girl?" The deputy pulled out a little book in his shirt pocket to check the names. "Jacob and Esther. You seen them around?"

The sheriff said nothing, though he was closest to us. He just looked at us through his dark glasses.

We looked at each other. Julian immediately answered for us: "No— I mean yes, we know them, but no, haven't really seen them, no. At all."

Julian didn't sound that convincing, but that may have been because we knew Julian, and we also knew the half lie he was telling—the lie that kept getting bigger and bigger.

The deputy continued: "Now, if you boys were trying to find them two Slough kids, where would you look?"

"Don't know," said Julian, again too quickly, and again adding more than he needed to: "Well, I guess there's plenty back roads just around her, and Jacob always wanders around all over places, you know, like that."

The sheriff kept his gaze on us. We could hear muffled talking in the background coming through the car's radio.

The deputy at last went on: "Well, you boys see anything—anything, at all—you be sure to let us know. Tell your parents we said so." We nodded. The two officers kept their gaze on us. Finally he said, "You take it easy, now," and then added, "and keep out of trouble, ya hear." The big sheriff slightly nodded.

The car slowly pulled away down Eastfield Road.

Arnold immediately said, "Geezus Julian, you're worse than Billy for blabbing. You didn't need to tell them all that stuff!"

"What d'ya mean?" asked Julian. "I didn't tell them nothing."

Arnold: "You mean 'anything'."

"What?"

"Never mind." Arnold sighed.

The presence of the sheriff's cars cruising around in Eastfield shook us up.

"I gotta get going home," I said, getting on my bike. "Lunch."

Arnold and I would be going up Eastfield Road. Julian would go in the opposite direction to get to his house.

"Me too," said Julian. "The game is on soon."

Arnold stood there as we were about to go our own ways. The mystery would have to stay put. But Arnold stopped us peddling off. His face suggested something deeper crossing his mind.

"Maybe," he said, "just maybe the Slagmann meat van was there all night. Maybe it was left there, so it is in the same place because it was parked there all night. Right in the same place where we came across it last night. It never left Lovers' Lane."

Thinking about it, the Slagmann truck did seem to be right about where it was last night. We talked about it. Maybe David Slagmann couldn't get the truck started. Dead battery or something. That happens. Maybe he had come back to try to get it started. That could be it. But we didn't see him. Our questions had to be left behind. The flashlight would have to be left behind. Lovers' Lane would have to be left behind—for the moment, at least.

Arnold, however, couldn't let it go yet. "Meet here, right here, after lunch. An hour." He turned to me. "Get you on the way down."

And that was almost that—except that Arnold added the specifics: "We'll see if the Slagmann van is still there, later this afternoon. Might mean something."

Julian nodded, then it dawned on him. "But the game is on. The Dodgers!" Julian looked helpless.

Arnold directed him: "Figure it out. Be here, blabber boy."

Julian made off, and Arnold and I rode up Eastfield Road. Neither of us said anything. I deliberately avoided all the puddles and potholes until I peeled off into my driveway. There was too much to think about this weekend, and it wasn't over yet.

"See ya," I said, half looking back over my shoulder.

"An hour," Arnold replied, and he was off.

TANG AND QUESTIONS

Mom, in the kitchen, seemed to have been expecting me, maybe because I was a little late. Dad was likely outside somewhere.

Though I had taken breakfast almost halfway through the morning, lunchtime was scheduled as usual. I was hungry, but even more thirsty. We had covered quite a bit of distance on our bikes in a short time. To the cupboard for a glass and then to the fridge. Anything would do. I settled for Tang, which I poured out while I stood at the fridge with the door open. A little spilled on the linoleum floor. I downed one glass immediately, filled another, then sat down at the kitchen table.

Mom looked me from the sink. "Soup and a sandwich?" she asked. "I've got vegetable. And a baloney sandwich."

I gazed out the window and thought about the hunt for Jacob and Esther and then about Slagmann's van up there at Lovers' Lane—and somewhere, the stupid flashlight. In the bushes? The stories didn't fit together, but I couldn't pull them apart. The last few hours had spun my twelve-year-old head. I thumbed aimlessly through some magazine on the kitchen table.

While mom waited for some soup to heat up on the stove, she put the finishing touches on the sandwich.

"Did you see any of the other kids this morning? Did you ask them if they remembered seeing Jacob or Esther?"

"Huh?" I said, surfacing from my thoughts.

"Did you ask any of the other kids if they saw Jacob or Esther?"

"Oh, yeah, well, I asked Julian. He didn't see Jacob any more than me last night. You know, we saw him earlier in the night. Not Esther at all."

Mom put the sandwich in front of me. "Did you talk to anyone else—any of the other kids you were with last night?"

I took a big bite, chewed, swallowed, and answered: "Yeah, I saw Arnold Rheinhurst, too. Doesn't know much either, except that he saw Jacob last night, kind of when we did." I swallowed the last bit sandwich. I was surprised mom hadn't interrupted to tell me not to talk with my mouth full.

"Anyone else?"

"Oh yeah, I went to Billy's house with Julian. He couldn't come out because he was sick. He was with us too—last night, when we were outside, on the road. For a while."

Even as I finished saying all this, it seemed like I had said too much. Not in terms of information, but that I was too chatty. Mom could somehow make me chatty without much effort—especially when I wanted to say nothing and she was after something.

Dad came in, got a cup of coffee and sat at his usual place. My vegetable soup arrived at the same time—it was vegetable alphabet soup. Mom took her place at the table. The feeling of being surrounded, just like at breakfast, came back. It would be hard to dispatch with the hot soup fast enough. More questions I did not need. I aimlessly moved some of the letters around in the soup to cool it down.

"Just been up to the Sloughs," dad said, taking a drink of his coffee and addressing his words to mom. "See if there was any news, or any way to help."

"Any news?" mom asked, immediately.

"No," he answered. "The sheriff and his deputies were up there earlier, up at the Slough place. They been looking around the Eastfield area the last couple of hours. Probably start going property-to-property tomorrow, searching, talking to people—if the kids don't show up by then. They're bringing in a few deputies to help."

"Mr. and Mrs. Slough must be worried sick," mom said, shaking her head. "Why would those kids just have taken up and left, just like that?" She drifted into a drink of her coffee before attempting to emerge with some hope. "Maybe they've gone to see some relatives, and didn't tell anyone."

"No," said dad, "No kin around these parts, none at all. And they wouldn't have had money, either. No sign of packing."

One part of me wanted to say that I had seen the sheriff and his guys also—twice, in fact. It seemed better, though, just to listen. Arnold's principle to "volunteer nothing" held me silent. I worked the sandwich, dipping it into the alphabet soup and dunking some of the letters.

Dad turned to me: "You see any of the other kids this morning? You ask them about the Slough kids?"

I didn't want to say that mom had already asked me that, since it might look like I was hiding something. "Yeah," I said, "but they don't really know anything much."

"No one saw them after you saw Jacob earlier in the night, out on the road?"

"No, don't think so."

"Who were you with when you saw Jacob?" dad asked.

I tried to remember if I had said anything this morning about who exactly I was with. I couldn't remember the details, so I started out cautiously. "Julian was there. Playing together. Catch and stuff. Up by the street light, later on. Hanging out. Talking baseball and stuff."

Dad said nothing, which made me a little nervous. "Oh yeah—and Billy and Arnold came by, for a while." Had I said that before?

Dad's silence suggested I hadn't said enough, and so I offered more. "Teddy Sullivan, too, came by." Yes, I had said pretty well the same thing earlier. So far, so good.

"Did Jacob come with someone, or was he on his own?"

I answered right away, mainly because it was the truth: "On his own. He was sort of around. You know."

Despite the information, mom and dad's concerns filled the air. That dad went up to the Slough place pointed to the seriousness of missing kids.

Dad came up with more, directed, it seemed, to mom—like he was saving it. "Seems the last time Esther was seen was at the high-school basketball game yesterday. The game started just after dinner. She sang the anthem. No one seems to know where she went, after the game. Mind you," dad went on, "no one at the game would know that she's even missing—not yet." Dad thought a bit. "The sheriff's deputies will probably start talking to kids who were at the game, see if they know where she went when the game was over, which was nine o'clock, thereabouts. Maybe she went to stay with someone after the game."

"That's when she was seen last?" mom asked.

"Seems so."

"And Jacob. The last time Jacob was seen was by the boys last night out on the road…"

We all sat there, we three. Outside it was clearing up a little, even if inside it seemed like fog had moved in. Mom held her cup in both hands. Dad finished his coffee and put his empty cup down.

He spoke slowly and carefully, finding his way as he went along, turning to me: "If you saw Jacob around, say, about eight-thirty last night, and the basketball game in Silverford was over at about, maybe, the same time or just later, then Esther and Jacob were not together then, or they couldn't have been just after that."

We all thought some more. Was it best now—right now—to tell them the truth? Just tell them? That Jacob was with us later than that? That would mean telling them about going to Lovers' Lane. About The Watchers' Club. My sandwich was almost gone. The alphabet soup was my only escape. Using my spoon, I randomly played with four letters that floated up from left to right: S, T, C, A. I floated them around and came up with "SCAT."

Dad went on: "How did they get together—where, when?"

Dad did not usually do this thinking-out-loud thing, but he returned his attention to me. "Did Jacob seem like he was going to go anywhere after you saw him? Did he have anything with him?"

I stopped and held my full soup spoon of "SCAT" half-way between the bowl and my mouth. The "S" noodle-letter slid off the spoon and into the bowl. "CAT." Of course, Jacob at about that time was going to go with us to Lovers' Lane, but there was only one answer I could give. The words crawled out: "No. Don't think so. He don't—doesn't—say that much."

"CAT" disappeared into my mouth like they were going into a tunnel, and I looked down at all the jumbled letters in the broth. No words. The lie was getting big. I had to add something that might lessen the guilt building into the deception. "Jacob—he may have been around later, too, maybe, but not with us." I shrugged.

Saying this last bit made me feel slightly better, so long as the extra thought didn't jeopardize what couldn't be told.

I now guzzled soup directly from the bowl, which mom did not like. But she had bigger business beyond my table manners. "You saw him only once last night, you said?"

"Yeah, I think so." Again, the lie and the truth were getting hard to keep apart.

Dad continued his verbal sleuthing. "You mean you think you saw him only once—a little later than about eight o'clock?"

"Yeah."

Oh, boy, I needed to get out of there, but I also needed to look like I didn't need to get out of there. My own story was confusing me. I asked if I could be excused. If I started to stand up with the plate, bowl, and glass, I might get permission by default.

Mom may have picked up on my hurried, unsettled sense. "We know you must be upset—confused with all of this," she said. "Jacob and Esther missing. The sheriff and his men looking around. Any information may help. It's important."

Dad was not so soft: "We need to let the sheriff's office know what we know. If you saw Jacob just after eight, eight-thirty, some time, and Esther was at the basketball game at about the same time, or just leaving it—this is important. At that point they would have been a ways apart." Dad was beginning to sound like he was on a case or something. "We need to phone the sheriff and let them know this. You understand, son?"

Dad saved "son" for important moments. "The sheriff may want to talk to you and your friends who might have seen Jacob last night. You kids may have been the last to see him before he disappeared, out along the road."

Those letters and chewed up words churned away in my stomach. I put on my reassuring face: "Yeah, okay." I stood there with my hands full. "May I go now—please?"

"Yes," said mom.

To the sink. To the possibility of getting out of the kitchen alive. To my bedroom. But on my way mom stopped me cold: "One more thing," she said.

I turned around, fearing for the worst. What now?

"One more thing," she repeated.

"Yeah?" I waited, expecting a final question that might just break me.

"Clean up the Tang you spilled by the fridge."

"What?"

"The Tang. You spilled some by the fridge. On the floor."

"Oh—oh yeah."

I never thought a request to clean up after myself might offer some relief. I took a cloth from the sink, rinsed it hastily under the tap, and gave the spill a quick wipe. My parents watched like it meant something.

Life was for that one brief moment was simple. Tang—what the astronauts used in outer space, and where, as things closed in, I might have preferred to be.

OUT THERE

I retreated to my bedroom and closed the door behind me. Despite the gloomy daylight, I left the light off.

I sat on my bed for a moment or two, then lay down, looking at the ceiling, dazed by mysteries and events going on out there, right now, beyond the momentary, simple quiet of my bedroom. Jacob and his sister were somewhere. When did they meet up? It must have been after we were up a Lovers' Lane. Out there—the sheriff and his deputies, searching Eastfield and asking questions. Radios crackling with information and exchanges: "ten-four" and "copy that" and "over and out." Out, yes. David Slagmann also somewhere out there, maybe waiting for us back at Lovers' Lane, or just trying to get his dad's car going. Why was the driver's door of the Slagmann van left open? The flashlight also had to be out there somewhere. By the clearing? Did David Slagmann have it? Had Billy's dad noticed it was missing yet? Did Billy confess to what we were up to last night? Arnold, Julian, and I had our stories straight. For the moment, Billy was probably safe beneath the covers of his bed, protected by the sudden fever or something that fell over him last night. We still had to get to him—tell him our cover story. Tell Teddy, too—that would be easy enough. Arnold lived close to him.

I thought about Mr. and Mrs. Slough in their brown old house that smelled like cat piss . . . all those pictures and little statues of Jesus on yellowed walls, waiting to hear about their two kids. Little Piggy Slough: the younger brother, probably rooting around in the junk in their yard or among all those rabbits awaiting slaughter, his runny nose drawing two wet, dirty lines between his nose and lips. Out there, right now, just beyond the walls of my room, my own dad probably talking to the sheriff's office about what I had said.

Suddenly nothing was simple.

Half an hour or so went by as images and questions passed through and around me in various combinations. I thought, too, of Arnold's attempt to at least solve one part of the moment's confusion—Arnold...I had almost forgotten! I was supposed to meet him!

Mom was still in the kitchen, tidying up. No sign of dad. I flew by her, throwing out some parting words about as fast as I could: "Just going out to horse around, down the road—back before dinner."

She called out her usual departing words, "Don't be later for supper." And she added, "And be careful!"

Colliding Worlds

I hopped on my bike and peddled to the end of the driveway, skidding to a stop in the gravel. Timing was about perfect: Arnold was coming down the road.

He pulled up beside me. "No sign of life at the Slough joint," he said.

"Nothing?"

"Nope—not a creature was stirring, not even a louse. One of the sheriff's cars was cruising around up by the school, though."

"Geez," I said. "They're all over the place."

"I talked with Teddy for a second. He's okay with the story that we didn't go up to Lovers' Lane, and that we saw Gumboot around eight o'clock, or around there."

This was a relief. Even though Teddy's parents didn't care or worry too much about what Teddy was up to, he might say something that could get back to our parents.

"Yeah" said Arnold, "and your crank-butt neighbor Old Man Bryer seems to be checking out everyone, watching who goes up and down the road. Sitting on his veranda inspecting everyone who goes by. Like he's some kind of security guard or something. He gave me the once-over. The guy's a certified crank."

"For sure," I confirmed.

Old Man Bryer didn't like us kids. He had little time for our shenanigans, and he let it be known that he didn't like anyone going anywhere near his tidy property. Teddy once told us that Bryer kept a shotgun loaded with rock salt just for trespassers. "How'd you know that?" we asked Teddy. "He shot me right in the ass with it, once," replied Teddy, almost proud, adding, "Stung like a bugger, too. But I'll get him back." We believed him.

That Bryer was now so suddenly concerned about the Slough family was weird, since they were the "riffraff" he so strongly wanted to rid the Eastfield of. Or maybe that's why he was so interested.

Arnold focused on what was happening and what he might do: "Yeah—everyone's got their knickers in a twist about the missing Slough munchkins. As if anyone would miss them. Probably got lost following some smelly brick road. Didn't the Scarecrow want a brain? Those two could use one, too." Arnold could be cold and funny at the same moment, though you could tell he was genuinely curious about their disappearance. No doubt he'd like to solve the mystery before anyone else, but not because he wanted to help the Sloughs. He just figured he was that clever.

"So," Arnold added, "we get over to Lovers' Lane again. See if the Slagmann meat truck is still there. Gotta be gone by now, since whoever was there earlier probably got it started up, or had it towed away, or if that wasn't the problem, they might have left by now. We can look for the flashlight, too."

"Yeah," I said, though going back didn't appeal to me. Arnold pulled out a pack of Juicy Fruit gum and gave a stick to me. We unwrapped in silence and flicked away the paper and foil. I started to tell Arnold about what my dad figured out.

"Esther Slough was at the high school basketball game in Silverford last night. Sang the anthem at the beginning of the game. And the game was over around when we were first with Jacob—you know, under the light along the road when we met up. You said he was there, right?"

"Yeah. He was there. In the shadows, like usual."

"No one knows where Esther went after the game or what—or who she was with, where she was going."

"What'd you say—to your dad?"

"Nothing. He thought Esther and Jacob must have got together sometime after that. Sometime after about eight-thirty. With the basketball game just over. He wondered how they would have got together, being, like, a few miles apart."

"Okay. He doesn't know—that Gumboot was with us for an hour or more after that, when we went to Lovers' Lane, right?"

Arnold was checking my story, since we had already agreed that our Watchers' Club outing last night was not to get back to any parents. "No way!"

Arnold did some figuring along the lines of my dad. Walking our bikes, we started down the road to meet up with Julian: "So, if Gumboot did meet up with her, it would really have to be at least, maybe, nine-thirty, or even a little later, getting on to ten, or something—'cause that's just about when I noticed he wasn't with us, when we were walking down The Trail."

"Yeah. After Billy started acting weird."

"But," calculated Arnold, "Gumboot was there when we spied on Slagmann and his girlie friend, right?"

"Yeah. He was closest to Billy. I remember. Remember, I thought he said something when we were yelling things out and running away."

"Yeah, you said that." Arnold was suddenly interested. "What'd you say he said?"

"'Horror,' or something. Teddy said he said 'horse'."

Arnold squinted. He seemed to conjure a partial thought. Arnold did like to have partial thoughts, so he kept it to himself.

No matter what we talked about, the two separate worlds kept colliding—Jacob and Esther's disappearance, and then the events surrounding our thing at Lovers' Lane. Maybe getting the flashlight back to its rightful place would restore things to their right places.

Arnold read my mind, or maybe I had read his: "We gotta get that flashlight back to Billy's," he said. "Then our story about last night stays with us. It's gotta be where Billy dropped it. We get it. Smuggle it into Billy's house. His old man won't go too nuts if he finds it in Billy's room—we're not going to be able to get into his basement and put it back exactly where it was supposed to be. But if he thinks Billy had it out to look at it, he probably won't be too mad and just tell Billy to put it back next time. Without it back, Billy will crack under his dad's questions about where it went. Then we'll all be in deep crapola."

No kidding. We got on our bikes. Arnold felt confident, even a little cocky. "I can probably get into see him again later today—tell his mom I have some homework or something for him that I need to explain. Then just sneak the flashlight in—leave it somewhere in his bedroom."

Arnold had one final, odd remark as we started to peddle to meet Julian:

"You ever eaten rabbit?"

"No. You ever?"

"Nope."

"What's it taste like? Chicken?"

Arnold smiled his cunning smile. "No. Like cat."

DING DONG BELL

Early afternoon: the morning gloom lifted to become an unexceptional dull autumn day, though nothing even close to normal had taken place this particular day.

Arnold and I peddled quickly down Eastfield Road to meet Julian— or at least as fast as Arnold permitted.

In a few minutes we intercepted Julian on his way to join us. He was out of breath. We pulled over to the side of the road to make our plans, but before Arnold could lead us forth, Julian spoke: "Guess what?"

"What?" I said.

"Well, okay. Well, two things, really."

"What?" I repeated, instantly impatient.

"My parents know about the Slough kids being missing. And they know the fuzz are looking for them. They asked me about it. They were talking on the phone to someone."

"Who was talking to who?" I asked.

"My parents! To the fuzz!"

"What'd you say to them?" asked Arnold.

"To who? The fuzz?"

"No, to your parents, you dolt!"

"What I was supposed to say."

"Which was—?"

"That I saw Jacob last night, up by the light, around eight or so, and that he wasn't really with us. Then he wandered off. That's what I said. So there."

Julian was flustered.

Arnold noted that he had told his parents without them even asking.

Julian and I were surprised, and even a little impressed, even if it broke Arnold's law to "volunteer nothing." He continued: "I told them what they needed to know: as little as possible." Arnold read our surprise. "You see, if I tell them before they ask me, they won't be suspicious of me for not telling them in the first place. Head them off at the pass."

Arnold passed on the one further bit of information to Julian that he had already told me: "And I saw Teddy. I asked him if we wanted to come with us, but he was working on some old car—some piece of junk he was trying to get running."

We stood and looked at each other. And then I remembered: "So what's the second thing?" I asked Julian.

"What you mean?"

"You said there were two things," Arnold impatiently piped in.

"Oh, yeah," Julian smiled. "The Dodgers are winning. They'll win! Four straight!"

Arnold groaned a little. "Who cares? A bunch of guys wearing short pants chasing and throwing and hitting a little white ball. Whoop-de-doo."

Julian didn't care, and for a moment he thought he was clever: "But the Dodgers do that better than anyone."

Arnold ended the conversation: "Yeah, better than my butt."

This matter settled, we moved on with our plan to get the flashlight. While we walked with our bikes, Arnold did our collective summing-up: "The flashlight is probably right where Billy dropped it, with the light turned on. Slagmann's butcher-mobile should be gone by now. If it's still there, then we vamoose. Old Slagmann will likely need it for his butcher business tomorrow, so it's got to be out of there soon. Even if he needs a tow truck."

Julian had an idea: "Yeah, we just sneak up. Not takes roads. If the truck is still there, we can check out what's going on."

Arnold needed to think about this. We continued down toward the turn off that would take us toward Lover's lane. We walked on the ditch side of Eastfield Road. There was still quite a run-off flowing down, even though the harder rain had given up a day or two ago. Arnold stopped us: "Check that out!" He was looking in the ditch.

"What?" said Julian.

"There," pointed Arnold. His finger took us to the body of a dead cat, half submerged in the middle-flow of the water. Hung up among some debris and with water spilling around it.

We put our bikes down to take a closer look. It was a skinny black cat—an adult—with a few random white markings.

"Seen it before?" asked Arnold.

"No," I answered.

"Me neither," said Julian.

With so much space around Eastfield, there were opportunities for strays to survive. "Feral," my dad called them. Some we came to know, or at least recognize, as they made their cautious way through the bushes and sometimes scooting across the roads. Some people blamed the number of strays on Mrs. Raskolnikov, the witch lady, who died a few years back. She had quite a few cats, and when she passed away, most disappeared into the fields and bushes around Eastfield, where they earned keep by catching birds, rats, mice, and accepting occasional handouts. A few still hung around her decaying, empty house, which probably sheltered them. So it was not such a big deal to come across a dead cat here or there. There had even been a case of someone throwing a sack of newborn kittens into the ditch up past my house not that long ago. No one found out who did it, but mom reported it to the Silverford SPCA, who could do little more than come and take away the sack. We kids were divided on who we thought might have done it. Arnold and Teddy guaranteed it was the bunny slayer, Mr. Slough. Julian and I thought it might be Old Man Bryer, whose property often seemed like a fortress. He would never have allowed stray cats to settle around his place. And he had that salt-shooting shotgun.

Arnold found a long stick and got part way down into the ditch, his feet inches from the water. He poked and pushed the cat corpse until it dislodged and began to tumble and drift in the ditch's current. We watched it swing around and then sink and rise as it slowly floated away from us.

"Hasn't been dead that long," Arnold noted.

"How'd you know?" asked Julian.

"Body isn't that stiff. Bodies stiffen up after they've been dead for a while." The poor cat continued its watery voyage.

"We'll follow it," said Arnold, who was more intrigued by the dead cat than Julian and me. "See where it gets to—a final resting point."

We picked up our bikes and walked beside the ditch. The cat's pathetic little face showed itself every now and then.

Once more it got hung up on some of branches in the ditch. Arnold again poked it along. "It's a mother cat," he said. "Just had kittens. See—it's got a bunch of new nipple things."

Yes, the underside of the cat was punctuated with pink, slightly swollen teats.

The cat moved in the small current again.

"How d'ya think it died?" Julian said.

"Road kill," I answered.

Arnold was not convinced. "Maybe some vicious dog—crushed its neck in its jaws. Maybe a racoon not liking competition. Or maybe it choked on a rat." Julian sort of laughed at this, but he stopped himself not knowing if it was supposed to be funny. "Or maybe there's a pussy slayer on the loose in Eastfield." This made us think. Arnold relished the moment by adding, "Even maybe—maybe even among of us."

For fun, Arnold and I both looked at Julian, who said, "What?"

Arnold added, "Could have been curiosity. Killed the cat, you know."

The cat's down-stream progress in the large ditch took us to a pipe that crossed under the road.

"Quick—to the other side!" said Julian. Despite my wish to get on with our other business, I went along. We got there and waited a few seconds. The cat didn't come out of the other end of the pipe.

I pointed out the obvious with the hope of leaving the scene: "Must have got caught up in the tunnel. Let's go."

"Yeah," said Arnold in his best, spooky voice. "We'll leave the pussy in the tunnel of love."

"No," said Julian, trying his best to be as dramatic as Arnold. "The tunnel of death!"

Arnold seldom allowed himself to be one-upped. "The cat was already dead before it went into the tunnel."

"Come on," I repeated again.

We began to move on, mounting our bikes.

"And no," Arnold said, remembering the suggestion Julian had made minutes ago, "we better go the road way. We won't be able to sneak up so easily in the daylight. We can move faster on our bikes, too, if we have to."

I agreed, and with the poor little mother cat stuck in its tunnel of love—or death, or whatever—we once more headed off, and I, at least, was thinking of the kittens of that sad, dead mother cat.

TRACKS

After one more turn, we were on the nameless secondary road that would take us to the Lovers' Lane clearing. Arnold, a little behind, stopped. Julian and I stopped and looked back. Something must have been up, or Arnold had second thoughts.

"Why we stopping?" I asked. Not another dead animal, I hoped.

"Look," he said.

"What?" questioned Julian.

"Tire marks," said Arnold.

He was right. There seemed quite a few tire marks in the wet dirt, especially for a road hardly ever used.

"New ones," said Arnold. "It rained lightly this morning, and the roads were already wet from harder rain earlier. Any marks made before then would have been washed away."

Again, he was right. The marks were definitely fresh.

"Were they here before lunch?" I asked. "When we were here earlier?"

Arnold pondered, speculated, and directed. "Don't think so. But then we might not have noticed. There would have been no need to look. Now there is."

This added seriousness to what we were up to—not that we needed it. "For sure," he added, "these are pretty new."

Julian tried to put it together. "So that means there's someone down at Lovers' Lane. Right now." This was less a conclusion than a question.

"Could mean that," said Arnold. "It looks like more than one car has come—or gone, or, more likely, come and gone."

Arnold scrutinized the road, as if trying to imagine what might be ahead. We three stood there, holding our bikes. This was suddenly creepy and confusing.

Arnold rescued us with a possibility: "Could be...could be that someone has come, or came, maybe, to help get the Slagmann van started, or to tow it out of here—if there was something wrong with it last night, if it couldn't get started. So they've gone down the road. They may have left already. That would mean"—he calculated for a second—"at least one new set of tire marks in, and one set out. Maybe two if they got the truck started, or if they were towing it out."

Our eyes returned to the road beneath our feet for conclusive evidence. But as Arnold quickly pointed out, it wasn't there: "The tire marks overlap. Whoever came down could still be there."

Arnold seemed baffled, which was not like Arnold. All at once he said, "I'm an idiot!"

If anyone one else in our gang ever said anything like that, the comeback would have been unanimous: "Tell us something we don't already know." Coming from Arnold, and coming at this point, we said nothing. He filled us in: "If these car tire tracks were made after we were here earlier, then they would be on top of our own tire tracks, the ones made by our bikes when we were here before."

This was almost complicated, but we got the idea.

"Yeah," said Julian, nodding slowly, and now looking behind at the clear tracks we just made.

Arnold looked ahead. "See. Our tracks from this morning," he said.

We could see some thin, twisting lines that must have been made by us earlier. Arnold approached them, walking his bike. We stayed beside him. He stopped. "Look," he said.

Parts of our clear tire marks had been erased by the fresher tire markings. His conclusion was immediate: "A car, or maybe cars, has been past here since we were here."

This still didn't answer the question about who it was, or if whoever it was had now come and gone—or even whether the Slagmann meat truck was still there.

"So, like, do we take a look?" asked Julian, "or do we just get outta here?"

Arnold worked on our next move. He smoothed his hair back. Unlike Julian and me, he was not wearing a baseball cap.

We were only a minute or two from final turn before the straight stretch, to the point where, this morning, we saw the Slagmann truck from a safe distance. We knew we could not be connected with being at Lovers' Lane last night. Unfortunately, with what we had been telling our parents, we were moving steadily away from the truth and from safety, and all the time it was getting harder to go back. All we could do, it seemed, was cover up, or try to repair the situation, but this was becoming hard. And if we were seen here now, maybe by David Slagmann, or someone else, the connection might be made. Yet what were the chances this might get back to our parents? David Slagmann had no connection with us or any of our families. Even if he saw us, he probably wouldn't know who we were. What was the proof? The flashlight! That stupid flashlight! That klutz Billy!

The idea of the flashlight brought me out of my floundering thoughts and back to the moment. We looked down the road. A decision loomed.

"We go," said Arnold. "Take a look." He looked to our responses, which were mainly empty. "We are, after all, The Watchers' Club."

I guess we still were, though this was shrinking as a good thing.

Something in me said this need-to-know was trouble. But we needed the flashlight. We needed to get the flashlight back into Billy's house, and then we could return to business as usual. Curiosity was winning over caution, and we obviously weren't too concerned about what it proverbially did to the cat, despite what we had seen in the ditch just ten minutes ago.

We readied to peddle ahead. Arnold spoke the obvious. "Try to keep it quiet. No hurry. Slow down before we get to straightstretch. We peek around the trees there, down to the clearing where the truck was this morning. If anyone's there, we don't want to be seen. If we hear a car coming, we go off the road and into the bush. Hide. Got it?"

We got it.

We peddled forward, following the old dirt road and the new tire tracks, and leaving behind our own new tracks.

More Than Enough

We slowed to the final curve, and kept to the extreme right-hand side so that there was little chance of being seen from where the Slagmann truck had been parked. When we got within a few yards of our planned vantage point, we put our bikes down off to the side of the road. Arnold signaled quiet. We kept to the very edge of the road. If there was nothing there, then we could go and hunt for the flashlight. All could be well. Arnold would get the flashlight back into Billy's house, and that would be that. Relief, we hoped, was just a glance away.

Arnold, crouching, edged forward a little ahead of Julian and me. When he got to the point where he could take a look down to the clearing, he held up his palm as a stop sign. He would survey the scene, and then we would get our turn.

Turning his face from us as he looked around the bend, Arnold went forward a few feet more. Then he held still. We held our positions. We had been actors in this scene before. If the coast was clear, he surely would have immediately let up on the stealth. His stillness, and the time he was taking, seem to mean he could see something. What? Slagmann's truck still there? Then what do we do? Do we still try to get the flashlight?

Arnold turned back to us, and his face betrayed something between confusion and astonishment. "Geezus murphy," he uttered.

"What?" whispered Julian. "What?"

I cautiously moved forward with Julian to where we could peek down to the clearing. Geezus murphy all right! Two of the sheriff's cars were parked on angles beside and slightly behind the Slagmann van, which still had one door opened. A couple of guys, deputies maybe, moved around beside the cars, pulling stuff from the trunk of one of their cars, looking around the clearing, and talking on their CBs. It looked like one guy was taking pictures. One of the cars also had its lights flashing, and there were a few flashes. The big sheriff with the dark glasses we'd seen in the Slough's yard was also there. He stood somewhat away from the activity, by himself, sideways to us, hands on his hips. I backed out from my vantage point. Julian was right beside me, and he got a quick view before I pulled him back.

"Holy Moses," Julian said.

Arnold gave immediate direction: "Julian—to your house. To the garage. Quick!"

We pulled our bikes out, mounted, and left the scene as fast as we could, crossing the road with the pipe beneath it, where the unlucky black and white mother cat found its wet, cold, resting place. The tunnel of something.

RETREAT

Our ride to Julian's was reckless. Potholes and puddles meant nothing as we retreated through the gray afternoon.

We pulled into Julian's yard, scrambled off our bikes, and headed to the safety of the converted garage. We could hear, faintly, somewhere on the outskirts of Eastfield, the sound of a fire truck or ambulance, or maybe a police car. More important was the dash for the couch, since it was the only prime real-estate in the garage. Julian got there first and stretched himself out full-length so that there wasn't room for anyone else. Arnold cared less, and we resigned ourselves to a couple of chrome and plastic chairs, catching our breath in the quiet that followed.

Though we were warmed by our bike ride, the garage felt cold and damp.

"Julian," Arnold said, "get that heater thing going. It's freezing. Colder than a—than a kitty-cat corpse in a ditch."

Julian got up to turn it on. The moment he was off the couch, Arnold and I seized the opportunity to take his place. The heater operated more or less like a large toaster. We watched the coils turn bright electric orange.

Then Julian suddenly yelled out "Crumbs!" and tore away into his house.

"What's with him?" Arnold asked.

I had little doubt. "Gotta be the baseball game."

In a few minutes Julian returned, with a smile bigger than his face.

"Told you!" he said. "Told you! Gonna be the Dodgers in four!"

He pranced around a bit, but our non-response soon settled him.

Julian eventually started going through one his many shoeboxes full of baseball cards. Arnold sharpened a chewed-up pencil with his pencil knife. I found a hot-rod magazine on the floor and haphazardly thumbed through it.

The silence could no longer hold Julian. "So what was going on there? Like, there were twenty deputies there, crawling all over the place!"

"Four," said Arnold. "Five if you count the sheriff."

Julian's exaggeration nonetheless hit home. It felt like twenty. It felt like one hundred!

"Okay," said Julian, taking a breath. "What they doing?"

Arnold continued to whittle the pencil down. "They've been out, driving around, since before lunch—out looking for the two Slough numbsculls, right? Looking down all the back roads around Eastfield." Arnold stopped and looked at Julian. "Remember what you said right to the sheriff, bright boy? When they stopped us on the road and asked us about where we might look for the Slough kids?"

Julian looked puzzled. Arnold reminded him. "You said, 'Hey, there's lots of back roads around here. That's where you might look. Go look around the back roads'." Arnold was a champion blame-dumper. "While they were looking around this morning for the Sloughs, they came across Slagmann's van—by accident. That's all. They weren't looking for the stupid meat-mobile. Now they're trying to figure it out. But—"

"Figure what out?" I interrupted.

"Figure out what Slagmann's van doing there. Middle of nowhere. On a Sunday afternoon," Arnold answered.

"But it doesn't have anything to do the Sloughs," insisted Julian.

"They don't know that," replied Arnold. He stopped working on the pencil and tossed it into an empty tin garbage can where it made a singular clang. "They could never know that Gumboot was up there last night. At this point they wouldn't know that the truck being there would have nothing to do with him—or his sister, what's-her-name."

Yes, that was some kind of relief, but temporary given Arnold's next three words: "But we do."

"So," said Julian, "now what?"

The question hung.

Julian put his baseball cards back in the box and took out the Monopoly set. He returned to the table and began to set it up. Arnold and I helped, organizing the plastic houses, hotels, and the paper money. The heater's warmth began to spread. Financial wheeling and dealing might cancel our questions.

"I'm the banker," Arnold declared.

As we put all the monopoly pieces in their proper places, I tried to put the story together: "Okay, they find Slagmann's van. No one there with it." Arnold didn't stop my already-plodding narrative, which meant he too didn't see anyone else other than the sheriff and the deputies. "And now they're probably getting hold of old man Slagmann, telling him about finding his truck. Maybe Slagmann even knows where it is. Maybe David Slagmann went home last night and told his dad he couldn't get the truck started. So finding the truck is no big hairy deal."

This felt a little better—that is, until Julian spoke up: "What about the flashlight?" he asked.

The hubbub of the last half hour had pushed the object of our quest out of my mind. But not out of Arnold's, who said that if they came across Slagmann's truck, with the door open, like we saw it, and they couldn't find anyone there, they'd wonder what's going on, and they would start looking around. Which—it looked like some of them were doing. "And they might have found the flashlight. It wasn't that far from the truck. Unless, not likely, though, someone took it earlier. Maybe Slagboy picked it up after Billy the Klutz Kid left it there."

"So they'd keep the flashlight?" said Julian, trying to imagine all of this taking place out there.

"Yeah," said Arnold. "They'd keep the flashlight."

"Why?" returned Julian.

"Evidence."

"For what?"

"For nothing. They'll just take it away. What they do. Collect stuff at scenes of crime. The flashlight would not look like a piece of junk that had been just sitting there. It was brand new."

"But," agonized Julian, trying to organize his money into tidy piles, "there's no crime or anything, right?"

"The sheriff's guys don't know that. They're looking for missing kids.

They find a parked truck. Slagmann's. They figure it's stolen, maybe. They find a flashlight." Arnold did his best to sound convincing. "They'll have to figure out that the Slough kids, the Slagmann truck, and the flashlight have nothing to do with each other. They may be fat-ass doughnut suckers, but they're not totally dopey."

This should have reassured us. But oh, man—the sheriff and his guys may have the flashlight! So much for trying to rescue Billy from his father's anger. So much for keeping ourselves out of trouble. Billy would spill the beans, no doubt!

Personal worries took a more practical edge. Arnold added: "Let's say they've got the flashlight. But they probably won't be able to figure out where it came from, or who owns it. Or even really care. Why should they? Someone dropped it—or lost it. Nothing too strange about that, maybe."

"What about Billy?" said Julian.

Arnold was tough: "Well, Billy boy is just going to have to tell his dad he lost it, that he doesn't know where he lost it. He'll have to soak up a little daddy wrath."

Despite Arnold's confident, inevitable tone, this didn't sound convincing. Would Billy's dad buy the story that Billy lost it? He'd ask where. He can't remember? Billy would get in trouble one way or the other. That was that. Could we get to him and fill him with resistance to his father's interrogation? Could he keep the rest of us out of the picture? As far as we knew, he might have already told his dad what happened. Maybe the illness that seized him last night after we left Lovers' Lane might temporarily save him—or buy some time.

Monopoly. The only business left was to roll the dice to see who went first.

Julian rolled a measly two.

Arnold smirked, "Too bad. Snake eyes," and he proceeded to roll a seven—a three and four. "Lucky seven." I picked up the dice.

Arnold came up with possible consequences: "What's the worst?"

Arnold only liked questions when he had the answers. "Billy gets into trouble. Or, he finks on all of us and we all get into trouble for going up to Lovers' Lane. That's the very worst. We could just say we were horsing around in the dark with the flashlight. Looking for owls or something. We don't have to say anything about how the flashlight was lost, what we were using it for. We just say we—Billy—somehow lost it on the way. All we need to say."

Strangely, "the worst" was beginning to almost sound okay. If only it would all go away! One other item popped into my head: "Jacob?"

"What about him?" said Arnold, dolling out the final round of starter money.

"Do we say that he was with us after we left the road?"

Once more, worlds collided. Jacob's disappearance. The lost flashlight. I rolled a five—a four and a one.

"Gumboot won't say anything about anything. The clod barely talks. Look, it will go like this: we get Billy to take the heat and say nothing, except he lost the flashlight goofing around up The Trail. Maybe even Billy's dad won't notice it's missing for a while. The Slough dolts eventually show up"—and for the moment, unusually, Arnold seemed stuck for words—"and, well, we'll just play Monopoly." He smirked: putting his finger on one corner of the board, he added, "Just make sure you don't end here: 'Go to jail'."

With this we began our game, which continued late into the afternoon. Arnold steadily acquired most of the property along the Boardwalk. I concentrated on Utilities. Julian's unthinking strategy was to see how fast he could get around the board, as if it was a baseball diamond and he was accumulating runs. Instead, the only thing he accumulated was rent debts. Typical Julian.

In the end, Arnold had a stranglehold on the game. Julian resigned himself to poverty. My Utilities didn't come through.

By late afternoon we were worn out. It was time to head home for Sunday supper. Nothing was said about our next move. Things would happen on their own—unless, that is, we were going to make one more try to go back to Lovers' Lane to check for sure that the flashlight was gone, or unless we might try to talk with Billy and convince him to take the heat by himself. But all of this was moving beyond us and anything we could control, just like this Sunday afternoon that was likewise slipping away.

Monday was not something we looked forward to, but there was something reassuring about the idea of school. The predicable; the safety of the morning roll-call; the routine of school work; recess; lunch time; the smell. Even the threat of long-division would be welcomed compared to what we had taken on since last night.

HOPE AND FEAR

We left Julian in the garage with a "See ya tomorrow."

Arnold and I slowly rode up Eastfield Road. No traffic. For once we were not in a hurry. The late afternoon light was falling away, and at the same time the sky began to clear itself of the gray clouds that earlier hung above us.

A raccoon slipped across the road twenty or so yards ahead of us, heading toward Mrs. Raskolnikov's run-down property. We liked them because, with Zoro masks, they seemed to be able to break into anything. Others hated them. Jacob Slough's dad set deadly traps in order to keep them away from his meaty rabbits. We'd seen a few coonskin tails hung up around his place. Old Man Bryer shot them dead on the spot with a .22 if he spotted them on his property, so we heard. Dad once said Bryer was a champion sharpshooter with a good collection of guns.

When we got to where I would turn into my driveway, Arnold and I stopped. Seriousness descended as we stood in the spreading cold: questions might be waiting for me when I stepped through the door—questions that, when you look back, force you to grow up just a little bit more, even when, like Peter Pan, and despite the freedoms that growing up offered, it wasn't something you were sure you wanted to do right away.

"What's gonna happen, you think?" I asked.

"Depends," Arnold said.

Arnold had been doing some thinking of the complications and possibilities as we slowly climbed to this point along Eastfield Road. "Depends on when Billy gets better. Whether his dad notices the flashlight is missing. Or if we get a chance to talk with him before his parents, or his dad, talks to him. Or what Billy says, or says he will say. Maybe even on what Gumboot says, if anything, which depends on when he shows up. The worst might be that Billy spills the beans that we were with him when he lost the flashlight, and that Gumboot was with us when that happened."

"Yeah, which for me means that, like, I lied twice to my parents. About where I was, and then about not seeing Gumboot last night, later on. That's trouble for me, for sure."

"Yeah," said Arnold, though I knew that despite a strong sense of discipline within his family, he often managed to get away with murder. "We can talk to Billy if he makes it to school tomorrow, and if he hasn't spilled the beans about the flashlight, it might be okay."

With split hope and fear, I returned a "See ya" to Arnold, and I wheeled my bicycle up the driveway, past the rockery where, many summers ago, I captured a huge swallow-tail butterfly with Rebecca, the girl who used to live across the road. We surrendered the butterfly to Danny, her older brother, who used a magnifying glass to burn a perfect hole though its wings before he let it go to some uncertain fate. "There is a hole in everything," Danny said when he set it free. I didn't want to think any more about Danny and his grave fate, or if there really was a hole in everything.

DUM DADADUM

I put my bike around back, and went straight into the kitchen. The smell of supper reminded me how hungry I was. Mom was at the sink. Dad probably in the living room reading the newspaper.

"Hi," I said.

My entrance startled her, which was unusual, since she usually had an uncanny sense about my arrivals.

"Oh," she said, turning. "You scared me."

She dried her hands on a dishtowel. We stood there for an awkward moment. It was as if we both had something to say, but couldn't think of it. She looked over at the stove and its simmering pots.

"Dinner ready soon," she said, strangely hurried. "Wash up, then help me set the table, please." She walked over and peeked into the oven.

I switched on the long florescent light that stretched across the mirror above the bathroom sink, and turned the hot water on full and let it run. I took a deep look at my face. The steam quickly fogged up and distorted my reflection, almost as if I was viewing some alien being.

I turned off the water, let it drain, put in the plug, and filled the sink with mixture of hot and cold. I slapped the water over my face. With my finger I drew a circle on the mirror—and then two dots for eyes and round mouth. Not good. The face looked like it was screaming. I wiped it away, revealing once more my own face. I dried off, and hunger sent me back to the kitchen.

Simon emerged from his bedroom, where, supposedly, he was working on some college assignment. These days he seemed to put in an appearance on his way out or in, or when his own food detector went off, or when he wanted to borrow the car. My parents gave him a lot of room to do his thing, which, when I grumbled about his privileges compared to mine, I was told that when I got to college, I, too, would have the same "rights." College? What did that have to do with anything?

Simon greeted me—"Hey squirt"—while he pinched a few boiled carrots from one of the bowls.

Mom gave his hand a playful smack: "Wait 'til the food is on the table."

Simon looked at me while I carried plates, glasses, and cutlery to the table. "Getting into any trouble with those friends of yours?"

He wasn't looking for an answer. Dad came into the kitchen just as I deflected Simon's question with a sarcastically meaningless response that, as soon as it left my lips, brought back last night's confusion. "Yeah, the cops are after us." My answer fortunately disappeared into the hubbub of kitchen activities, though dad gave me a glance.

We launched into supper. Bowls and dishes made the rounds. These days the only noteworthy item at the table was the huge amount of food my brother managed heap on one plate, and then how fast he could eat it.

"Do you have to put so much on at once?" mom asked.

Chewing and swallowing like there was no tomorrow, Simon replied, "If I put it on the plate all at once, I won't have to ask for seconds. Save you the trouble of passing more stuff around or having to deal with leftovers. Conservation of mass and time," he added.

Dad just watched him but commented, "Slow down, buddy boy."

"Can't," said my brother. "Got to go to Ken's house to study. Quiz tomorrow. First one of the year."

I knew mom and dad were quietly impressed with my brother's apparent interest in the courses he was taking at the new community college, since, when he was in high school, he tended to goof off a little, and was more concerned with girls, music, and a little basketball.

The rest of us mere mortal eaters were probably less than halfway done when, with an empty plate, Simon stood up and declared, "Better get going. I can use the car, right?"

Mom and dad looked at each other as Simon looked at them. They had no reason to say no.

"That's fine," said dad.

Before he left the kitchen he asked, "They find the Slough kids?"

"No," said dad. "I might go back up after dinner to see if they're back."

"Weird," commented Simon.

"Dessert?" asked mom, changing the topic.

"Save some for me." Simon disappeared to his bedroom.

While Simon was at the table, he was the center of attention. I now uncomfortably inherited his place. We ate in silence, until Simon made a pit stop on his way through to pick up the cars keys. "See ya," were his parting words. Mom barely had time to get say, "Don't be too late—and drive carefully."

"I won't be and I will," Simon chirped. Simon of late had become increasingly impressed with his own wit. The outside door closed, and he was gone.

We returned to supper.

"So what did you do today?" mom asked.

I chewed. "Biked around with Julian and with Arnold. Played Monopoly at Julian's."

"Hear anything more from your friends—about either of the Slough kids, I mean?"

"Nope," I said. "They heard that Jacob didn't come home last night. Esther, too."

Dad piped in, "And they have no idea about where he went, after you saw him—or anything about his sister?"

"No, don't think so."

I picked up the pace in order to finish up dinner. I didn't want to hang around any longer than I had to. I, too, wanted to pass on dessert for a quicker get-away. But unlike my brother, I had nowhere I had to go.

We ate in silence, but not the kind that issued comfort. The silence directed my own thoughts to worrying about what my parents were thinking about, which seems to have been the missing Sloughs, which was not what I wanted to think about, and this in turn it brought me back to the flashlight that might shine its way to my lies about last night, to where simple mischief became serious trouble. *Whew!*

I stood up, chewing and swallowing at once, with my empty plate in my hands. "May I be excused?"

"Yes," said mom, "but don't talk with your mouth full."

She looked at dad who was judging my performance.

I stood and chewed a few more times, then swallowed.

I walked over to the sink to put in my plate and glass.

"Dessert?" mom asked.

"No. I'm plugged. Thanks."

I made for the exit.

"Any homework?" mom called after me.

"Nope."

"Okay, practice a little piano then. You have a lesson coming up."

"I'll do it right now." This may have sounded too good to my parents—that is, I didn't want to give them the wrong impression of complete cooperation, so I added, "So that I can watch TV later, right?"

I had begun lessons the previous year, somewhat reluctantly, but with a growing acceptance—so long, that is, that it didn't cut a chunk out of the time I could spend with my friends and in front of the boob tube.

I went to the spare room where the piano was and closed the door behind me. Faint sounds drifted from the kitchen. My parents would be cleaning up. Dad might soon be off to the Sloughs to see if the kids had come back. I warmed up with a couple of chord cycles which I could repeat mindlessly—A A A, D D, Em Em Em, D D... stubborn questions fell into wordless images...Billy producing the flashlight from beneath his jacket ...David Slagmann's weirdly frightened profile when the light from the flashlight struck him...A A A, D D, Em Em Em, D D...the sheriff talking to Mrs. Slough in her front yard...Arnold mutating a toy soldier to put a bloodied silver screw club in its hand...the open door of the Slagmann truck we saw this morning...the dead mummy cat in the ditch...the sheriff again, this time standing with his back to us at Lovers Lane...A A A, D D, Em Em Em, D D, A A A...

After vaguely working through was I supposed to practice, I went straight to my bedroom, turned on the radio, fished out a few magazines, and parked myself on my bed. Not quite seven o'clock yet, which was when Disney started. Sunday was the best TV night. Outside the rain started up again, and it sent a shiver through me. I eventually wandered into the living room. Mom was still in the kitchen. I plunked myself on the sofa, and waited for Jiminy Cricket to croon, *When you wish upon a star, it makes no difference who you are.* The bug's words were hardly consoling.

Disney ended, and Ed Sullivan stiffly introduced his regular fare of jugglers, comics, dancers, and singers. I asked if I could stay up to watch *Bonanza*—permission was granted on the basis of getting ready for bed.

As usual, the Cartwright brothers with their dad—"Pa"—solve everyone's problems while sorting out bad guys, thus making the Wild West a little less wild. Hoss finds a Mexican kid wandering around. Hoss coaxes a few words out of the kid while filling him with Hop Sing's cooking.

The boy has witnessed something bad. Pa sends his sons to check it out. They figure the kid's parents were robbed and were then shot by bandits. In the end, the robbers get taken out by the Cartwright boys in a blaze of bullets and bundle of fists. They find the kid's relatives, who, despite their broken English, are eternally grateful to the Cartwrights. *Dum dada-dum dada-dum dada-dum dada-dum-dum.* Once more, the Wild West is tamed. The end. Click.

I made my way to my bedroom via the bathroom and barely picked up part of a conversation between my parents. They were definitely keeping their voices down.

Mom asked dad, "The Slough kids back yet?"

"Not sure," he answered. "The sheriff's car was there, at their house. A deputy outside. I asked if the kids had been found. He said he couldn't say."

Mom hesitated. "What do you think is going on?"

"Not sure. Something's happened."

They continued their business of clearing up or whatever they were doing, and I retreated to my bedroom. Moments later I fell into bed just as mom poked her head into the doorway for a "Good-night."

"G'night," I responded, and turned to the wall.

Sleep quickly and heavily passed over me, but through it, I thought I could hear, out there, mixed with the wind and the rain against my window, the voice once more calling out from the dark, "JA-cob, Ja-COB."

4
TO SCHOOL

Despite slow-motion dreams of running blindly though dark fields with Mexican bad guys chasing me with a torch or flashlight or something, Monday morning came quickly. I had to be stirred from sleep, first by dad's "Rise and shine," and then, and few minutes later, by mom: "Better get up, mister. We all slept in a bit. School day."

She opened the curtain to let in what little dim light there was.

I dressed and then galloped through breakfast. Mom sat close to the radio, listening to the morning news. Dad had just left for work.

Teeth brushed, nose blown, jacket grabbed, lunch nabbed. My bike was around back, so I had to pass through the kitchen to say good-bye. Mom was still by the radio, having a cup of tea. She stood up as I came in.

"Bye," I said.

She stopped me with a look that might have meant she had something more to say, but she just came out with the usual, "Bye. Don't be late coming home from school."

I put my hand on the doorknob. She added, "And be careful."

The morning air was cold and damp. I stopped at the end of the driveway to see if I could spot either Billy or Julian coming up the road. No one in sight. But I was a little late.

I mounted my bike again, and turned up the road, head down, trying to get some momentum for the slight incline. When, in a couple of minutes, I was up to the Slough's property, the weekend came back, slowly at first, but then with a sudden, confused heaviness. I got off my bike, right in front of the Slough house.

A small cat, with coloration not unlike the dead one in the ditch we saw yesterday, huddled motionless by one of the old posts that supported the frayed gate to the Slough property. It looked as cold as I was beginning to feel.

The Slough house showed no signs of life. The morning's dullness was enough that you might expect to see some lights turned on from within their house, but there weren't. Nothing from their usually smoking chimney, either. I looked back to the cat. Gone.

I shivered. Needed to get going or I would definitely be late for school. On my bike to fight the uneven wind and the incline. I didn't want to clean blackboard erasers at recess, which is what Mrs. Easterbrook often made you do if you didn't get seated in class on time. Pulling away, I took one glance back toward the back of Slough property. Nothing. A few motionless crows over the rabbit pens. I set my will to the pedals.

Early Dismissal

The warning bell sounded, which meant I had a few minutes to get to my class. I rammed my bike into the bike rack and sped to the school's side door. One of the annoying girls in my class, Betty-Anne Travinash— or "Traveling-ass" as she was sometimes called—was, like me, also on the verge of being late, but she didn't hurry. She was always late. When we passed through the double outside doors together, she gave me a kind of scrunched-up nose greeting. I returned the face with what I hoped was bad attitude. She smiled back too nicely. The boy-girl thing had, this last year, become a little more complicated. But there was no time to dwell on what this all meant. Girls. Weird.

I raced up the stairs, leaving her in my wake. Stuff chucked into the cloakroom and to my desk just as the final bell went off. My desk was two seats from the back in a middle row, so I didn't draw too much attention getting there from the cloakroom. With the bell, the general noise level of the class went down to a whisper. Despite being a rag-tag bunch, Mrs. Easterbrook had us pretty well under control.

Mrs. Easterbrook was not at her desk at the front of the class, which is where she usually perched when the bell went so that she could pick off latecomers. I could see her through the partially open door to the right of the front of the class. She was in the hallway talking, or listening, to Mr. Orewell, the principal. His presence anywhere produced an immediate improvement in behavior.

I looked around the class. Arnold and Julian were off to my left, and we made eye contact. Arnold pointed to the front of my row, and I had to slip a little out of my seat to see what he was pointing at. Billy's desk. He wasn't there. I looked toward Arnold and Julian. Arnold made a throat-cutting gesture with his index finger. I wasn't exactly sure what it was supposed to refer to. Billy was, it seemed, still not well from Saturday night.

Mrs. Easterbrook returned to the class, closing the door behind her, though we could still see Mr. Orewell through the small window in the door to the hallway.

"Class"—she took a deep breath—"I…I just have to speak with Mr. Orewell for a few more minutes."

She looked out at us and seemed to forget what else she wanted to say. Then it came to her in rush when she was halfway to the door: "Grade six: take out your Social Studies readers and turn to the chapter on Christopher Columbus. The rest of you"—and here she stopped again before finding the words—"the rest of you take a piece of foolscap and begin writing a short story or poem with a picture about Halloween. I'll be back in a moment or two." She left the room, closed the door, and returned to talk to Mr. Orewell.

I foraged and found my Socials book, but Arnold again caught my eye. He pointed behind me, to my right, in the corner. An empty seat. Jacob, too, was not in class.

I turned back to Arnold. His face showed little expression beyond a kind a what-do-you-think look. Truth is, I didn't know what to think. Jacob hadn't returned home yet? Or maybe he came in late yesterday and was sick or something. I returned Arnold's look with a shrug.

I turned to the chapter on Columbus, though still wondering about Jacob not being there—and Billy, too. I started to read to myself: "With the support of King Ferdinand and Queen Isabella of Spain, Christopher Columbus set sail in 1492, hoping to…*wonder if Billy's dad noticed the flashlight was gone*…hoping to find a speedy trading route to the riches of India, Japan, and China. He bravely set forth in his three ships, the Pinta, the Nina, and the Santa Maria, out into…*did Billy mention to his dad that Jacob was with us*…the Santa Maria, out into the vastness of Atlantic Ocean. His trip…*and where is Jacob, and his sister*…His trip would not be easy, but his determination led to the discovery of America...*where did Jacob go after Lovers' Lane*...to the discovery of America. In America, Columbus Day, a holiday that celebrates Columbus' accomplishment, is normally held on the second Monday of October…"

Mrs. Easterbrook re-entered the class and sat at her desk. Normally, she would sit down after she had paced the rows to check how we were doing. But now she just sat at her desk, looking, without much expression, at her sea of motley faces, a cough or a sniff here and there, a whisper, shuffling feet, and once in a while a sigh. More strange is that we didn't do the roll call or our other regular morning rituals.

Mrs. Easterbrook just sat at her desk, looking out at us and then at the door.

By the time I got to the place in the Socials Studies reader about Columbus' other voyages, complete with colored dotted lines across the Atlantic showing his watery routes, concentration had sunk. The only thing keeping me from squirming to death were the pictures in the book—drawings of the old ships and weapons—and the occasional gaze out the window, where I could see the playing field and the surrounding old pasturelands that pushed into the more wooded areas of Eastfield.

Then a knock on the door and the unexpected entrance of Mr. Orewell, who couldn't have gone too far. Mrs. Easterbrook stood up and instructed us to stop what we were doing.

"Good morning," he said.

Mrs. Easterbrook, looking a little nervous, put her hand on her chair. He looked at us, and began, slowly: "The Silverford Sheriff has just made a visit to our school, and has informed me that, because of"—and here he held his words for a long moment—"because of a serious situation that has been…discovered in Eastfield, we will be asking you to return to your homes at first recess, rather than after school."

A buzz went through the class. Mr. Orewell quelled it by increasing his pace and mustering more authority: "At that time, some teachers and staff will be walking with you to your homes. Parents are also being contacted to come to the school to pick up students. Those of you who do not have parents at home during the day will stay at the school, and will be supervised in the gym. You are not to leave the school grounds unsupervised."

Mr. Orewell nodded to Mrs. Easterbrook and left, probably to pass the same message on to other classes.

Mrs. Easterbrook sat down and finally gave some direction: "Grade six—remember to take your Socials book home and continue reading to the end of the chapter. The rest of you—take home your drawings or poems and try to finish them."

We tried to carry on with our work, but there was too much in the air to settle down even one bit. The two school secretaries with clipboards came around, double checking attendance and trying to organize how people would get home. Recess did come soon enough, and then, in small groups, we were escorted outside by our teacher. Some parents were already waiting, and a few cars began to pull up.

Teddy, Julian, Arnold, and I managed to exchange some words while we waited. Julian, as usual, and in the absence of Billy, was the most hyper: "What was Mr. Orewell talking about? Why we supposed to go home? Weird, huh? And not by ourselves? Why can't we just walk or bike home, if we have parents there?"

Arnold's theory was at the ready: "The Slough kids. They're not back yet. And the sheriff and his posse are taking it serious."

"I don't give two rats' asses," added Teddy. "Thank the Slough dopes for getting us out of school. Okay with me. I can work on my jalopy."

Julian trotted out his own half-baked explanation: "Maybe there's, like, a disease or plague, and they don't want us to get plagued. So they're sending us home. Maybe what Billy's got. Killer disease."

We all looked at Julian and let a silent moment pass so that his dumb theory had enough time to choke itself.

Arnold put it to rest: "You see any doctors or nurses around, Einstein? Look over there." Arnold nodded in the direction of the front of the school where the flagpole was, about fifty yards away. We hadn't noticed. The sheriff's car. Mr. Orewell was leaning over, talking to someone in the passenger's side of the car. Mrs. Easterbrook beside him, arms crossed. Of all the teachers, why her?

"Like I said, Arnold continued, "something's up—more than just a couple of missing dimwits or"—here he looked at Julian with a touch of disdain—"or some contagious disease you get when you sneak up on people making out in cars and yell out something about cutting up meat." If we hadn't been so interested in the reasons for the dismissal, we might have had more fun at Julian's expense.

The schoolyard began to slowly empty. I began to think that wherever we went, the sheriff seemed to be there: there on Eastfield Road, there in front of the Slough place, there up at Lovers' Lane, and here, now, at our school. Like he was trailing us, though I knew this was stupid. I let fly by kicking a rock that, until this moment, my foot had toyed with. I connected, and the thing whacked against the nearby wooden fence that marked the perimeter of the schoolyard, making a pretty good noise that, just for a moment, got a little attention. I even surprised myself.

"Nice one," Teddy noted.

At the same time I saw mom from the corner of my eye. "Maybe we can do something later. Meet or something." This sounded half-hearted.

They echoed a "See ya."

Mom, walking quickly, met me halfway to the car, and gave me an embarrassing hug. She called over to Julian: "Julian, you are to come with us. Your mother asked if I could give you a ride home."

Julian hustled over. Just before we got into the car, I remembered our bikes. "Your father will come and pick them up later," mom noted. And, in silence, with the happy yet uneasy prospect of no school work for at least the rest of the day, we left Eastfield Elementary and Middle School.

The News, Oh Boy

We dropped Julian off and continued toward Silverford. "You can do some shopping with me," said mom. "Pick up a few things for dinner. Won't take too long."

Mom usually pestered me with questions about school and such, but she was quiet. Not good quiet. I wanted to ask if she knew anything about why we were getting off school, but, with the awkward involvement with Jacob on Saturday night at Lovers' Lane, I figured that less said, the better.

At the bottom of Eastfield Road, we turned on to the main road to Silverford. The new mall—the only mall in the area, but still not completely filled or completed—was a little more than halfway to Silverford. Shopping for food with mom wasn't a favorite pastime, though better than shopping for clothes. There was always the opportunity to sneak in a few treats or comic books into the shopping cart.

I turned on the radio, which was tuned to the local station. When Simon was in the car, he made sure we listened to stations that originated beyond Silverford—in particular, those that carried the music he needed to hear and that my parents didn't need to hear. "How can you listen to that racket?" dad would ask. Simon would answer, "'Cuz it's cool. Coo-ull. Get with it." Mom would shake her head in mock disapproval and add, "But just turn it down a little, please."

It was about time for me to exercise such power, and so I made a motion to switch stations, but at the same time my attention was called to the voice on the radio: "…and in this morning's breaking news about the apparent tragedy in the Eastfield area, just outside of Silverford." The mention of "Eastfield" got my ears up.

The voice continued. Mom seemed to grip the steering wheel. "There are reports of the bodies of two young persons found in the Eastfield vicinity by the members of Silverford Sheriff's Office. No other details have been released at this time, though an official statement is expected within the next twenty-four hours. Our reporters will be there when further news breaks. Stay tuned to radio KONO 1410, the daily smile on your daily dial, for all the late-breaking news, weather, and sports."

Mom turned the radio down, then off. Her hand returned to the steering wheel. I looked to her face. Her bottom lip pulled back, tightly. She gazed ahead at the road. She looked like she was about to cry. The obvious question was out there. I didn't want the obvious answer. What did I hear? I couldn't put images to the words that began to race through my mind and run down into my body. No. No! Unthinkable! Jacob and Esther—the bodies of two persons. In Eastfield! Could it—? No.

In a few slow, silent minutes we were in a parking place at the mall, beside the supermarket. The car idled. Mom's hands remained on the steering wheel. The hurried parking lot, with cars coming and going, shoppers loading their cars…all offered no clues—about anything. Jacob and Esther. Was it? How? When? No, couldn't be.

Mom at last turned off the engine, put the car in park, and pulled on the emergency brake. She took a deep breath. Her lip loosened, but her eyes carried every ounce of a mother's caring weight. She must have had heard something of this news before.

"I should have told you," she said. "Before you heard it. I'm—so sorry. Sorry."

She reached over and hugged me, which I now allowed—and maybe even needed. Maybe it was the only thing at the time that made sense. "I hope we can—that we can—can talk. Later, maybe later, we can. When your father…"

We shopped in silence. I didn't sneak any treats into the shopping cart—not even the new *Mad Magazine*. It didn't seem quite right to attempt to get away with anything so small. But then she asked me, like she was trying to make the world go away: "Would you like, maybe, a magazine or a comic book? It's fine."

I thought of the motto of *Mad Magazine* that was always attached to Alfred E. Newman, the hopeless mascot of the magazine: *What, me worry?* Not worry? Not likely.

MONDAY, MONDAY

The rest of Monday was painfully quiet. I shuffled through old magazines, tried to find radio stations, and watched some TV, which had a couple of game shows with contestants who all acted like genuine lunatics.

Dad came home early from work. He had the evening newspaper with him, which he usually saved for after supper. Judging how quickly he found mom at the kitchen table and was sharing the front page with her, no doubt there was some news. While I foraged in the kitchen, I overheard one short sentence, uttered by mom: "Think it's them?" Dad said nothing.

I carried on with listless activities, while my head uselessly groped with what seemed to have happened.

Simon arrived home from college not much later, where the news of the two bodies had apparently spread quickly. At the dinner table, neither Simon's new-found wit nor his huge appetite showed up. He was a bit older than Esther Slough, and even though they were never friends, she was part his life's landscape, from being in school with her and just by their family living fairly close to us. At one moment, toward the end of the meal and without any context, he dropped his fork and burst out, "We still don't know for sure—that it's the Slough kids who they found." My parents, startled, looked at each other, then nodded in agreement, but these were nods with little conviction. The nods said it couldn't be anybody else.

Simon left the table without finishing his dinner and without taking his dish and glass to the sink. Mom, with worry pressed into her face, watched him leave. She clenched a napkin. My only thought was that all of this was making Simon upset in some way deeper than my own understanding, and this made me think about what I should be feeling— and in truth, I didn't know. I just sat there and picked away at the meatloaf and creamed corn, waiting for something to say, or something said. All I could come up with was that I would help clean up after supper. Mom thanked me. Dad looked back and forth from the table to the window.

Through the trees beside our house, you could see a little of Eastfield Road. It wasn't very far along the road from where The Watchers' Club met just two nights ago. Billy showed us the flashlight. That stupid flashlight that impressed us so much, leading us to—who knew what? The recollection allowed me to follow the windings of a smaller but useless thought: Was Jacob a member of the club? He was always there when we carried out missions. We didn't always treat him like he fully belonged, but we didn't tell him to "get lost" either. He was with us—but now?

That we had been with him on the night he went missing, and that I hadn't owned up to being with him up at Lovers' Lane, and that he was—what? Dead? How? All those times when we didn't say hello or good-bye . . . those times when we sort of ignored him. What did we really know about him? The mindlessness of cleaning up the kitchen did not make any of this go away. I fussed over a few things that normally would have been shirked, like putting away the glasses neatly, right-side up, rather than just fitting them in the cupboard willy-nilly. Mom thanked me. I could tell that she wanted to say or do something. Instead, she awkwardly looked at me and smiled weakly, and she gave a final wipe around the sink.

Getting Tight

Later Monday night, after watching Perry Mason win another case and solve yet another crime—the murderer turned out to be the victim's conniving half-brother who hoped to get more than his fair share of a large inheritance—I wandered off to my bedroom. This offered little escape from the gloomy confusion that seemed to sit on our house, and even, for that matter, on Eastfield.

As usual, the radio and some magazines were my only possible retreats, but nothing could hold off that last picture of Jacob returning every few minutes. There on the slope at Lovers' Lane, off some few yards beyond Teddy, below Slagmann's truck. Waiting for Billy to turn on that stupid flashlight. Then the confusion of running to the Old Orchard—and, after saying something that was not quite clear, Jacob is just not there anymore. And earlier, another picture of Jacob on the way up The Trail, when Arnold suddenly aimed the flashlight in his ghostly, god-help-me face. The frightened look, sort of like the look on David Slagmann's face when he too was caught in the blinding glare of that flashlight. And then the darkness.

How many more times would I have to rehearse this?

An hour or so went by, and dad came into my room. Normally, mom took the lead role with touchy-feely issues. Dad usually reinforced the important stuff, letting me know that I had better follow up, buck up, or smarten up. But tonight mom was probably too upset.

"What you up to?" he asked, sitting on my bed. I was propped up with a couple of pillows, thumbing through some car magazine. Dad didn't usually sit on my bed.

"Nothing, really."

"Son, I know you must be upset with the news," he began. My eyes kept to the magazine.

"This is tough. A shock to all of us, so it's okay to feel upset. Mixed up. We're all confused."

Dad looked around the walls on my room, which was hung with a few pictures taken out of wrestling and car magazines. He stood up and went over to the window, making sure it was locked. He also closed the curtains to the darkness.

He continued: "Tomorrow, or the day after, the sheriff will probably want to talk to you, and to your friends, about Saturday night. About seeing Jacob. You kids may have been the last to see him out there on the road before he—he disappeared. I phoned the sheriff's office, and told them that you saw Jacob on Saturday night. I told them what you told us."

I kept my eyes in the pages, but the print began to swim away. "Son—you understand?"

"Yeah," I answered, trying my best to sound okay with things. Inside I was tight, but also swishing around in uneasiness.

"Anything else we should know—I mean about what happened on Saturday night? Anything else you remember? Did Jacob say anything?"

I pretended not to hear. I didn't want to hear. I finally said, "What? Huh?"

Dad was patiently firm. "Anything you can remember about Saturday night and about Jacob?"

"He was there, and then he wasn't. He didn't say anything. You know what Jacob is—you know, what he's like."

Dad didn't respond, but he knew. A few times mom corrected comments to say that Jacob was, yes, a "slow learner," but that it wasn't nice to think anyone was better than anyone else. I thought of Arnold and Mr. Bryer, who, it was clear, felt that some folk were clearly better than others.

"So somewhere around eight, or a little later, that you last saw Jacob—that right?"

We had been over this before. I was trying hard to believe my own lie.

"Yeah, some time around there, I think."

"You didn't see him any later than that, out there on the road?"

"Yeah, I think so."

"You think you did, or you think you didn't?"

"I don't think I saw him later."

"Well," dad said, "you better be sure about that, so think carefully. The sheriff will want to know everything you know. He's going to ask lots of questions. And to the other kids as well, I would think—the kids who were with you."

Dad spoke slowly. A warning lurked in his words. There was no way that we—our gang, The Watchers' Club—wanted the sheriff to know all that we knew about or did Saturday night. No way. But bury the idea the best I could, the inevitable crept up: one of us would surely have to tell about what we did that night. You just can't lie to a sheriff. We would have to say we were with Jacob at, maybe, nine-thirty or so, and where we were and what we were up to. Maybe Billy had already given in to his father, who by now was sure to have noticed his missing flashlight. Teddy would hold out, just like he did at school when he was in trouble: "Uh, I dunno." Arnold, as usual, would try to find a way around the truth by making sure that he would not have to take any blame. As for Julian, well, he too might cave in pretty easily—not to his parents, who were soft, but maybe to the sheriff. One part of me knew that I had an opportunity, a big opportunity, right now, with dad here, with him somewhat sensitive to how he thought I was feeling, to clear the fog and the questions with the truth about Saturday night, though it still didn't make full sense why it might matter.

Silence passed between us. Dad wasn't one for much talk, so he wasn't about to ask me about my friends or how I doing at school. He stood up: "Probably won't be any school tomorrow, not until this gets sorted out. Get some rest. Don't stay up too late."

This was probably the best moment for the truth, and my confession—the truth—almost moved forward, but suddenly the moment was too heavy to move forward. "Yeah, I'm a bit tired."

He went to the door, and, in my failure to speak up, relief sunk into guilt. But this was short-lived. Dad stopped and turned with one hand on the doorknob: "After you saw Jacob around eight or eight-thirty, did you go anywhere? What time did you get home?"

I thought for a moment. What had I said before, if anything? I had to keep my head in the magazine and keep cool, though I was beginning to burn.

"Not sure. About nine-thirty, or maybe, not much, maybe a little later, I think."

Dad stuck around for a few more seconds, either waiting for me to say more, or just watching me. Then he left: "Goodnight."

"Goodnight," I echoed, though it was anything but good.

I waited a few minutes for dad to get to wherever he was going. I hoped he had gone to the basement, which would then allow me to check out the newspaper. I got up out of bed and quietly went into the living room, where I expected it to be on dad's reading chair. Not there. Maybe the kitchen. The lights were still on—the paper was on the table. I picked it up, but where the story should have been—it had been cut out of the newspaper. Must have been mom, who sometimes tucked clippings and other odd things away in a shoe box, for, she said, "a rainy day." But why this? It wasn't a very big chunk of newspaper that was missing, so it couldn't have been much of a story. Maybe Eastfield did not figure that importantly in the greater picture of Silverford's bigger, busier business. Or, more likely, maybe not much was yet known. The paper was always a day behind.

I retreated to the bathroom, then back to my bedroom, closing the door behind me. It wasn't that late. The house was quiet, though I knew dad was still up. My brother vaguely stirred around in his room down the hall. Mom was probably in bed, listening to the radio.

With the lights out, and with the protection of sheets and blankets pulled over my head, there was a momentary possibility of thoughtlessness, but the darkness only took confused regrets to a starker place. I should have told him. Why didn't I tell him? What will happen now?

As I reburied my head into the pillow, a hiccupping sob, unannounced, rose up from down within my throat, and a sob forced itself despite the hidden, inner protests to hold it all back. The sob rose like possible relief, but it was not a letting go.

Two kids found dead in Eastfield. Two kids I knew. No, no, no.

5
FOUL PLAY

Tuesday morning moved slowly and, despite the cancellation of school, without much enthusiasm.

I woke up into darkness and silence. Slowly sounds emerged: the familiar traces of my parents' voices filtering to my room. Dad getting ready for work. They would have coffee together before he headed to Silverford in the company car.

I managed to restlessly slither into an extra hour or so of sleep, but it was hardly peaceful. Take a pee and forage for breakfast.

In my t-shirt and underwear, I made my way to the kitchen.

Mom sat at the table thumbing through a magazine and listening to the radio. "G'morning," she said. My response was to scratch myself. "You can get yourself some cereal. I haven't made anything special. But go wash and tidy up." I couldn't really figure out why I need bother—after all, I wasn't going anywhere—but resistance was too much to muster.

I dressed, washed, and returned to the kitchen. The radio was still on, but mom wasn't there. I could hear she was down in the basement, probably doing laundry.

I poured a bowl of cereal and went over to the kitchen table and added sugar and milk. A few mouthfuls of thoughtless chewing and looking out the window was cancelled as my attention was drawn to the radio, which had finished with a few boring items about some elections and a fire somewhere: "—and there is no further information available about the discovery and identity of two bodies found in Eastfield area on Sunday. An official statement from the sheriff's office is expected later today. The question of foul play has not at this time been ruled out. When other details become available, KONO 1410, the daily smile on your daily dial, will be there. Stayed tuned for all the weather and all the sports."

The radio moved into some blathering commercials. What had I just heard? *Foul play*? The Slough kids missing…*two bodies*…Jacob and Esther. Mom was suddenly right behind me with small basket of laundry in her arms. We both made some kind of quiet noise of surprise in seeing each other.

"What?" I said.

"What?" she said, almost at the same time.

"Oh—you just scared me a little. That's all."

How long had she been standing there. She turned and left the kitchen, and I was left to my cereal, which, in silence, I ate.

The rest of the morning was spent in my room, cleaning it up a little and looking at one of my brother's music magazines that I found in the kitchen. Mom told me Julian was coming over for the afternoon since his mom had been called into work. Simon, a little unusually, poked his head into my room on his way out to college, and he told me about some good FM radio stations, but I couldn't seem to pick up any on the old radio. The only station coming in loud and clear was the local one which I crossed over a few times while searching around on the AM band, but I didn't feel much like listening in. He said it might need a little antenna, which he said he could hook up.

ACCIDENTS HAPPEN

About halfway through lunch Julian arrived. Coming into the kitchen, he put his beloved baseball mitt on the table and sat down beside me. He seemed full of energy—or at least a lot more than what I could work up. While mom tidied, she asked him the usual questions about his parents, school, and even baseball. Julian was on a high because the Dodgers were winning the World Series. Today, more than usual, mom enjoyed Julian. She offered him a glass of milk and a brownie while I finished up my macaroni and cheese. Julian accepted and wolfed down the offering enthusiastically. "Thanks," he said, wiping his milk moustache on his sleeve. "That's really good."

After we finished, Julian grabbed his mitt and we went off to my room where he immediately became interested in my meager collection of baseball cards.

Nodding to the wall above my bed, Julian noted, "You still got that old Yankee's banner hanging there? Waste of space."

"It was my dad's," I said.

After some quiet moments and shifting our focus to some comics, he got closer to me and asked in a low tone. "Hey, heard more about the Slough kids?"

"What?" I answered, my face screwing up a little. I heard what he said, but the way he said it caught me off guard. His mild curiosity didn't suit what had taken place right here in Eastfield in the last couple of days. Maybe he didn't know. "What?"

"The Slough kids. Anything more?"

He must not have heard, so I looked right at him and didn't hold back. "They're dead, Julian. They found them—dead!"

I waited for some kind a look of disbelief or shock. Or something.

"That's what everyone's saying," he said. "I mean, d'ya know any more about it? My mom was mental about the whole thing."

Again, Julian's manner put me back. Didn't he get it?

"More about what?"

"You know, like how they died and all that."

I just looked at Julian, and so he kept going, jacking-up scenarios: "You know what I bet? I bet they were walking around, stumbling around and all that at night, late on Saturday night it must have been, and they got hit by a car out there somewhere, or walking on the railroad tracks, hit by a train. Or they fell over a cliff or something, or fell into a river and drowned. Or fell down a well, like the well at old what's-her-name's witch place down the road—"

"Mrs. Raskolnikov."

"Yeah her. So maybe they weren't found until Sunday night, or maybe Monday morning. That's what I bet happened. Some accident. They're klutzes, you know."

I could only look at Julian. He was as befuddled at my reaction as I was to what he said—and the way he said it. Yet—yet maybe he had a point. Maybe they were in an accident. The Slough kids were stunned, for sure, and if anybody could get into a freak accident, it was them. Despite Jacob's great strength, we had seen him fall out of trees, break through ice, slip off logs—stuff like that. Even the few times he went swimming with us, he did more sinking than floating.

"So, you don't think that they were, like—murdered or anything?" I asked, skeptical of his take. I elaborated: "Like what the radio said, then? Like about the 'foul play' and that—because that's what they said, you know. I even heard it today, this morning, on the radio."

"No. That's what they say when they don't know what happened. They investigate and all that kind of stuff. That's what my mom said about it all—and she used to work in a law office, you know. For a real lawyer."

What Julian said offered a little relief, though I usually didn't buy into his deeper ideas. It didn't change anything, but, for the moment, a weird accident was easier to deal with than some kind of crime. Or at least that's how it was for Julian. Maybe because I lived closer to the Sloughs than Julian, or that I had known them more or less all my life, I felt more upset than Julian—Julian, after all, had only moved to Eastfield a year to two ago. Yeah, for sure: accidents happen. And if you were walking around at night, and you were the Sloughs, well, anything was possible.

"Let's go outside," Julian suggested, "maybe play catch or do something up The Trail."

I grabbed my mitt and we made our way to the kitchen, passing mom in the hallway listening intently to someone on phone. I mouthed, "Going outside to play catch," and held up my mitt as a sign in case she didn't get my words. She turned partially towards me with a distracted nod, and then turned away.

We grabbed a couple of more brownies on our way out.

WILD PITCH

While we started to play catch, dark, low clouds began to move in. The cool, wet air was dropping. It wouldn't be too long before the rain started up again. But there was no stopping the game. But it did feel good to be outside doing something.

We tossed the ball around, challenging each other to throw a little harder, put a more "stuff" on the ball, or hit the mitt perfectly by holding it up as a target. Julian was good, and he loved talking baseball trash.

I tossed him a pretty good one, quite hard and almost straight into his glove. He came back with, "That all you got? Your low on ammo or what? Come on—burn one in! Can't expect to win the World Series tossing in cotton-candy softies!" He lobbed the ball back to me, mocking my throw.

While I enjoyed his challenge, and knew that it was in fun, I did try to throw harder and harder, until, with one attempt to break both the sound barrier and Julian's mitt, I lost control and the ball flew feet above him and bounced its way into the bush at the base of The Trail.

"Wild pitch!" shouted Julian, and he turned to get the ball. "Batter," he shouted out, "take your base!"

In a few moments, it was clear that Julian couldn't find the ball, and so I jogged over to help him. "You see where it went in?" I asked.

"About here, somewhere, I think."

We kicked away at the bushes and felt around with our feet, and we used our gloved hands to push aside the branches, high grass, and the occasional prickles growing here and there. No ball. This was not the first one to be lost around our yard, and it wouldn't be the last. We gave up, looking at each other and shrugging. There were more old baseballs around in my basement if we wanted to continue, but the momentum of the game was as lost as the ball.

Julian immediately had an idea. "Hey—what say we cut over to Mrs. Raskherface's shack?

"Raskolnikov."

"Yeah, I'm pretty sure I saw some small cats—wild ones—out by her place a few days ago. See if we can find them. No one will be around. Just for a bit. Nothing else to do."

We weren't supposed to, but we sometimes prowled around the back reaches of the Raskolnikov property to explore the odd junk that was piled here and there. We tended to stay away from her deserted, old house, mainly because it was fairly close to the road and we might get spotted. There was also something creepy about the place.

Although the old lady died a few years ago, a few of her cats survived and proliferated in and around the old farmhouse. They may have been living under the wooden floors, or maybe even some had moved inside by getting through holes that were beginning to appear. Many of the windows were also broken. An old NO TRESPASSING sign nailed to her fence meant little to us. We could easily cut across some heavily-bushed land to get around to the back end of her property. It was only about five minutes away after turning off about a third of the way up The Trail.

"Should we leave our gloves here?" said Julian, whose mitt meant more to him than mine.

I tossed mine to the ground without much thought, but Julian went over, picked it up, and placed it around his own as best he could, and then put them on the ground, mine more or less on top of his. I watched him with a little amusement, and he knew it.

"That's a Louisville Slugger Black Diamond Extra-Deep Pocket, and I don't want to get it wrecked up."

I looked at him. "Julian—it's just a baseball mitt. Dead cow skin."

"Yeah," he retorted, "but it's top-of-the-line dead cow skin."

"Cows are all the same."

"No. Some cows make better baseball-glove cows than others."

"And you would know that, right," I sarcastically asked.

Julian looked at me with a final comment: "Moo!"

With this final dumb-ass exchange, I left it, and gave him my you-gotta-be-nuts raised eyebrows. He returned the look with gusto.

"Come on," he said. "See what we can find."

I couldn't resist one more shot: "I bet your mitt is made out of pussycat leather!"

Julian's come-back was lame, but oddly enjoyable: "So's your butt!"

With our baseball cow-skin mitts left on the ground at the base of The Trail, we headed out in the hope of finding or seeing anything. But it didn't really matter. We were doing something.

While we moved quickly through the bushes, I couldn't help think of the dead, black-and-white mother cat we saw in the ditch on Sunday afternoon, tumbling and rolling slowly in the dirty water of the ditch before it got stuck along the pipe somewhere. Thoughts, too, of Jacob Slough crossed my forward path, but these were pushed aside while we made our way to the back of Mrs. Raskolnikov's crumbling old place.

Hands Held Out

We were around the back of the old place in hardly any time.

Like Saturday night with The Watchers' Club, we were quick and stealthy—though in this case we didn't need to be. But still, we didn't want anyone going along the road to see us. Officially, the deserted property was out-of-bounds, but the chances of being seen were slight, and most people around Eastfield wouldn't have cared. Since the old house would probably be demolished as soon as the property was sold, no one worried too much about damage or vandalism, or even thought much about the place—well, except for the permanently irritable Mr. Bryer, who said it was a "disgrace" to the neighborhood. "A vermin trap," he said.

One other thing made our outing a little more tense: though we were beyond the age when we thought that old Mrs. Raskolnikov actually was a witch and that her shack was haunted, it was still a little creepy to be around her dark, deserted place. Creepy that she was dead. Creepy she died in there. We had all heard tales of weird noises coming from the house, and of white smoke rising from her chimney on nights with full moons. Some kids said that, since her death, they had even seen her at the windows, beckoning them in with her hands held out. We knew these stories were kind of like fairy tales, but still, they held us.

We crept up behind the house, crouching by a patch of some tall weeds. We were about ten yards from the back door, which had a board nailed across it, though it looked like it had been partially pulled away. A broken window was to the left of the door. All dark within.

We looked around, and except for a solitary crow cocking its head and looking down at us from the roof, things were still.

"Shhh," I said. "If there's any kittens around, we might be able to hear them meowing."

Julian nodded, and we listened and watched for a few minutes. Nothing.

"Let's just go peek around the side," suggested Julian.

I had a better idea. "Hey, why not take a look in through that busted window. By the back door. I've never looked in, have you?"

"No."

The only kid I knew that had ever been inside was Danny Caine, the older boy who used to live across the road from me, and who, one hot, unforgettable summer, when I was six, showed me many startling things about nature—and he went in and actually talked with Mrs. Raskolnikov, all the time. I remember what he said when asked what he saw in her house: "Many wonderful things." He mentioned pots of healing plants, fossils, a bowel of broken glass, and pictures that she painted or drew or something. "And a room full of bread crumbs," he added. Danny also said that the old lady could look at the stars and tell the future. She told him that up in the woods there would be light in the dark, but not a good light. It also occurred to me that I was now about the age that Danny was when I followed him around as his second self. And then I thought about what happened to him, and I didn't want to think any more. It had been the worst thing to happen in Eastfield, and, six years ago, it almost caused my parents to move. The Caine house was gone now, and a new place built with new neighbors who liked gardening, which helped with the forgetting.

I made a dash to the back porch, which was only two steps up from ground height. I wasn't exactly quiet with my approach, mainly because the porch planks were loose and cracked. But there was no cause for alarm, since we were way out of earshot for anyone who might be vaguely interested in our innocent mischief. I went down on one knee by the back door. Julian arrived a few seconds later. We didn't say anything for a couple of seconds. We would have a look inside the shack. We weren't expecting to hear or see anything, but faintly, somewhere, I thought I heard a faint meow.

"Hear that?" I whispered

"What?" he said.

Julian was readjusting his baseball cap.

"Meowing. Somewhere."

"I didn't hear anything."

"Shhh," I said.

We knelt and waited. Julian sniffed. The temperature had dropped, and we were cooling off from playing baseball and our quick trek. Light rain began to fall, making it a little more difficult to pick up any sound.

Again I heard a meow, and it didn't seem too far away.

"You hear it this time?" I asked, still whispering. "You had to hear it."

"Yeah. I did, for sure."

"A cat, right?"

"Yeah, think so. Must be."

We both looked around, trying to figure out where the sound came from. We heard it once more, this time maybe even closer.

"I think—it came from inside," Julian whispered.

Then another meow, and I nodded slightly. Lowering my voice even further, I confirmed: "Yeah, from inside. Just behind the wall or door, it sounds like. Keep the noise down. It might be scared of us."

The adventure was turning out better than we had thought. The idea of finding a stray cat or some kittens in Mrs. Raskolnikov's old witch house was cool. What if it was a black cat!

I focused on the broken window a few feet away and to our left. "Let's take a look in. Through the window. Sounds like its right there."

I barely finished this idea when we heard still another meow, closer, and now that we were fixed on the window and the darkness inside, the sound clearly came though the opening.

"Shhh," I said, standing up. Julian stood up too. The rain began to fall more heavily, and with the low overhang of the porch roof above us, the noise of the rain might help to disguise our few steps to the window. We didn't want to frighten off the cat. The idea was clear: if we don't at least see a cat, our mini-mission would be a failure.

As we closed in to the window, Julian leaned his back to the wall and looked away from the shack into the expanse of the deserted property. "Rats!" he said.

"What? Rats? Where?"

"No, I mean, look. It's beginning to rain like mad."

"Yeah. So?"

"So we left our baseball mitts on the ground. They're going to get soaked! Not good for the leather!"

Julian and his stupid baseball mitt! Moo. I could see how badly he wanted to save his precious mitt from drowning, and so I accommodated him, but not without some sarcasm: "Okay. We'll just take a quick look, and then go. And don't worry Dodger-boy. My glove will protect your sissy-mitt from the rain."

Julian's impatience heightened the intensity and sped up the quest. Edging closer to the window along the porch...should easily be able to poke my head through the window into the shack's darkness.

Another meow. This one really close, and definitely through the window. I ducked beneath the window frame. I would slowly straighten up and look in. Don't frighten the kitty with any quick movement. The unspoken plan would be for me to look, and then Julian. He still gazed out into the rain. "It's really coming down," he said again. I ignored him. I wanted to see inside the place, and I wanted to see the cat.

Crouching below the window, I slowly stood up until my eyes were about even with the window. At first I couldn't see much at all beyond the inside windowsill. The dull day, the overhang, and the darkness within made it difficult. My eyes needed to adjust.

Then I saw it! The transparently green, glowing eyes of a kitten, reflecting the little light that came through the window—and that was about all. I strained to see more, but then the cat, remarkably, as in dream, seemed to float, float slowly, slowly towards me, waist-high, out of the darkness. What? I was mesmerized by the impossibility of what I was seeing. I stared at the cat's eyes. Then, as the shape of its head and body began to show into the light of the window offered...a pair of hands! Dusty, dark hands that seems covered in soot or charcoal or something. The hands were holding a little white cat with black paws. Hands! The cat looked at me and meowed feebly.

Beside me I could hear Julian sigh, move away a bit, and continue mumbling something like, "It's going to get soaked, I'm telling you."

Hands! Someone was holding the cat. Someone right there, right inside the house! Just a couple of feet from me! What? Who? My breathing stopped, and, for the moment, the sound of the rain pounding down faded. I was stuck for any kind of thought, but my eyes found no choice but to follow the arms up into the darkness, where I could make out the shape of—someone. Then the shape whispered as it stepped closer: "Milk. It needs milk."

Astonished, confused, petrified—I turned, then I heard the shape say, "I drew'd it." My legs were finally able to move, and I bolted past a surprised Julian into the pouring rain. I could hear him behind me, and when I reached the heavily wooded area that led to my property, I could hear Julian, "Wait for me!" I didn't. "Slow down!" Julian called out. I didn't.

WEIRD, MAN

At my back door, one hand on the doorknob. I stood and turned. Julian was quite a bit behind me, even though he was the faster runner. He had stopped to pick up the baseball mitts at the base of The Trail. I stood there, winded and soaked. Julian, clutching the mitts, caught up, and we went in, but instead of going up to the kitchen, which, for the moment, did not feel like a safe place to be, I went down the stairs and into the basement, where I flopped onto an old sofa that was the main piece of furniture in our unfinished rec room.

Julian tossed my glove on to the sofa, and then, after finding a couple of old towels by the washing machine, joined me. He was more interested in drying out his mitt than anything else. He passed a towel to me. I draped it over my head, covering my face. I was numb.

Julian finally disturbed my escape under the towel: "What was with you? You took off like you saw a ghost. You see the cat? I definitely heard something."

A ghost…a cat? What did I see? The towel remained. I leaned back into the couch.

"You didn't see?—or hear—?" I asked.

"What?"

"Him."

"'Him'? 'Him' who?"

What I saw…it didn't make sense…the green eyes floating across the room, the dirty hands holding the cat, the arms, shape stepping into the light toward me? Then he stood there, looking at me.

I remained beneath my cover and repeated the words: "He—he said it needed milk."

"Milk? 'He' who?"

It didn't make sense. Maybe if I didn't speak it would all go away.

"What the sam heck you talking about? Who needed milk?"

I murmured, "The kitten. The little kitten…and he said, 'I drew it', or something."

"What? Who said it needed milk? Drew what? What you talking about?"

Upstairs we could hear mom walking around.

Julian finally said, "You're acting too weird, man. Ga-ga."

It was still too clear in my head.

Julian could wait no more. He grabbed the towel off my head and looked at me. "What you saying? You pulling my chain or what?"

I returned his gaze and then looked at my rain-soaked glove that was making a dark, damp spot on the sofa. "Jacob," I said. "It was Jacob. Jacob holding a kitten. There, in the old house."

SPOTS OF TIME

Within the strange mix of time and memory, there are moments, spots here and there, that rise out of seemingly forgettable events, out of ordinary and trivial occupations that otherwise fill our days and nights. And in that rising-up, these spots of time sometimes cast some light upon surrounding time and events, restoring memory with a clarity that can, in equal measures, be both surprising and disturbing. Saying Jacob's name, then and there to Julian, in my basement at my old house on Eastfield Road, on that rainy, October afternoon, was such a moment.

"Jacob?" said Julian, squinting with disbelief pressed into his face.

I nodded slowly, and took the towel back from him.

"You saw—Jacob Slough?"

I nodded again.

Julian continued. "In the shack?" he asked.

I nodded.

"You, like, saw Jacob Slough when you looked through the window?"

Julian needed to get this right. He probably still wondered if I was jerking him around, which, of course I was perfectly capable of doing.

"So you saw Jacob in the old place, just now, when we were there?"

I waited a few seconds, "Yeah."

Julian now sat back as well, thinking, probably trying to gauge my intention. Then he sat forward again and tried to continue: "But—but he's—"

"I know," I said, though I didn't know anything.

We waited, we two: "But what about the cat?" Julian. There was a cat—a kitten?—that we heard? Right?"

Same word: "Yeah."

Julian was trying hard. I didn't help. I couldn't quite come up with more.

Julian attempted to plough forward: "So you saw a cat, a kitten, through the window, not Jacob Slough?"

Time for a different word: "No."

"So you didn't see a cat? Then—what was doing the meowing, then?"

While I slowly came back to myself, Julian became a bit peeved. He looked at me with something more than a little frustration, then sat back in the couch and started to restlessly shape the pocket of his mitt by punching his fist into it.

I finally tried to share the scene: "I saw them both. A little cat and Jacob. Jacob stood there, holding the cat. Inside. He said the cat needed milk. That's what I saw, and that's what I heard." Julian stopped working on his mitt and stared at me. I added, "And I'm not kidding."

Julian realized this called for absolute confirmation: "Pinky swear?"

"Pinky swear."

"Mother's grave?

"Mother's grave."

"Stick a needle in your eye?"

"Stick a needle in my eye."

"But he's dead!" Julian stated. "It said so on the radio! Missing with his sister, and then they found them. That's why we got out of school. Why the sheriff and his guys were all over the place—looking for them, and they found them!"

Julian was now more uneven than me, and he wasn't even the one who saw Jacob standing there in the half-darkness inside Mrs. Raskolnikov's spooked-out old joint.

"I know," I said, thinking this through as best I could. "But—but it didn't give any names or anything on the radio, or anywhere else, did it? It said, like, 'two bodies were found,' or something like that."

Moments passed as we tried to process, until, with a seriousness Julian didn't usually muster, he said, "You sure you saw him?"

I looked at him. "I'm sure—it was Jacob. I'm not making this up. And I'm pretty sure he said, 'It needs milk.' He wanted to get some milk for the kitten—or me to get it, or something. A little white kitten with black paws, I think."

Julian and I began to settle down again.

"We need to figure this out," I said. Arnold's powers of deduction would have been useful. But I tried to begin with what we knew: "Jacob is not dead."

Julian reluctantly agreed then added cautiously, "Well, unless he's a ghost."

I gave Julian a look, but he at least came up with something that suggested his brain did work: "That means"—he suddenly looked optimistic—"that it was two other people who were found dead."

This was good news of a sort, though it felt weird to suddenly kill off a couple of new people with some simple reasoning.

"Yeah—but," Julian continued, taking his time, "his sister—?"

"Don't know. Like they were probably together, the two of them, going missing like that. Like, what are the chances—?"

Then it hit me.

"She's in the shack, too, I bet. Bet they both been hiding out there! That's where they've been. Who would bother to look there?"

"Yeah," echoed Julian, liking the idea so much that it was well on its way to being a certainty. "But you know they're searching around right now, you know. Looking for them."

"I know," I said.

We were unofficially congratulating ourselves, mainly because two kids, our neighbors, were not dead after all. And now they were not missing. We knew where they were! We brought them back to life. And now—now maybe all the stuff about Saturday night would go away. This was good news. Minor questions, however, still hung.

"Why'd they be in the old house?" I asked.

"Who knows. They're kind of out of it, right?"

I agreed, and, being on a roll, came up with a possible answer. "Maybe their dad was really, really upset at them for something. I might take off, too, if that guy was mad at me!"

"No kidding. Look what he does to those rabbits!" Julian made a kind of crunching noise that was supposed to sound like a rabbit's neck snapping. Julian brought up another little memory: "Remember when Jacob brought that pet rabbit of his to school, and then he told us how his dad would be killing it?"

"Yeah…"

Despite the unpleasant picture we conjured, we decidedly felt better, having solved at least one part of the big mystery that had been following us around.

"So do we tell somebody?" Julian asked.

"We should, I guess. Yeah—we should."

We looked at each other and felt pretty good, considering.

"We should tell your mom," said Julian.

Still soaked in our clothes, we marched upstairs into the warmth and light of the kitchen to tell her the news. Jacob and his sister were alive!

Two Persons

Mom was not in the kitchen. We could hear her speaking somewhere in the house, so we figured that she was probably still on the telephone, where, an hour or so ago, we had left her on our way out of the house. Instead, when we rounded the corner of the hallway, we could see she was talking with someone at the front door. We stopped, waited for a second, and when she shifted aside, we could see she was talking to one of the sheriff's men. We retreated into the kitchen and sat at the table. The thought crossed my mind that we should let them know about what we discovered in the old house.

But then the front door shut. We waited, and mom came into the kitchen.

"Oh, you two," she said in an odd, distracted way.

We stood up, and began, "Mom—"

She stopped me: "That was one of the sheriff's men—at the door. They're going around talking to everyone."

I could tell she wanted to continue, and I couldn't push myself to interrupt. She sat down: "They've begun to search around the neighborhood, up and down Eastfield Road. They're beginning to do it now. They want us to let them know right away if we notice—see—anything unusual."

"What they looking for?" I asked. "They've already found—and we—"

Mom cut across my words. "You know. They found two—two persons. You know this. Around in Eastfield. A horrible thing. And they are letting it be known that it was probably not an accident. He said this will be in the news and on the radio, but they wanted to let as many people as possible know right away—if they lived in the general Eastfield area, because they think—."

She took a drink from a cup in front of her. She grimaced. She was shaken. "He said they found some possible—evidence, they said—and a weapon or something, and now," she said, "they have to find—they're looking—." She stopped, looked up from the table at us, as if trying to read us so that she could find the right words. "They are looking for—who—for who might have done this."

Who? Who might have done this? The murderer. She didn't say it. She couldn't say it in front of us.

"I better phone your father right now," she said, standing up quickly and looking at me. Then she noticed: "You're soaking wet—you too, Julian. What have you two been up to?"

"We were just outside, playing around," I said. "It started raining. And we—."

"What?" You were outside—just now? You are not to leave the house! At all! Who said you could leave the house?"

"You said it was okay."

"I said what—when?" she challenged.

"When you were on the telephone, you said it was okay."

"Young man—I said no such thing!" Now she was upset. "Get to your room right now and get on some dry things, and don't leave." She made for the phone in the hallway, but before she disappeared, she turned: "The sheriff's office wants to make it clear that they don't want anyone wandering around. On their own. You understand?"

She stopped and changed her tone, as if catching herself. "Julian, your mom called. I said we would drive you home—in an hour or two."

"Thanks," said Julian.

Then she was gone. Julian looked at me and was strangely impressed. "Never seen your mom like that before. Geesh!"

"Neither have I," I said.

GRAVEYARD MURDER

Back in my bedroom we put on some dry clothes. I found pants and a sweatshirt for Julian, who, though a bit smaller, was a close enough not to look stupid in my stuff.

"Maybe we wait for my dad to come home, then tell him about Jacob," I said. "I don't think my mom is sort of ready to hear about this right now."

"Yeah," said Julian. "They think there's a madman on the loose, and he might get us or something."

"Yeah, guess so." For the moment we were more unsettled by mom's marching orders than the possibility of danger lurking in Eastfield.

I fiddled with the radio. I passed over our local station a few times. I didn't feel much like any more news—at least for the moment.

We had some time to kill. Waiting made us feel like prisoners, even though we had a free day away from school. We had information, and we wanted to get rid of it. We'd better do it soon, or get yelled again. I continued to fuss with the tuner. Julian, meanwhile, found a model car kit under my bed that I had been building sporadically for a month or so—a '57 Chevy 2-door hardtop. "Can I work on this a bit?"

"Fill your boots."

Julian, sitting on the floor, organized bits and pieces around him.

I gave up on the radio, and, with my stash of comics exhausted, I took up a book to pass the crawling time. Mom was a member of one of those book clubs that sent you "A Golden Classic" every two weeks for the rest of your life or something, and always left some of these books around my room. "Reading is a key to success," she'd said. "Books enrich you," she added, though I had no idea what she meant. "Maybe one day you'll be a writer." That would be dumb, I thought. Sit around and write all day? Yeah, right.

A pile of three book-club books had been on my bureau for a few weeks. I picked one I had heard of: *Tom Sawyer*. Propped up a pillow against the headboard, I made my way into the action. A few color illustrations made it a little easier. I soon got to the part where Tom and Huck, sneaking out on a moonless night, find themselves in a graveyard, debating whether the dead can hear them. Three shadowy figures come toward the boys, but they turn out to be men from town who they recognize. The boys keep out of sight. They witness a grave dug up and a body loaded onto a wheelbarrow. A fight breaks out between two of the men—Potter, a ruffian, and Robinson, the town doctor. Robinson hits Potter, who falls to the ground unconscious, while the third, Injun Joe, waiting for the right moment, stabs the doctor with Potter's knife, killing him. The boys, horrified, run away into the dark. Joe then puts the knife into Potter's right hand. "That score is settled," says Joe, who wants revenge on the doctor for something that happened years before. Potter comes to, sees the knife in his hand and the bloody body beside him, and asks, "Lord, how is this, Joe?" and Injun Joe asks back, "What did you do it for?" Potter, stunned, believes him, and falls for the set up, then runs away, leaving the knife behind.

I took a breath. Would Tom and Huck end up telling about what they had seen? If they did, would the killer Injun Joe come after them? Would innocent Potter be caught and hung? That they were out sneaking around in the night without permission made their situation more unsettled, especially for Tom, cared for by his Aunt Polly.

Tom and Huck's fate was infused with the strong, sweet smell of modeling glue. Julian was making progress with the car. I watched him, biting his tongue, fiddle with a few small pieces. I put the book down, relaxed my eyes, and must have even dozed off for a minute or two, since I slipped into a passing dream of being followed through long, tangled grass by a shadow on a moonless night.

The dream shuddered aside with the far-off sound of the back door closing.

"Geez, what's with you?" asked Julian.

"Huh? What?"

"You just kind of spazzed just now for a second."

"Huh?"

"You made a little moany sound just now, and your body spaz-jumped."

"Oh," I said, as if I knew what he was talking out, though I found I had to make an excuse. "A cramp."

Julian let it go. He preferred to admire his progress on the Chevy.

Noises came down the hall and from the kitchen. Dad was home early. Julian started to clean up the spare bits and pieces from the model and put them in the box. He liked this kind of detailed work, just like he loved organizing baseball cards and tracking player stats. These were safe, closed worlds. And then came an unannounced thought that, for a second, surprised me for being so peculiar: In what world was Jacob Slough safe? Right now he was probably freezing in that creepy, broken-down shack with his sister—and maybe waiting for me to bring some milk for the hungry kitten he held out. I didn't like this picture at all. The way to get rid of it was to report what I saw. Yet if I repeated this, would it send Jacob and his sister back to Old Man Slough, who would no doubt give them a good thrashing. But they were probably used to it. I had to report what I had seen, and I confirmed with Julian.

"We should go tell them, right?"

"Yeah," said Julian. "We should."

TAKING IT ALL IN

Mom and dad sat in the kitchen beside each other, studying the Silverford newspaper. But despite concentrating on the paper, dad was in the middle of saying something to mom: "—two cars from the sheriff's office. Out in front of the old place now," he said. "I passed them, on the way home. They pulled me over and asked me who I was and where I was going, then waved me on. Something's up. Looks like they just got there."

My parents noticed we were in the kitchen, and they went silent.

"Oh, hi," dad said. "Hi Julian."

We returned his greeting.

Mom was still quietly upset, and even though dad moved away, she looked to the newspaper, as if there might be something more, something she missed.

What did dad just say about cars from the sheriff's department caught my attention, and so, for the moment forgetting about our resolve to tell him about seeing Jacob, I asked him, "Two sheriff's cars? Where?"

He looked at mom, thought, and then addressed us matter-of-factly: "Just down the road. In front of the old Raskolnikov place. Couldn't see all of what was going on." He slowed down a little to finish up: "But it looks like something."

Mom turned and noted to dad, "Well, when they came by, they said they would be searching around Eastfield, all the properties, today."

"This was more than just a search," he said. "One car had its lights flashing. Something was up."

Dad returned his look to us. We knew what the "something" probably was. Though neither dad nor mom had a clue about this, it was hard to figure if this was good news or bad news.

Dad picked up on our barely-hidden stupor: "You boys must be pretty upset by all this. This is all a—tragedy. Your safety is our first concern. We don't know what any of this will come to. But we do know that—something bad—has happened right here in Eastfield, and it seems like it involves people we—you—we all know. The sheriff and his men will solve it. Meanwhile, we need some caution, until this clears up. Keep out of the way of things. That's why you are off from school, and why you can't go wandering around without some supervision."

Dad seldom strung so many words together. Last night his words sought information. These were different. Caring words, official words, serious words, words of the wise. Words of warning. Words, too, that avoided the unthinkable details of what had happened, and words also that were unaware of just what Julian and I, standing silently there, knew—who the sheriff and his men probably found in the old Raskolnikov place .

"Maybe, with what is going on right now down the road, some of this will be cleared up," he added. We still didn't move. "You understand?"

We nodded our heads.

"Good," he said.

Mom listened with visible pain. Dad took another breath and tried to return us to the safe, predicable world: "So, what did you boys do today?"

"Nothing, much," we both said at once, hurried.

Dad nodded, vaguely. An awkward moment rose up between mom and dad who, on one side of the kitchen, gave us thoughtful gestures of reassurance, and Julian and I on the other side, feigning grateful reception of such reassurance. In truth, there was little comfort on either side of the kitchen.

"Well, maybe we'll just go back to my room," I said.

"We'll take Julian home in a bit," dad added.

We returned to my bedroom and closed the door behind us.

Tom Sawyer

"Looks like we won't have tell about seeing Jacob after all," said Julian, who seemed both relieved by and casual about what we just heard. "The fuzz must have found them—so maybe that's something."

"Looks like it." Without saying it out loud, my thoughts returned to the dark beginning of all that had happened. There were still two bodies, weren't there? And foul play.

Julian sat on the bed and picked up the book I had been reading. I stood with my back against the door.

Julian opened to the title page and read aloud, "'*The Adventures of Tom Sawyer* by Mark Twain.' You reading this?"

"Yeah."

"It says 'Samuel L. Clemens,' too, after 'Mark Twain.' Who's he? The guy who did the drawings?"

"Guess so," I answered.

Julian flipped through the pages, stopping to look at some of the pictures.

I walked over and sat on the bed beside Julian. He lingered over the picture showing what I had just read about: two boys hidden behind some bushes seeing another guy—with a knife in his hand—confronting the doctor. "Cool," he said.

At last he looked up, "What you think will happen to Jacob and his sister—Bessie?"

"No—her name's Esther."

"I bet they take them to the sheriff's office, for questioning. Then take them home."

I could tell Julian liked his last pronouncement. It looked differently to me: "Don't know. My dad was thinking that who they had down the road had something to do with the missing persons—the ones found dead."

"Okay, yeah, but they'll figure out that it has nothing to do with all that other stuff—the murders or whatever. They're the Sloughs, not the Boston Manglers."

"You mean 'strangler.' The Boston Strangler. There was only one, butt-brain."

Maybe Julian was right. Maybe I was getting too wrapped up in things, making them too complicated.

Julian put the book down. "Wanna play cards—play War?"

War: the dumbest card game of all time. The deck equally divided.

Players turn over single cards at the same time. The high card wins the mini-war and takes both cards. The loser eventually runs out of cards.

"It will take too long. And its bore ring."

"You're 'bore ring'."

I gave in, and War it was for the next five or ten minutes, until dad knocked on door and stepped in.

"Julian, we'll take you home now."

"I'll come, too," I said.

Julian grabbed his beloved mitt and pile of wet clothes.

On the way though the kitchen we crossed paths with my brother, Simon, who had just been dropped off by one of friends on the way back from college. "Something serious going on down the road at the old Raskolnikov property," he said with some purpose.

"We know," said dad. "Don't go nosing around there."

Simon gave the kind of dirty look older teens give their parents when they don't need—or want—advice.

"We have to take Julian home," said mom, looking at Simon. "Stay put. We'll be back in half an hour or so. We'll pick up some dinner. Anything you fancy?"

"No," he said. "Just get something good. I'm famished."

"Lock the door behind us," added mom, a little embarrassed, but also firmly.

Simon returned another of his looks, but slightly less defiant this time.

With this parting exchange, we made our way to the car, hoping, of course, to see what was going on down Eastfield Road.

Move Along, Please

Mom and dad took the front seat while Julian and I piled into the back, with me on the driver's side. Normally mom would have taken home Julian on her own, but maybe dad didn't want her in the car alone, or maybe, like us, he just wanted to see if things were still going on down in front of the Raskolnikov place.

As soon as we pulled onto Eastfield Road, making a right-hand turn out of our property, we could just make out the lights of the sheriff's cars way down the road. Dad straightened out and very slowly headed toward them. A deputy was on the road, a big flashlight in his hand waving us forward. No other traffic. When we were even with him and more or less right in front of Mrs. Raskolnikov's house, dad came to a stop and wound down his window.

"Everything all right, deputy?"

The deputy leaned over with his big flashlight and looked into the back seat where Julian and I sat. He looked familiar. It was the guy who talked to us on Sunday afternoon from inside the car when Julian blabbed on.

"Everything under control, folks. Move along, please." He said this with some authority. Dad did up the window and began to slowly pull away.

The deputy's look from behind the flashlight temporarily froze me, but Julian brought me back with a quick, quiet pinch of my leg. He signaled with a frantic pointed finger that I look behind and slightly back through the rear window, and I caught a quick glance into the back seat of one of the sheriff's parked cars that we passed. A light in the cop car had gone on for a second or two, revealing at least one person sitting in the back seat on the side closest to us. I didn't need more than a moment of light to recognize who it was: Jacob Slough. They found him. He had the same look when, on Saturday night, on our way up The Trail, Arnold blasted Billy's flashlight into his helpless, winced face. The light in the sheriff's car went out, and we pulled further away and headed down into the darkness of Eastfield road.

Though we expected something like this, the look on Jacob's face in the back of police car was unsettling. Julian and I looked at each other, but then quickly turned away.

We drove down the road in silence until dad said, "You see anything?"

The question, we could tell, was addressed to mom.

"No," she said. "Hard to see what was going on. Looked like they may have been searching the house, or around the property."

"They found something," said dad in a low but certain voice. "Something, for sure."

Julian and I looked at each other and said nothing, and we continued toward his house.

We dropped Julian off. His mom came out, thanked us, and hurried him in. We did a quick shop and returned home.

§

After dinner, Tuesday evening faded into an unsettled, slow quiet. Dad was edgy. He went to the basement a few times, almost secretly. I couldn't hear him down there, which was weird. What was he doing? Looking for something? I thought it best to just keep away, and besides, I had my own junk to figure out. What did I really know? Only that Jacob was with us up at Lovers' Lane. That he wasn't missing or dead. That the cops had him. That wasn't much. No doubt he had been taken home by the sheriff's guys by now. Maybe his sister was found as well. Everything else remained a mystery.

I went to bed thinking of Jacob's face frozen by the sudden, bright light, both on The Trail that night, and now, earlier, in the light in the back of the sheriff's car. Jacob's ever-hapless face. And then him standing in the darkness of Mrs. Raskolnikov's house, holding the kitten in his large, sooty hands. As I sunk into uneasy dreams, his words played over me...*it needs milk...I drew it.*

6

ARRESTING

Except for watching a couple of stupid game shows on day-time TV, Wednesday was as restlessly uncertain as Tuesday night. Not even enough energy to pay attention to World Series game that was on. But in the house, worry followed mom around. Anticipation of any news kept her near the radio. She also spent a fair amount of time on the telephone, talking in low tones, always just out of my hearing.

Julian didn't come over. When I asked if he might, I was told his mother took the day off from work. Mom said that maybe she would drive me down to his place later on. What bugged me was not talking with the other kids. How much did they know about what was going on? About what was happening with Billy? Had he told his dad about the flashlight and about what we had been up to on Saturday night at Lovers' Lane? That Jacob was with us? If so, would this get back to my parents?

Despite everything else that had happened, then, we remained on the verge of getting in trouble for not owning up to being with Jacob later than we had said—not to mention what we were up to at Lovers' Lane. Maybe because he wasn't lost any more it wouldn't matter. But this was beginning to look like small beans.

Somewhere around the middle of the afternoon I wandered to my bedroom and returned to *Tom Sawyer*. Maybe Huck and Tom would escape their troubles and have adventures on some raft, which I knew was going to happen since I had already gone through the pictures in the book. I settled on my bed and into the story: the day after the murder, along with others from the town, Huck and Tom watch as the innocent man, Potter, is arrested, and the murderer, the intimidating Injun Joe, pins the crime on Potter. Huck and Tom, horrified, and having sworn secrecy, watch. This story was getting pretty good in an edgy way, but was interrupted by the arrival of dad, who came through the back door into the kitchen. Home early again. A few minutes later I heard mom's voice go up, then nothing. Despite Tom and Huck's predicament, curiosity got the better of me, and I made my way to the kitchen.

I entered in time to hear mom gasp, "It just couldn't be—just couldn't!"

Dad placed his arm on her shoulder, and then she sat down. They weren't looking at any newspaper, and the radio was turned down. Dad must have brought some news home from Silverford.

"What?" I said.

Dad turned to me. Mom looked up, and her face suggested he shouldn't say anything. He read her face and said, "He'll find out soon enough. Better now."

"What?" I said again.

Mom didn't move. She looked white. Dad turned to me. "Sit down, son."

He waited until I settled.

"I've heard from town, son," he began slowly, "from people who know—about the case of the—bodies that were found—not all that far from here. And more, too."

Dad was taking his sweet time getting this out. Mom's color returned, and was replaced by a look I hadn't seen from her before, ever. Call it shock, call it fear, call it being fully drained. What was going on? "It's—it's not good news, and—it seems, I guess, that—" Here he stopped, picking up on something else. "It's—on the radio." He walked over and turned it up.

Mom tried to intercept him, but he already hit the volume dial. She said, "He shouldn't hear it on the radio. It should come from us, because—"

"No," dad said. "He'll hear it. There'll be questions. It's out there now."

Mom backed off. They talked as if I wasn't there.

The newsreader's words broke in: "—on what is now being viewed as a possible double homicide in Eastfield." We all quit fidgeting. "After an extensive search, a suspect was arrested yesterday evening and is being held for further questioning. He was apparently found hiding out in a deserted Eastfield residence. While he remains a suspect, his name is being withheld. A decision about holding him will likely be made early next week at a preliminary hearing. According now to the official statement from the Sheriff's Office, two teens were found dead Sunday afternoon in a deserted, wooded area of Eastfield. It is believed that the victims may have been attacked Saturday night while parked in a vehicle. The parents of the deceased have been notified. Any connection between victims and the suspect has not been clarified by the Sheriff's Office while the investigation continues, but sources suggest there may be evidence that ties the suspect to the crime and the victims. The Sheriff's Office is calling on anyone who may have information. More on this later, with news on the hour and every half hour, here on KONO 1410, the daily smile on your daily dial."

Dad turned the radio down. Mom looked at dad, "It can't be. I can't believe it. That poor boy wouldn't hurt a fly!"

I fumbled with my question: "That means what? Jacob?"

Dad spoke plainly, though he cut short some of what he said: "Son, it's Jacob Slough who's been arrested. They found him in the Raskolnikov place yesterday—hiding out. They figure he must have—. That was the fuss in front of her place when we drove by, it seems."

Any voice, any words I had, disappeared and sunk inside to a swirling, sick-feeling place where jumbled images started to crash into each other. I knew Jacob had had been found. But arrested? Then the utter jolt: two teens murdered on Saturday night? What? When we, The Watchers' Club, were all there. David Slagmann with his date or girlfriend in his dad's meat truck...we were there...we heard them moaning around in the truck, making out...Billy dropped the flashlight after turning it on the truck...we saw David Slagmann's face for a white, ghostly second...we shouted out and ran away into the darkness...we met up at to the Old Orchard. And Jacob. Jacob? Where was Jacob when—no, that's not right.

"You all right, son?" said dad.

For a moment or two we three just stood there, until mom approached and put her arms around me. Some of the next few minutes disappear, but I know I fell into, maybe retreated into, in my mother's arms until, sometime later, I found myself back in my bedroom. *We were there. We were all there.*

COLLECTIVE WORRY

Thursday. School cancelled again. Another dull, dark day. The rain held off, but it always threatened. A day of reckoning. I would have to say things, things that I knew about but weren't clear what place they now had in the grim, confused story growing around us. No. Surrounding us.

I wandered around the house, watched a little TV, picked away at some breakfast, but spent most of the time on my bed looking up to the ceiling. I didn't have enough willpower to get back into *Tom Sawyer*. The book, with its green and gold cover, sat quietly on the side table near my bed, waiting for me to move Huck and Tom beyond their sworn silence, and perhaps their fear of the murderer, Injun Joe.

From bits of conversation I heard from mom while she talked on the telephone, the word was out that Jacob had been found, and that he was suspect in the murder.

Still my head refused to hold the idea that David Slagmann was dead—and someone else, too—his girlfriend, the other person in the van?— and that Jacob could be involved. How? Jacob was a big, dumb, strong kid and all that, but he couldn't have done what everyone was thinking. The sheriff's guys would surely figure this out. In the wrong place. At the wrong time. That's all.

Unthinkable: the idea that we were part of the scene where it took place. We must have been there earlier, since when we left David Slagmann and his girlfriend, they were there—making out. What we saw. And what we saw the next morning, Sunday, before the sheriff and his men got there, was Slagmann's meat truck with the door open but no one around—what did that mean? Had the truck been there all night? And then—now that we knew what took place—the murdered persons could have been, must have been somewhere right there! Right where we were looking! What if we—? What if we were we the last to see them alive, and then, without knowing it, the first to discover them dead—murdered?

I was startled by mom knocking on my door. She came in and sat on my bed.

"How you doing?" she said quietly.

"Oh—okay, I guess."

I wanted to forget what I knew. But I also wanted to deny Jacob's guilt, offer some help. I wanted to say what we saw that night and the next day.

"We'll have lunch in a while."

The events of the last few days had clearly taken something out of her—even in my own state of confusion I could notice that much. Because she was one of the more active members of Eastfield's community, being a past president of the Eastfield Elementary School PTA on more than one occasion, and a member almost every local organization, she seemed to know or get on with everyone. She never had a bad thing to say about people. She often used to censor us kids with one of her many proverbs: "If you don't have anything good to say, don't say it." People would often call her to let her know things, or even for a little advice—neighbors, other parents, and particularly the mothers of other kids at our school. Now, by the number of calls that came in, it seemed she was trying to reassure many of those who phoned, or she was just hearing whatever they had to say. She must have, then, been taking on some of the collective worry of Eastfield. She was also one of the few around who had some contact with the Slough family, so maybe it was thought that she knew more than what was on the radio and in the newspaper. Maybe she did, but if she did, she kept much of this to herself.

"After lunch, this afternoon," she said, "someone from the County Sheriff's Office will be coming around to talk with you. About Jacob. About Saturday night, when you last saw him. They called this morning again."

Was I supposed to react to this?

"They need to gather information. They want to talk with anyone who saw Jacob on Saturday."

She imagined my fear, and she imagined right. "Don't worry," she repeated. "I'll be there—with you. They only want to know what you know."

I didn't want to know anything! I didn't want to say anything! Now a pile of questions from some guy I didn't know. Will he have spoken with some of the other kids? Billy? Arnold? Julian? Teddy? What would he know? Would it be the big sheriff guy?

"You okay?" she asked, giving my knee a light squeeze.

"Yeah," I nodded, though it felt like my head was shaking "no."

"Come on," she said. "Help me make lunch."

I wanted to resist, but not because I wanted to be disrespectful.

"Come on," she said again. "It'll take your mind off things."

The she noted *Tom Sawyer* by the side of the bed.

"You reading this?" she asked, picking up the book and flipping through it.

"Yeah. A bit."

"I read it around your age. I remember. Some kids witness—" Then she put the book down, suddenly choked. "Well, I shouldn't, I wouldn't want to . . . to spoil the ending for you."

Together we headed for the kitchen.

Cutting cheese and stirring strawberry jello powder into hot water did little to settle any thoughts about a visit from the sheriff's office. What did I know? What should I say? What did I see? I wasn't so sure anymore.

Two Paths

Mom and I sat down for lunch. Usually the radio would be on in the background in the kitchen. Not today. My brother passed through on his way to afternoon classes at the college. He gave me one of his various greetings: "Hey there, squirt face." Mom walked with him part of the way outside where his ride was waiting. She probably wanted to say something to him.

Mom returned and sat down: "Simon seems to like his classes at the college."

We picked away at our food while time ticked away until the doorbell rang.

"Probably it's that person from the sheriff's office to talk to you," she said, giving her mouth a nervous dab with a serviette. "Go into the living room. I'll bring him in. Didn't think they would be here so early."

I didn't want questions. I only wanted to say that Jacob couldn't be the murderer.

To the living room. Mom said a few words at the door, and there was another voice speaking—a man's voice. The sheriff?

Then, not one, but two men came in to the living room. The first was small and slight—a deputy maybe, given that he was wearing a kind of uniform. The other guy was indeed the County Sheriff—the large, creepy guy with the dark glasses we had seen a couple of times during the week.

The two men took off their hats. Mom introduced me to the sheriff, whose name was Berg—Sheriff Gaper Berg. The other guy was a special deputy brought in from the next county to help out with the investigation—Deputy Vernon Newberry. He had a fine, thin moustache that perched perfectly level between his top lip and his nose. But why two? Was this that important?

"Have a seat," mom gestured, and she directed me to sit, too.

Deputy Newberry sat beside me on the chesterfield. The sheriff sat partly across the room in my dad's reading chair. I didn't like him sitting there.

"Can I get you both a cup of coffee?" asked mom.

"That would be nice, ma'am," said Newberry.

Sheriff Berg nodded.

"How would you like it?"

"Cream and sugar, if it's not too much trouble," Newberry answered.

Mom looked at Sheriff Berg.

"Black," he said. "Thank you."

Mom hurried away. Deputy Newberry finally broke the silence: "You follow the World Series?"

"A little," I nodded.

"Two fine teams. Fine pitching for both teams—especially for the Dodgers. Who you pulling for?"

I had to say something. "Um, don't really have a favorite." I felt I better say a little more. "My best friend is crazy about the Dodgers."

"And that friend of yours?" he asked, pulling out a small notebook and a pen from one of his shirt pockets. He also put on a pair of gold wire-rimmed glasses and clicked his ballpoint pen to attention.

The deputy looked up at me, pen poised, waiting. He repeated, "Your friend—his name?"

"Oh. Julian," I said. He looked at me, waiting. "Julian Weissman," I added. He scratched away once more in his book, and cocked his head, waiting again. "He lives down at the bottom of the road—Eastfield Road."

Why did I open my big mouth? But it wasn't like they didn't already know the names of the kids around here.

Newberry cleared his throat and took on a phony, sympathetic tone: "We know this…this situation must be very tough on you and your family and friends. All these things going on and such. Being away from school and all. Not good. This kind of event can be bad for a community if it isn't cleared up quickly." He stopped and looked right at me. I couldn't tell if he wanted me to add anything. He finished his thought with certainty: "And that we aim to do. Clear it up."

He spoke slowly, quietly. His eyes wandered while he spoke, but his gaze always settled on me just when he reached the end of his sentences. He also had a little twitch or something around one of eyes that at first looked like a wink. Sheriff Berg, unmoved, and seeming unmovable, looked at me the whole time.

Newberry continued. "You've heard, I'm told, that Jacob Slough has been—is being held for questioning about this terrible crime."

I nodded.

"We just need to ask you a couple of questions, about Jacob, and about last Saturday night, if that's okay. We'll wait for your mom, then begin."

I took a deep, unsteady breath that I hoped was hidden.

"You know," he continued, leaning toward me slightly, "sometimes it's hard to figure out what's going to be important. Investigating this unfortunate case…well, everything, every detail, is has to be there. Pieces—all the pieces—need to be in place, and you never know where you might find them. So, it is important you tell us what you know. We've talked to some of other persons around Eastfield, and we told them the same thing." He twitched. "We need to add up all the information we get—compare, compile details and the like."

Sheriff Berg, who until this moment hadn't moved, crossed his arms and let out some air through his nostrils. Who had they talked to? My friends? And what did they say? Billy, maybe? Billy! He would have just gargled it all out, in one fast, hiccupped sentence. Would the others have said anything about going to Lovers' Lane and seeing David Slagmann and the girl parked there? Maybe so. Maybe not. But Billy. There was no hope!

Mom temporarily rescued me with a tray and three cups of coffee. She gave one to Berg and the other to Newberry. There were also a couple of her homemade cookies on a plate. "Help yourself," she said, placing the plate on the coffee table between us. She sat down on the other single sofa with her own cup of coffee. Newberry readjusted himself and took a sip before putting the cup on the coffee table.

"Fine coffee, ma'am," he said.

Berg nodded his approval.

"Thanks," mom nodded.

"We were just telling your son here that it's important he tells us what he knows. We want to get this situation cleared as soon as possible so that we can all get back to normal. A preliminary court hearing is coming up soon involving Jacob Slough. The County Prosecutor's Office needs as much information as possible."

Mom nodded.

"So, Saturday night," Newberry began, shifting back to me. "Last Saturday night. Can you tell us what you were doing, who you were with?"

Deputy Newberry readjusted himself so that, it seemed, it might be easier to take notes. His pen was cocked.

I wasn't sure where to begin. My mouth dried up. "Well, I was out with Julian, throwing a ball around, for a while after dinner."

"When would that be, and where were you?" he asked, writing at the same time.

"Might have been about—maybe seven-thirty or so, or a bit later." I looked over at mom, as if the time had something to do with her, with supper being finished. "Out on the road. A little up the road."

"Now," said Newberry, "it gets dark earlier these days. Starts to get bit dark even around, say, around six-thirty, seven."

I nodded, though I didn't really know.

"So, how'd you throw the ball around in the dark?"

Mom shifted in her chair. What did this matter? Didn't he believe me?

Sheriff Berg took one of the cookies, considered it, put the whole thing in his mouth, crunched down on it, and sat back. The whole thing.

"Pardon me?" I said.

"How'd you throw the ball around in the dark?"

"We go out to the road, under the streetlight, if it gets too dark."

"That what you did Saturday night?"

"Yes, sir."

"You and—", he looked at his notes, "Julian?"

"Yeah. Yes, sir."

"When did you quit playing catch under the streetlight?"

"Maybe around eight or so. Around there."

"Then what did you do?"

"We went up the road some, and sort of ran into some of the other kids who were just hanging around."

"Who?"

His questions let me know that he would not let go until he had the details. Could I resist? Should I?

"Billy—Billy Luckhert, and Teddy Sullivan, and Arnold Rheinhurst." I stopped for a second, like I was finished. Everyone in the room seemed to freeze. Why? Deputy Newberry stopped writing.

"No one else?"

I knew—could feel—what they were after, and I had to oblige: "And then Jacob Slough was there—I think."

"You 'think'?"

"Well, I didn't see him right there—then, like at that time. One of the other kids noticed he was there, kind of away from where we were gathered—where we were talking and stuff."

"Who? Who was the kid who 'noticed' him when you didn't?"

"Arnold, I think. Arnold a little later…he said that he saw Jacob hanging around the road where we were, when the rest of us didn't really notice him, then."

Newberry paused. "Arnold said a little later on he noticed Jacob earlier?"

"I think so."

"Why would Arnold say later that he noticed Jacob hanging around? Why would he—why did he—mention this later, do you think?"

This threw me. Newberry again wrote like a madman in his little book even though I really wasn't saying much.

I could only say, "I—I don't know."

"Okay, I see…I see. You didn't see him, then, Jacob Slough—at that time when you were one the road, earlier?"

"No, sir."

"But then you did notice him later on? That correct?"

Did I just say I saw Jacob later? Newberry didn't wait for an answer.

"When was that? And where?" he asked.

This wasn't what I had told my parents about Saturday night. My troubled mind began an anxious countdown. Four friends out there with their stories. Three adults with me in this room. Two people dead. One kid sitting in a jail…4-3-2-1…A sickly truth rushed up. Then Sheriff Berg made it crash right into me with the only question he asked that afternoon: "Where'd you go then, boy?"

He leaned forward. I could see myself, very small, reflected in his sunglasses. Why was he wearing sunglasses? His hand came forward. I thought, for a second, he was reaching toward me, but he was going for another cookie.

Newberry stopped writing.

How do you resist the truth not knowing if it will set you free or take you hostage? This was a question I couldn't, sitting there, begin to quite articulate, but it was felt without words. Two paths. Take one. You don't know where either goes, but both seem to lead to a place from which you can never return.

Two paths. Take one. So it began—again.

"We," I said, "we went up The Trail, walking around, after we were on the road for a while." I glanced at mom. She hadn't moved. She was holding the arms of the chair. This was new information for her, and she had no way of knowing where it would go. Neither did I. She must have wondered why I never said anything before—to her, and to dad.

"'We'?" said Newberry.

Berg seemed to look at me, but it may have been at the cookie, which he held out in front himself. Would my answer determine whether or not he crammed it into his mouth?

"Julian, Arnold, Billy, Teddy. And me."

Berg still held the cookie.

"And Jacob Slough?" Newberry asked.

Would Berg ever eat that thing?

I answered, "Arnold saw that he was following behind."

"Arnold said so, that Jacob was following behind?"

I nodded.

"What did he say—Arnold, I mean?"

"He said that Jacob was there on the street earlier and we didn't notice him."

"But you saw him now?"

"Yeah. Yes, sir."

Newberry knew not to give me time to think.

"Following behind when you were on your way—up this trail?"

"He—yeah, he just kind of follows up behind, follows us around, sometimes, when we do stuff."

"Everyone else see him that night?" Deputy Newberry drew a little closer to me.

"Yeah—I guess so. Not sure."

In one munch Berg finally demolished the cookie and sat back. Newberry looked over his notes. Did they both already know this? Or was this all new?

"And you were going up this trail?" he continued.

"Yeah. The Trail."

"This is the trail that goes to—where does it go?"

"It starts in my backyard here, and goes right through to the top of our property. A ways up."

Newberry again didn't immediately follow with another question. He wrote more in his notebook. I was now in deep. Real deep. A path where words began to leave my body behind, like I didn't own them anymore.

"Where were you going on Saturday night?"

"We were going up to this other area. Way up by the old slag piles."

"To do—what?"

"We—", I searched for some air.

Newberry pushed: "To do what?"

I took a big breath that could never be deep enough: "We were thinking about, about going to sneak up on people parking, you know, making out and stuff, just sneak up and then run away."

Sheriff Berg shifted, slightly. Newberry re-crossed his legs. Did this mean, *Caught you!* or, in the case of Berg, that was he maneuvering for another cookie?

Deputy Newberry sped up. "And you did this?"

"Yes, sir."

"Did you approach a parked vehicle?"

"Yes."

"And did you see the vehicle you approached?"

"Yes."

"You all saw the vehicle you approached."

"Yes."

"And did you recognize this vehicle?"

"Yes."

"What vehicle was it?"

"Mr. Slagmann's butcher truck, or van."

"You all saw this vehicle?"

"Yes, sir."

His quick, short questions stole away time to think, repeating what he already asked. Or was he? And he kept saying "vehicle," which was weirding me out.

"Though it was dark?"

"I guess it was light enough, I guess."

"How did you know it was Slagmann's vehicle?"

"I've seen it before. It comes—I think it still comes—to the Slough place sometimes. To pick up rabbits—rabbit meat, I mean. It has writing that says 'Slagmann's Butcher' on it."

"And Jacob Slough was there, right then, when you approached the vehicle?"

"Yes."

"And the others would have seen him, too?"

"Yeah. Yes."

"And you were close to the vehicle?"

"Yes."

"How close?"

I had to think. *Think.* Close to the vehicle. How far? "Uh, maybe five, six, seven yards, or something like that, when we were closest. Not sure."

"You hear anything?"

"Hear?"

"Yes, did you hear anything? Noise, coming from anywhere—that you remember?"

"Some kinds of noises coming from the van."

"Noises?"

"Yes, sir."

"What kind of noises? Describe them."

Here I had to take a deep breath, not just to remember, but to find a way to describe what was awkward to put into words. "Kinds of noises, like, you know, groaning noises, moving around."

"Groaning noises..." Newberry nodded, twitched, and seemed to scratch under what he had just written, like he was underlining. "What time would that be?"

"Not sure."

"Your best guess. Your very best guess."

How far, what time, what next? "Nine. Nine-thirty, maybe. Bit later, maybe."

"Okay. Then what'd you do?"

The only thing that came to me was the shortened account of what we did—shortened because I just wanted to move on: "We yelled out some stupid stuff and then ran away."

My mom stood up suddenly and said, "Let me get you a glass of water."

Things stopped for a moment until mom returned. I took a big gulp and squeezed the glass. I managed a "thanks," but could not look at her.

While Newberry had fired these questions, he had been creeping toward me and writing like mad. His twitch-winks sped up. I caught a glimpse into his little black notebook. What I saw made me feel even more unsettled: he had been writing in shorthand, which I recognized because mom knew shorthand from when she was a secretary. She'd even taught me a few of the squiggles. I didn't think guys knew shorthand. But this Newberry—he knew shorthand, and it looked like he was good at it. He leaned back, took out a hanky and gave his glasses a quick clean.

I still didn't dare look directly toward mom. I had no idea what she might be thinking, but I figured that at the least I was going to be in big trouble—not just for messing around on Saturday night, but also for not saying what I had been up to. For not saying I had been around Jacob later. Mom moved into the short silence with something for me: "You okay?" she asked.

I didn't get a chance to answer.

Newberry broke in: "Don't worry. Just a few more questions, ma'am, and we'll be done. We've got to hurry on, too. We've got a lot to do this afternoon," he added. "He's doing fine." Berg looked at his big, shiny pocket watch.

Newberry replaced his delicate-looking glasses and said, "For the time being we're going to pass over some details, I think, but certain information is essential—important, I mean."

Here Berg stopped for a few seconds and looked closely at me. "Did you see who was in the vehicle?"

"Yes."

Sheriff Berg leaned forward again, and this time he did so with clear intent and anticipation. Newberry kept going.

"And, and who did you see, could you see—in the vehicle?"

"David Slagmann."

"You certain of that?"

"Yeah."

"You know him?"

"No. I mean yes, I've seen him around—with his dad, sometimes, and a couple of times playing basketball at the high school when my brother was there last year."

"Your brother knew him, then?"

"They used to be on the school team. Basketball."

Newberry scribbled like mad for few seconds before going on.

"Anyone else—I mean anyone else in the vehicle with him?"

"Yeah."

"Who?"

"Don't know. I don't know who it was."

"You don't know?" he stopped.

Newberry seemed uncertain, or maybe disappointed. The answer put him out of his rhythm. Berg even turned his head for a moment.

"You mean you don't know if you saw someone, or you didn't know that person, or you couldn't see?"

"Well, I couldn't see, only the back of the head, sort of. Against the side window."

"The back of a head?"

"Yes."

"Against the window. Passenger side. The side of the vehicle you were on? That what you mean?"

"Yes."

"So, you're sure there was someone else in the vehicle with David Slagmann, and you think—do you think—it was a female."

I didn't say that did I, but I nodded. "I don't know, but I thought."

Newberry didn't care about this: "But could you identify this person?"

"No."

Newberry, nodding slightly, continued: "I see. I see. Okay." He registered something like disappointment before continuing. "Then where did you go?"

Robbed of energy, I answered, slowly, and in lower tones than before, as if, somehow, I had been defeated by an irresistible force whose triple name was Guilt and Newberry and Berg.

"We met back down The Trail. At the Old Orchard."

"The 'Old Orchard'?"

"About half-way down The Trail."

"You all met back there?"

"Yes."

"All of you?"

"Yes."

"Jacob, too?"

"Yes," was my automatic answer.

Newberry looked at me carefully. "So, he—Jacob—was there, then, with you when you gathered after running away from the parked vehicle?" Newberry twitched and waited.

Then I remembered. "No—he wasn't there. I don't think."

"So, let's be clear here, to make sure. Jacob wasn't there, then, when you and your other friends met up in this orchard a few minutes after running away from the vehicle?"

"No, don't think he was there."

"You're sure? Absolutely sure?"

"Well, but Jacob could sort of be there, without being seen, sometimes. He tags behind, usually." Newberry twitched and scribbled for quite a long time.

"But you didn't see him then. Then, after that, you also didn't see him following you all back down to this trail you came up?"

"No."

"You're sure?"

"Pretty sure."

"But you saw him up by the parked vehicle?"

"Yes."

"And you didn't see him at all after you ran away from parked vehicle to meet up?"

"No, sir. No." Why was he asking this again?

Newberry edged toward me: "So, he didn't run away with you and meet up with you like you arranged."

Again, it was hard to tell if this was a question. I answered, "No. I don't think so. I don't know."

Newberry leaned back again, tapping his notes.

"Did Jacob say anything? Up there, when you were up there, by the vehicle?"

"No." Then I remembered that Jacob did say something, and was about to say so but Newberry did not wait.

"And then you went home?"

"Yes."

"What time would that have been?"

"I don't know. Maybe ten, maybe."

Newberry looked over at mom for confirmation. "That sounds like about the right time, ma'am? When your son, here, came home on Saturday night?"

"Yes," she said, shaky. "Around ten, if I remember. He was out a bit later than usual for a Saturday night."

Deputy Newberry closed his notebook and put it on his lap. "And this was the night that Jacob did not return home."

Deputy Newberry reached over and took a few more sips of the coffee, which must have cooled down. "Fine coffee, ma'am."

With that, Newberry stood up along with Sheriff Berg.

He thanked me and added, "There may be details to fill in later—but for now this is helpful. You may be called into the hearing to answer a couple of questions." Here he seemed to be speaking more to mom than to me. "That will be up to the County Prosecutor, and will be at a preliminary hearing—early next week, I reckon. Maybe mid-week. To see if there's evidence enough for a trial."

Despite the uncomfortable idea of having to answer more questions later on, right now, with the prospect of Newberry and Berg leaving, I could at last come up for air. I felt a little dizzy.

Mom asked something that could have meant just about anything: "Then what will happen, if there is a trial?"

Newberry turned directly to her: "Not clear yet. There could be, maybe, a problem, ma'am, of your son here being under age—problem in testifying, I mean, even at the hearing. That will be up to a judge to decide. They don't always feel that a young person should be put through this kind of thing. Not to mention the accused. There may be an argument of him being tried in adult court or juvenile court."

None of this meant much, but mom gave her view: "Jacob is just a boy. Surely this will be taken into account."

"Don't know, ma'am. Sometimes the nature of an alleged crime gives the judge reason to try the accused as an adult in an adult court. Up to the judge at the hearing."

Just when I thought I wouldn't have any more to say, Newberry turned to me as if somehow he had been waiting for this moment, even though it also appeared he wanted get going:

"Oh—one more thing. Did you, or anyone, take anything with you—did you have, say, anything with you, when you went up The Trail."

What? Like a baseball mitt? A candy bar? I couldn't think of anything, and so I said, "No."

"You're sure of that, then?"

"Nothing, I think."

"You think on that a little, okay?"

I nodded.

For a second or two they looked at me. I felt some wobbling doubt, but couldn't think why. After a few words to my mom at the front door, they were gone.

She picked up the empty coffee cups left behind by our visitors, as well as the empty cookie plate. She said one thing to me: "We'll talk with your father about this when he comes home."

I left for my bedroom. The rest of the afternoon ground into me. Mom moved around the house. The phone rang a couple of times. I tried *Tom Sawyer* but couldn't concentrate. I needed to quit thinking about what I said, and what it all meant for Deputy Newberry and Sheriff Berg as they put "the pieces" together.

SECOND RECKONING

Jacob in jail. I suddenly felt like I was in jail, too.

Get outside. Some cold, fall rain on my face, if just for a few minutes. Mom was in the kitchen, preparing supper. I asked if I could go outside for a while, to throw a ball against the side of the house.

"Okay," she said after thinking for a second or two. "But don't—don't—go anywhere else. Don't go out on the road, or around the bottom of The Trail. Your father should be home soon."

I grabbed my mitt and found a hard, rubber ball under the back porch. Around the side of the house the cement foundation came up above ground a few feet beside our driveway, and I started to throw the ball and catch it on the rebound. The trick was to hit the wall at just the right place so that you got a clean one-bounce return. There was some kind of pleasure in the repeated rhythm of throw, hit, bounce, catch—throw, hit, bounce, catch. But in the midst of my inner game, somewhere behind me, a faint meow—or maybe not. I stopped, looked around, but nothing. I waited a little longer. No second meow. Was this a haunting from when I saw Jacob holding the little kitten inside the Raskolnikov place? I thought back… after I followed those plaid-shirted arms up into the darkness of his helpless face. For a second I was seeing a ghost! It freaked me out, and I ran. No ghost, just flesh and blood Jacob, hiding out in the old house…saying that the kitten needed milk.

I continued the game of catch with the wall with even more intensity, and perhaps with wanting to simply not think. Throw, hit, bounce, catch—throw, hit, bounce, catch.

After about ten more minutes, back in the house and to the fridge to get something to drink, and just as I did I heard dad arrive. Again, he was home early. I fell into worry once more, knowing that I would be in trouble having lied about Saturday night, and knowing that what we, The Watchers' Club, did that night was now deeply entangled with events that seemed to have taken Eastfield into dark uncertainty. I took my drink to the kitchen table and waited for the day's second reckoning.

Dad, carrying a rolled-up newspaper in one of his hands, came into the kitchen through the back door just as mom entered from the hallway. Closing in. They exchanged greetings. Dad cast me a look. He knew.

He didn't beat around the bush. After taking off his coat, he sat at his regular place at the end of the kitchen table, which was almost set for dinner.

"Your mother called me this afternoon. She told me about your conversation with the sheriff and the other fellow, the deputy, and I gotta say"—here he took a very deep breath and shook his head—"we're not pleased—not at all. You hear?"

I nodded.

He took a moment or two to look at me, like he was reassessing my net worth, which didn't feel like much more than about two cents.

"Son, you should have told us what you and your friends were up to on Saturday night—especially after you knew that Jacob had gone missing. Do you know how upset, how worried, people have been? Maybe, if you would have just told us, things—" He stopped and looked at mom before beginning again. "And now, with this latest news, well, we don't know what to think, quite honestly. We are all—we're just—this has become very big news. A serious matter, and you kids are right darn smack in the middle of it, one way or another."

Dad could be intense, but he seldom looked this uncomfortable. Somewhere between anger and worry. Mom sat at the other end of the table. I couldn't think of anything to say except, "I'm sorry." This fell short: "We were just fooling around. We weren't stealing or breaking stuff or hurting anyone."

The words hung in the air.

"And now they have Jacob," dad added, "who was with you, there, Saturday night—there, where it—this—all seems to have taken place. It now involves you and your friends."

Despite his driving words, and despite repeating himself, I didn't connect with all he said. I could only reply to what suddenly felt closest to me: "Jacob couldn't have done it!" The moment this came out of my mouth, the strength of my feeling surprised even me.

Dad answered flatly, "We don't know. There's evidence. Him hiding out and all. Him being there."

"But why? He wouldn't hurt a flea. He never fights back! Even when he gets picked on, which happens all the time!"

Mom came in here. "We don't know what has…gone on for Jacob."

"It's not right. Jacob probably didn't even really know David Slagmann—or his girlfriend he was with!"

This stopped my parents for a more than just a moment.

Like he hadn't quite heard me, dad questioned, "'Girlfriend'? What do you mean?"

I didn't get the confusion. "Well, you know, who David Slagmann was in the van with, parked up there."

Dad looked at me, still confused: "You mean his sister?"

Now I was lost the lost one: "David Slagmann…with—his sister?"

"No," dad said. "Jacob's sister. You know."

"What? Jacob's sister? Esther? Where? She was there, too? What was she doing there?"

"Slow down," dad almost ordered. He began again, slowly, plainly: "It was Esther in the van with David Slagmann that night. That's—that's who they found."

Esther? What did she have to do with any of this? She was in the van with David Slagmann and his girlfriend?

"What'd you mean?" I asked. It felt like there was knocking at my door and I didn't know how to turn the doorknob.

My parents looked at me and then at each other. Mom said, apologetically, to dad, "I didn't tell him. I thought—maybe he—"

Mom couldn't say more. Dad began. The story was simple yet confusing—and unthinkable: "She, Esther, was there—that night. Saturday night. When you were there."

"There? Where?" I was falling into a big hole, quickly, with no way to stop.

My parents looked at each other again.

Mom walked away a few feet, her arms crossed, but more like she was holding herself. Dad looked at me plainly: "Esther was the other person in the van. Parked with David Slagmann. Saturday night, when you and your friends were there. She was—she was the other person found—dead."

Mom turned away and looked out the window. I didn't know where to turn.

7
UNIMAGINABLE

Back in my room, my head blurred with the impossible. Esther Slough dead. David Slagmann dead. Two bodies. Esther in Slagmann's butcher truck. Just not right. Esther was who David was making out with? Didn't make sense. She wasn't the cheerleader type who the golden boy of Silverford High School would drive to Lovers' Lane with after a basketball game. Back to that brief flash of light when we glanced into the cab of the truck…David Slagmann's strained, surprised face, and then the back of the girl's head up against the window. Was it sort of reddish hair, long? I now remembered—yes, maybe it was, like Esther's. No. And then Jacob, who didn't show up after we ran away. And then him not showing up at home, hiding out in the old Raskolnikov place where, unknown to anyone, I saw him first, holding out the kitten…

Later that Thursday night, after a quiet supper with my brother not yet home from college, I helped to clean up the kitchen. "Simon should be back in not too long," mom noted. "He has a late afternoon class on Thursdays. We'll put some supper away for him." She loaded up a plate with about as much as it could hold and put it on the counter. After a few minutes of cleaning up, we heard the back door open.

It was Simon of course. He came into the kitchen, moving oddly. He crouched over, holding something close to himself under his jacket. He had an odd, soft look on his face.

"Look—look what was around on the back stairs, outside," he murmured.

He held out his hands and straightened up. I felt like I was seeing things. A kitten. *The* kitten! For sure: the little white one with black paws that Jacob held out when I saw him through the window of the Raskolnikov place! And now that I thought about it, probably the kitten I heard outside when I was throwing the ball against the wall.

Mom stood up and went over to Simon and the kitten. "Oh my, my," she almost cooed. "It doesn't look good at all," she said "Must be a stray— out there in the cold. Poor little thing." We watched the kitten, maybe frightened, in Simon's hands.

Finally, after we could look no more, mom got a clean tea towel and gently took the kitten from Simon's outstretched hands. She began to dry it off. It offered a few weak meows. "It's shivering," she said. "Poor little bitty thing."

I was no longer the center of attention, but I said, "It needs some milk."

"Yes," mom agreed. "Yes, some warm milk."

The distraction of the forsaken kitten was momentary relief for all, though I kept thinking of it in Jacob's outstretched hands, which were just now my brother's hands.

"If we feed it," said dad, ever practical, "it will stay around. We should take it to the SPCA. They handle this sort of thing."

Simon, not usually a soft touch, noted, "You know what they'll do with it, don't you—destroy it."

Dad saw where this was going.

Mom dried and rubbed the kitten. We watched as its fur fluffed up. "Wonder where it came from?" she said. She lifted the cat and talked to it like a baby: "Where did you come from, you little one?"

I could have answered, but that would have opened up just another hole for me to crawl into.

Simon, since he felt like the cat's proprietor, asked dad, "Can we keep him?"

Dad looked at us. We looked at him. He looked at the kitten. He was out-numbered and out-maneuvered, and he knew it. But just in case, Simon headed dad off at the pass: "Cats are easy. No trouble at all, not like a dog."

Dad felt obliged to put up a little resistance. "But if it's a female, we'll have to have it fixed, and that costs money. And kitty litter while it's young."

Mom, who was still working away on the kitten, held it over her head and pronounced the answer. "It's...male," she said. "And kitty litter isn't expensive. In no time at all it will be doing its business outside."

Dad steadied his unconvinced face, until finally he let in with the strongest statement he could muster. "Your mother and I will have to talk about it."

Mom nodded a small smile, and we knew what this meant.

"Okay," he said, "but if we keep it, you kids are to take care of it."

Simon and I nodded—and suddenly, just like that, we had a kitten.

"We'll have to name him," said mom, holding him so that we could take a good look at him. "How about 'Boots'? He has these little black paws that look like boots."

Simon wasn't so sure. He had this confident attitude since he started college, even though he had been there just over a month. I wasn't sure if I liked this slightly new version of him, since it showed up my relative immaturity. I liked it better when my parents used to tell him to act his age. Simon replied, "'Boots' is okay, but lots of cats are called 'Boots.' Like 'Puss'n'Boots'." He noticed mom was a little disappointed. "But 'Boots' is good name, given how he looks."

Since Simon brought him in, it seemed fitting that he confirm the name. "Gumboots," he said proudly, "He's wearing little boots, out there in the rain where he was found, so he should be 'Gumboots'—or 'Gumboot'."

Mom nodded her approval. Dad too nodded but could probably care less. Then Simon turned to me. "And what about you, Squirt. 'Gumboot' okay with you?"

I gave a lying nod. And I thought of Jacob.

Uneasy Dreams

The rest of Thursday evening revolved around little Gumboot, who, with a little food, warmth, and attention, seemed less uncertain than even just few hours ago when Simon brought him in from the cold.

At one point, later in the night when things began to settle down, I took him back to my room to play. At first, the kitten was shy about moving around, but after he got his bearings, he began to tussle with anything dangled in front of him. Then he quickly lost interest and wandered around the perimeter of the bed, sniffing this, rubbing that. He managed to get from the bed to the headboard and then to the windowsill. There he stood for a few moments, in part, maybe, because he saw his own vague reflection in the window, but perhaps also hearing the rain outside falling in the darkness. He meowed a few times, paced back and forth across the sill, turning always to the window. I didn't like the sound he was making. It reminded me of when I first saw him in Jacob's hands. Those outstretched, sooty hands, the plaid shirt. I had a little shiver. What was Jacob doing there? Why didn't I say something right away? I couldn't help but feel somehow responsible—but for what, exactly?

I picked Gumboot up, closed the curtains, and took him back into the kitchen where, waiting for him, was a cardboard box lined with a couple of soft, old towels. The sides were high enough that he couldn't escape. I put him in. He looked up at me as soon as he touched down. And as I walked away he meowed once more. Gumboot, I said to myself, and I continued to my bedroom and to more dim thoughts and, then later, to more uneasy dreams.

THEY CASTRATE THESE PEOPLE

The next few days were shapeless. Nothing happened, or seemed to happen, perhaps because so much had taken place over the last week.

My parents kept me busy around the house until school was back again. I didn't have contact with any of my friends during the end of the week and over the weekend.

On Sunday before lunch, dad had me working with him in the front yard, raking up leaves. From the little talk that I heard around, there was a feeling that, despite the shock of Jacob's arrest, Eastfield was safe again. I was no longer so sure of Jacob's innocence, but something did not seem right. Last Saturday night, just more than a week ago, felt like too many disconnected things—a dream, a bad trick, an accident, a mistake.

While we raked in the silence of the autumn morning, with small talk about how the Dodgers won the series so easily, Mr. Bryer, Eastfield's unofficial watchdog, pulled over in his spotless car. He probably saw us and took it as an opportunity to offer an editorial. His wife sat in the passenger seat of the car, but didn't get out. Their hyper little dog jumped around in the back seat, yapping like it would tear us apart if only it could get out. Mrs. Bryer finally took hold of him and put the drooling little beast on her lap, where it calmed down.

Mr. Bryer got out of the car and exchanged greetings with dad. He said he was out for a Sunday drive "with the Mrs." There could only be one topic.

"That's the trouble," I heard Bryer say, "when you got people like that living right here among us."

Dad offered nothing. Bryer, who you could tell liked the sound of his own voice, went on.

"Riff-raff like that ought'a be encouraged to, well, move along. Do good for our property prices. You know, a few more new places and clean subdivisions, and full amalgamation with Silverford. Get the road paved. Sidewalks, water, sewage. Right?" I had heard this all before.

His head nodded with certainty. I continued to rake over the same spot.

"And now look at the mess. What will developers think of Eastfield? Would you want a nice place in a neighborhood with people like that around? And after what some of us have done to clean the place up, we're pulled right down—a damn shame, I'm telling you. A shame."

He continued like he was sharing some big secret: "The only good that'll come out of this is that the Sloughs, with the two kids now—now not, well around—sad, yes—that they might pack up and leave. I mean, they couldn't really stay now, right. That old place of theirs could be—should be—ripped down, the property cleaned up. And all that filthy rabbit business."

At once Old Man Bryer's words got to me. He was a crank-ass. I knew he didn't really like us kids much, like we were some kind of threat to him and to his perfectly manicured property and all his new, shiny things. But now, at once, I saw him as something else, as something propped up by stupid hate. Suddenly I despised Bryer.

Dad replied, "Yeah, it would be hard for them now."

"You know," Bryer said, lowering his voice further, "in some parts they castrate these people. Or used to."

"What do you mean?" dad asked.

"Well, criminal types—like imbeciles and the such. Well, they, the law, used to sometimes castrate them so they couldn't have offspring—so they don't get any ideas about things, if you know what I mean, right? Don't know if they do it much anymore. Damn safer if they did."

Dad nodded—not, I hoped, in the spirit of agreement, but in understanding what Bryer meant. I pretty well knew what he meant. I had been around enough rural life to know what "castrate" meant.

Mr. Bryer, now talking a little out of the side of his mouth had one further comment: "It's something, though—though it probably means nothing—that Slough had been selling his rabbits to Zoran Slagmann for his butcher's shop. Don't know anyone who eats rabbit much anymore, though." Bryer must have thought he was funny now, and he added, "Probably tastes like chicken," and he chuckled.

Dad didn't respond much more beyond a vague nod, and with silence opening up between the two men, they exchanged a parting, but not before Bryer, upping his voice, noted, "Your yard, here, looking good. Those trees you planted are coming along nicely. See you've painted that gate, too. Good to see your son helpin' out. Idle hands: the devil's tools."

This last part was said in such a way that he probably intended that I give him some kind of approving look. I didn't, and then, with the dog put into the back seat where it started yapping again, Old Man Bryer was off once more on his Sunday drive with his Mrs.

I could tell dad was looking at me, and I was sure he wanted to say something about me being rude by not acknowledging Mr. Bryer. But he didn't. Instead, he asked me to bring the wheelbarrow around. I didn't say anything, but my dislike for Old Man Bryer was percolating away. Then I thought back half a dozen years or so to when I was Danny Caine's sidekick, to when he blew up Old Man Bryer's big pile of compost with his homemade bomb, and, for the moment, I felt a little better. It was really something, and only Danny and I knew about it. We did a pinky swear never to tell.

Danny's gone now, done in by the other explosion he manufactured. It was by far the worst thing that had ever happened in Eastfield. Until now.

BACK TO SCHOOL

School solemnly returned the next day, a cold, clear Monday. Everyone except the real young ones must have known about Jacob being arrested. Word may have gotten around that some of us had been with him that Saturday night when all that stuff took place.

At recess, Julian, Billy, Arnold, Teddy, and I listlessly kicked rocks around behind the wooden backstop at the far corner of the playing field. We discovered that Sheriff Berg and Deputy Newberry had visited all of us. We figured we all said more or less said the same thing, except Teddy, who told us that he said, "Don't know" to most of the questions. That got an uneasy laugh.

"Why did you do that?" asked Julian.

"Don't know," shrugged Teddy, this time getting a bigger laugh.

Arnold mustered some bravado: "I didn't give them much," he said. "Only what they needed to know. You could tell they thought Gumboot was guilty. But they have to collect and put together evidence."

While we carried on talking, Billy said nothing. In fact, he had said almost nothing in the morning before school as well. He barely lifted his head.

Arnold noticed. "What's with you, Billy boy?" he asked. "Berg and Newberry spoof you or what? Kill you with their charm?"

Billy didn't say anything for a second, and then mumbled, "Yeah. Sort of. I just had a bad time answering."

Teddy countered Billy's apparent worry with attitude. "And anyway, who the butt cares. They're all a bunch of saps. They're gonna put Gumboot in jail and throw away the key."

Billy's head went back down and he picked up a couple of rocks.

"You have to go—to the hearing?" Julian asked Billy.

"Yeah. Wednesday, I think."

"How come just you?"

I piped in. "They said I might have to go as well."

Arnold, somehow knowing, said that we'd all find out for sure today, after school, whether or not we would be questioned at the hearing. "Likely all of us," he said, again sounding casual and confident. "We're all evidence," he said, using the word for the second time.

Except for Julian babbling something random about "the Dodgers being the best baseball team of all time," silence worked its way around until Arnold broke it: "Just think what Gumboot Slough must have done, up there, in Lovers' Lane, after we went? The kid's a psycho, for sure. Killed his sister. Probably didn't even know what he was doing. He's burnt toast."

Julian asked, "You think he did it, for sure?"

Arnold liked being deferred to. "Must have. He'd kill a mockingbird."

It wasn't clear what Arnold meant by this, but Julian added, "His sister, though?"

Arnold, almost gloating, answered: "That's what the evidence points to."

Again with the "evidence."

Billy started walking slowly toward the school. He was still acting strange, a little like he was on the Saturday night after we met up at the Old Orchard. We let him go ahead.

Julian, nodding in the direction of Billy, wondered, "Hey, what's with Billy? He's like a zombie or something."

Arnold offered one of his patented put-downs: "No, zombies are cool. And they kill people. And eat them. Billy's got something stuck his head. Probably his dad's wrath. The flashlight, remember? That he dropped."

My thoughts, at least, turned over what Arnold said earlier: Everything points to it.

We all in our ways agreed—it didn't look good for Jacob Slough, the idiot boy of Eastfield.

The bell went to end recess, and we headed back to our class. A few of the other kids looked at us suspiciously as we made our way across the school ground. Word was getting around. Teddy said "Boo!" to one of the smaller kids named Radley, who then ran away.

Just before we were about to enter the school, Arnold stopped us all but looked squarely at Julian: "And you're wrong, you know."

"Wrong?" Julian stammered, taken by surprise. "About what?"

We are all confused—and curious.

Arnold put us out of our misery: "About the Dodgers being the best team of all time."

"Huh?" Julian almost moaned. "But they are. The best."

"Every heard of the 1927 Yankees? No team ever had a hitting record like them. Not—even—close."

Arnold startled us with this, since, first, Julian's earlier comment seem to have been lost in the ether; and second, Arnold had never mentioned baseball before, or, for that matter, any sport. He usually said sports were a waste of time.

But Arnold wasn't done. "You know what the 1927 Yankees batting line-up was called?"

Julian asked, "What?"

Arnold left a little time before he tossed us the answer: "Murderers' Row."

KITTY LITTER

Julian had to stay behind at school on Monday to catch up on some work, so I left for home alone.

Speeding on my bike down Eastfield Road, I mulled the prospect of going to some kind of hearing thing where I would have to answer more questions about Jacob and Saturday night. In front of a bunch of people? Who?

I passed by the Slough property on the way home and didn't glance in its direction. Feelings crept up about what I said to Deputy Newberry, and what might have to be said at the hearing that wouldn't do Jacob any good. Could he have done the unthinkable? I steered my bike recklessly and flew into our driveway.

Into the kitchen through the back door, breathless. Our new kitten. "He's in the sewing room," mom said. "I've put some kitty litter in there and closed the door, just so he gets a chance to feel more at home in a safe place."

The kitten curled up, sleeping on an old, fuzzy blanket mom must have put on the floor. I picked it up. It didn't seem bothered by the handling, even though I must have disturbed its sleep. Mom came in a minute or two later.

She smiled. "Gumboot's doing fine," she said, "considering all he's been through."

"What?" I said, taken off guard. "Doing fine?" I didn't get this at all.

"Yes. He's had some milk. I'll have to get some proper food for him."

"Oh—oh yeah," I said.

Mom pretended to be looking at the kitten.

"You okay?"

"Yeah, okay."

While I stroked the kitten cupped on my lap, she told me that the County Prosecutor's Office called, and that I would have to go to the hearing on Wednesday in Silverford. I would likely be made to answer some questions in the court, in front of a judge, mainly the same questions that Newberry asked me. Some of the other kids could be called in as well.

Mom explained that the preliminary hearing was to figure out if there was enough evidence to go to a full trial, which is what Newberry had said as well. If there wasn't, Jacob would be let go. There would be lawyers on both sides, she said, and the whole thing might last a couple of days.

"But I might not have to answer any questions, right?" I asked.

"They said this would be up to the judge after he hears some of the case. Juveniles don't usually have to answer in court. But it sounded like it you will."

She was trying to be open, and also trying to sound calm. She couldn't hide her worry. "You okay with this?" she asked.

I wasn't, but I felt I had to make her feel a little less upset, so I said as strongly as I could, "Yeah, I guess so."

Safely curled up in my lap, Gumboot purred while I stroked him. And I don't know why, but I suddenly thought about Deputy Newberry's moustache, and then I wished that I felt as safe as our new little kitten.

8
OPENINGS

Following a dull Tuesday at school, evening at home was quietly anxious while the hearing coming the next day loomed. Sleep that night was anything but restful.

Wednesday morning.

While we got ready to leave for the courthouse in Silverford, mom ran nervously around making sure we would leave on time and that I was dressed and well groomed. She kept saying little reassuring things like, "Don't worry," "Just be polite," "It will be fine." It felt like she was talking to herself.

Dad took the day off work, and he readied himself with a tie and jacket. The only discussion between my parents about the hearing I picked up on was when I passed their bedroom just before we left. Mom: "Will the Sloughs be able to afford a good lawyer?" "Don't know," dad answered, "but if they can't, the Court will appoint one."

We parked near the courthouse, a large, square, stale-looking building. With one hand on my shoulder, looking me firmly in the eyes, dad said one thing to me as we got out of the car: "Tell the truth." The words fell somewhere between advice and a warning.

We entered the through a waiting area but went straight ahead into courtroom as it began to fill. All these people. I recognized a few, but lots of strangers milled around. Were all these people here for the hearing? I hadn't known what to expect, but the talk that hummed and echoed was hard to ignore.

We stood a few feet within the courtroom, waiting to figure out where we were supposed to sit. I had time to look around. Except for Teddy, The Watchers' Club was here. To the front of the courtroom: on the left and right, behind where the lawyers would sit, were the two families, squared off, so it seemed, against each other, despite sharing the loss of their children. Zoran Slagmann, David's father, sat rigidly with a tall, stately woman with blondish-gray hair—must be David's mom. They were motionless. Mr. and Mrs. Slough sat in the same row at the other side of the room. Two slouching lumps almost joined together, holding each others' arm, they looked frightened, sad, worn.

Off to one side and further back sat Sheriff Berg and Deputy Newberry. These two reminded me why I was there.

We were escorted to seats near the front, and, while settling in, I again looked around. Arnold caught my eye and smirked. Billy sat between his parents, looking alternately at his feet then up to the ceiling. Looked like he was holding his breath. Julian was in the row behind us. I also noticed Mr. Bryer sitting at the back by himself, his arms stiffly crossed. Why was he here?

The room suddenly went quiet—Jacob was brought into the courtroom through a side door. He was escorted by a deputy and a thin, middle-aged guy wearing a plain brown suit and carrying a number of folders. The thin man's hair was pasted down flat and straight, but you could tell by haphazard curls that spun out here and there that his hair was not straight by choice. My Perry Mason TV courtroom training came in handy: this guy must be Jacob's lawyer. He somehow looked as out of place as Jacob, who kept his head down so that it was almost impossible to see his face. He passed not too far away from us, and for a second I was sure I caught a glance from his dark eyes. The two sat down, and the lawyer immediately started sorting through his folders and pockets.

A minute later, from the same side door, two middle-aged men wearing dark suits also came across the front of the courtroom. The second man, the taller of the two, carried a cardboard box, while the lead man carried a black case. His red bow tie and deliberate walk made it clear he was the leader.

A very large lady wearing glasses also came in at this time. She squeezed into a chair with a small table at the front of the courtroom. Looking bored, she readied what looked like a small typewriter.

After a short wait a fellow looking like a deputy stepped in from the front of the room and announced, "All rise for Judge William J. Leyland."

The judge, a short man with full, white hair, hurried to his place above and in front of us all and, sitting, put on his glasses and started moving things around on in front of him. "Be seated," he said without looking up.

The lawyers then introduced themselves to the court. Special Prosecutor Raymond Trotter stood up and pronounced loudly who he was and that he represented the People's case against Jacob Elijah Slough. Jacob's gangly lawyer followed and quietly introduced himself as Mr. Theodore Winnlow. He cleared his throat in the middle of his introduction to get more volume.

Judge Leyland looked up and took off his glasses: "Precede with opening statements—and, counselors, keep it brief. Keep in mind that this is a hearing, not a trial. And keep in mind there are young persons in this court."

Trotter stood up: "Thank you. I will be brief, Your Honor, because there is not a lot to dwell on that demands fancy reasoning. The case is clear, and the People will show that the evidence is overwhelming and unambiguous, and that a full trial is warranted." Trotter stepped forward a little closer to the judge.

"What we have, Your Honor, is a crime of the worst nature, one that has shocked and appalled a quiet, rural community. The kind of crime that make people afraid to leave their own homes. A crime that caused schools to be closed."

"Get to it, counselor," the judge interrupted without looking up. Trotter didn't seem to notice the judge's words, almost as if he expected them.

"Two Saturday nights ago, at approximately nine o'clock p.m. or a little thereafter, and after a high school basketball game at Silverford Senior Secondary School, two young people, teenagers—one of them the star of the basketball team that played that evening, the other, a girl gifted with a special singing voice, who that very night had sung our national anthem before the game—well, these two were out parking after the game, in a secluded area of Eastfield known locally as Lovers' Lane, just outside of Silverford City, innocently, doing, you know, what teenagers do." Here he paused to glance in the general direction of Jacob. "Little did they know. They were being—watched."

He turned toward the courtroom before turning again toward the judge.

"And then this—why we are here! What we have, Your Honor, while they were parked that Saturday night, is the brutal murder of these two young people. And what the People will establish and produce, Your Honor, is both hard evidence and clear circumstances—probable cause—

that point directly to the accused, and that is what will be presented at this hearing. The People will show that there is no doubt—no doubt whatsoever—that, based on the facts, evidence, and testimony collected already, some of which will be heard here today—that there is no doubt that the Court should move swiftly to a criminal trial of the accused." Trotter was just getting warmed up, and worked up.

"Now—now the Defense here, the Defense may argue a couple of things, one of them being that the accused is only a juvenile. That he should tried in juvenile court where, well, certain lenience and softer conditions will come into play. But the accused is fifteen years old, almost sixteen—a young, fully developed young man—not some innocent child who, by misfortune or accident, found himself in difficult circumstances. The other argument likely put forward by the Defense is that, mentally, the accused is not fit to stand trial. They may even suggest that there were no witnesses to the crime. Well, the People will argue this, Your Honor: the evidence, circumstances, the way events unfolded that Saturday night—and the motive—are the witnesses in this case. The heinous nature of this crime point directly to the absolute need to pursue a trial suited to the crime. And the fact that the accused, this strong, quiet, young man, is not some kind of an institutionalized escapee, but attends regular school and regularly socializes with others just like anyone else—all this suggests that he face the full criminal process—just like everyone else.

"And, Your Honor, you can guarantee this: the trauma that the community has been put through warrants—no, demands—that the accused be tried in a fashion that puts this community at ease. Justice, the People's justice, Your Honor, must be dealt. As you know, Your Honor, to move to a criminal trial the People simply have to, in reasonable degree, remove the idea of innocence with sufficient evidence. And this the People will do in the spirit of truth, justice, and the swiftness that due process will allow. Thank you, Your Honor."

Trotter sat down.

Trotter's quiet but clear scorn, direct focus, and sense of righteousness was hard to miss. That I might have to answer questions from him did not feel that great. Judge Leyland took some notes.

A few seconds passed. The expectation was that Winnlow would now speak, though it seemed he had not been paying attention in the way he was going through his scattered papers. Judge Leyland prodded him: "Counselor Winnlow. Opening statement?"

"Yes, yes, Your Honor," he said, standing up. "Yes, Your Honor." He cleared his throat.

"The circumstances will, yes, I suppose, very well end up showing that the defendant here, young Jacob Slough, was, that Saturday night—that at some point, he was in the vicinity—maybe even close to—to where the two young persons, one of them the defendant's older sister—a sister he was close to, no doubt—were murdered."

Winnlow stopped and looked down at his papers, but did pick up any. Was this jumbled sentence all he was going to say? The judge scowled.

Winnlow finally continued, abruptly: "That's all they might show—some circumstances. Not much reason for a full criminal trial to proceed. I—the Defense, I mean—will show that there was no motive for Jacob Slough, a young man—I mean, a young teenager, and one with no history of violence—to have committed this crime. No motive. The evidence is, again, just circumstantial. Yes—he was there that night, trailing along with some other neighborhood kids, out on an innocent prank. And he just happened to not come home after the group of young friends broke up that night. Given that Jacob Slough is a, well, something of backward sort—and this is well known, Your Honor—this should not be surprising."

Winnlow paused, like he had forgotten something, and after some fuss, and with some relief, he managed to pull a crumpled paper from his jacket pocket, from which he read slowly: "The law states, that if someone is not mentally competent, and might not be able assist in his or her own defense, then they cannot be tried, convicted, or sentenced." The paper was shoved back into his pocket. "So you see, Jacob Slough cannot, should not, be tried. And he is too young, too, to be in adult criminal court. To put him through a full criminal trial, and his family—poor, simple folk, as they are—would be, well, devastating and—and not deserved."

Winnlow petered off, walked back to where his papers were scattered, then fished one sheet out and read it to himself, nodding his head. He looked up, attempting to raise his voice to a pitch of some authority, and then he read directly: "You don't go to a criminal trial just because some people are anxious for some kind, any kind, of unthinking retribution—especially when that person is vulnerable and at the mercy of events he might not even be competent to understand. That is more like a…like a witch hunt!"

For a moment, it looked like Winnlow had finished, but he bumbled forward a little more: "I would also please like to say to the Court, so that it is on record, that I, I mean the Defense, feels that all of this, these proceedings, I suggest, have moved quickly, too quickly, to this preliminary hearing since the time of arrest of the accused—it's been just over one week—so that there appears some pressure to hear this case as quickly as possible, and because of this, the Defense has not had ample opportunity, nor resources, to thoroughly, well, review all the information that the County Coroner's Office and the Office of the Sheriff has, I think, come up with in what seems to be record time. It's—"

Judge Leyland cut him off: "Thank you. The Court will take this into account, Counselor Windy."

"Um, Winnlow, Your Honor."

"What? Oh, yes, apologies. Counselor Winnlow."

Winnlow abruptly sat down, then stood up, forgetting, it seemed, to finish off: "Thank you." He sat down again, but then half stood up quickly once more, to add, "Your Honor."

Jacob has no chance, I thought. None.

WINNLOW'S WAY

"Call the first witness," the judge said.

Trotter stood up. "I'd like to call Special Deputy Vern Newberry to the stand."

Newberry quickly came forward across the front of the courtroom to an elevated chair to the left of Judge Leyland. Before sitting down, Newberry was sworn in.

"Could you tell the Court your name, your role relative to this case, and something about your background, qualifications, and experience."

Newberry, looking crisp and holding a notebook like the one he wrote into when he interviewed me, could, it seemed, hardly wait to start: "My name is Vernon Stotes Newberry, Special Deputy appointed by the county to gather and coordinate evidence in the murders of David Gilbert Slagmann and Esther Ruth Slough. I am an acknowledged expert investigator in felony cases with over ten years of experience working in the field. I also completed training with the FBI in interview techniques and in the interpretation of forensic evidence."

"Very impressive, Deputy Newberry."

Newberry nodded, ever so slightly.

Trotter: "Now, Deputy Newberry, you come to this case—to all cases—with an open mind. That correct?"

"Yes, I do, sir. That's my job."

"Excellent. Now, could you tell the court what you have thus far done with regards to the case? What do we know? What have you found out in your dealings with those involved with this brutal tragedy?"

"I have worked with the local sheriff and his men on this case almost from the beginning. I was contacted when the two bodies were discovered, and I have interviewed a number of the key persons associated with the incident and with the accused. I have also supervised searches of and examined the areas relevant to the investigation."

"Excellent. Deputy Newberry, could you kindly provide a brief account of what we know about this case, and to the circumstances leading to the accused being at the scene of the crime that Saturday night?"

"Certainly. The two victims were found by the sheriff's men in a parked vehicle on an off-road in a deserted area of Eastfield, two Sundays ago, in the afternoon. The sheriff—Sheriff Gaper Berg—and his deputies were searching Eastfield for two missing teenagers, reported missing the previous night—Saturday night."

"Were the two victims found in the vehicle the missing persons the sheriff and his deputies were looking for? Were the two missing teenagers the same people as the two victims?"

"No. Only one. Esther Slough, age sixteen, almost seventeen, the older sister of the accused, Jacob Slough. The other missing person being looked for was the accused. He was not there."

"Who was the other victim you found, and could you describe the scene in some detail for the court?"

"The other victim was David Slagmann, age seventeen. Both David Slagmann and Esther Slough were found in the vehicle, which belonged to David Slagmann's father, a respected business owner in Silverford. It was his work vehicle. David Slagmann had borrowed this vehicle from his father after the basketball game on Saturday night. When it was found on Sunday afternoon, the front driver's side door was open. Both victims were inside the vehicle."

Trotter kept the questions to Newberry rolling. "Could you describe the victims factually, as they were found in the vehicle?"

"David Slagmann's appearance show that he been assaulted with a weapon and had received blows to his head and to the side of his face.

There was significant bleeding from these areas. He was on the driver's door of the vehicle, slouched over."

The Court was quiet, though low gasps filtered throughout the room. But Newberry went on, full ahead.

"And Ether Slough?"

"Marks on her neck were consistent with having been choked—strangled—and this is consistent with the findings from the Coroner's office, which I consulted with while the autopsies were completed. I have the report here for the Court, which confirm extreme pressure points and bruising of that area around the neck. She was found with the back of her head against the inside of the passenger door window. Some tearing of material around the blouse neckline—consistent with a struggle."

The judge nodded to the officer of the court standing to the side, who took the reports from Newberry and gave them to the judge, who quickly went through them.

Trotter continued: "So, Deputy Newberry, it appears that David Slagmann was bludgeoned into unconsciousness, and then likely bled to death, and Esther Slough was strangled. In the vehicle. Is that correct?"

Once more, lows gasps rose from around the room.

"Correct, though it is somewhat difficult to determine if the trauma to the head or the bleeding was the cause of death."

The image was left to hang in the court. Newberry's words and Trotter's summary seemed to call for silence, but some stifled sobbing came from Mrs. Slough. The Slagmanns remained motionless. Mom held my hand and squeezed it.

Trotter walked around the front of the court, shaking his head, and letting the words and the pictures sink in. Newberry finally gave in with one small twitch, but, up on that chair in front of all of us, he was a picture of cold, credible clarity.

"Deputy Newberry: Do you have any other information from the investigation or from the coroner's office that you can pass on to the Court? Can it be determined when the victims died? Were there footprints? And what information do you have relevant to the case that you have gathered in interviews?"

"It appears the victims died sometime that Saturday evening. An exact time cannot be determined. But the bruising and the state of the dried blood suggest that the bodies were found sometime between twelve and twenty hours after the assault, putting the time of the crime some time mid to late Saturday evening."

"Mid to late Saturday evening. And footprints?"

"Yes, footprints, a couple very clear footprints, right beside the opened door. Much of the clearing is a muddied area."

"Can you tell us anything about those footprints?"

"Likely size twelve. Simple treads to trace."

"What kind of treads? Why 'simple'?"

"The prints are from common, inexpensive rubber boots. The black ones with reddish orange trims. Galoshes. Gumboots, more commonly called."

"Have you been able to trace these boots?"

"Yes—they belong to Esther Slough's brother, Jacob Slough."

"And you can tell that? After all, lots of these boots are sold. Every five and dime store carries them. I may even own a pair myself."

"Yes, examination of the prints revealed that the treads were worn down considerably—in a distinct, unique way."

"And you found the matching boots?"

"Yes, as the judge will see in the third section of the report, they match perfectly with the treads of the rubber boots belonging to and being worn by Jacob Slough when he was found two days after the incident. This matching is, in a way, almost as distinct as a fingerprint matching."

"As distinct as fingerprint matching?"

"Yes. The boots worn by Jacob Slough were the same boots that made footprints around the vehicle."

"Thank you."

One more, Trotter moved around, letting the words sink in.

"And finally, Deputy Newberry, based on the information you have collected, can you tell us about events leading to Jacob Slough being at the scene of the crime that night?"

"Yes," Newberry answered, as if this was the moment he was waiting for. "Through extensive interviews, we have determined that, on the night in question, Jacob and some of his friends went up to the area where the crime took place. To spy on parked couples—to an isolated spot, a clearing known as 'Lovers' Lane' in the district of Eastfield. They came upon the parked Slagmann vehicle there. They saw that David Slagmann, one of the victims, was in the van. They could see he was with a female, but from their vantage place, they could not see the face of the female, who we now know was Esther Slough, the second victim and sister of the accused. After their short escapade, in which they yelled things out in an attempt to surprise or rile up the parkers, the group of friends ran away and then met up at an agreed place. But it appears Jacob Slough was not there when they met up."

"Not there? He didn't meet up with them?"

"No. No. Everyone else left Lovers' Lane, then met up, and after went to their respective homes—but they did notice that the accused, Jacob Slough, was not there when they met up, and we know that the accused did not go home that evening."

"And the time?"

"The best estimate is around nine-thirty to ten-fifteen. We can base this on the interviews with Jacob's friends, and based on when the high-school basketball game was over—David Slagmann played in that game— and the time it might have taken him to get to the area of Lovers' Lane."

"So, we can confirm that Jacob was at the scene of the crime—but, unlike his friends, he did not leave it?"

"That is correct."

Winnlow shot up, which surprised us all, since we were all so caught up in Trotter's account: "Objection. Objection, Your Honor. He can't know that. Whether Jacob stayed or not. Maybe he went somewhere else. Maybe he just went for a walk. This is speculation."

Leyland didn't even look up. "Sustained."

"Thank you, Deputy Newberry. No more questions."

Trotter seemed done, but he turned to Judge Leyland: "Your Honor, the People would like to reserve the right to recall Deputy Newberry to the stand later in the hearing, since a few items may require clarification. The People would, with the permission of Your Honor, prefer to call a few other witnesses in the interim in order to get and confirm, for the court, a first-hand account of the circumstances leading up to the incident itself, and, in particular, a linking of an alleged murder weapon to the accused."

Winnlow shot up. His chair almost fell over. "Your Honor, if, if Counselor Trotter is allowed to bring Deputy Newberry back to the stand a second time, the Defense requests that it be allowed to question him a second time—also. If the prosecutor and the deputy have further information, shouldn't this come out now? Why should we wait?"

Trotter immediately, but coolly replied. "With respect, Your Honor, the choice not to bring up the other details and incidents, including those leading to the identification of a possible murder weapon, is, I believe, at this point, best represented from first-hand sources. That is all."

Both lawyers waited for Judge Leyland to settle the issue. He took a few moments: "I agree with the Defense that it would seem fitting to bring up details of an alleged murder weapon and other details, especially if Deputy Newberry is in possession of these details and while he on the stand. But full disclosure of evidence is not necessarily a requirement at a preliminary hearing. Overruled."

The judge stopped for a second and looked down at his notes, then continued: "However, so long as when, or if, Deputy Newberry returns to the stand, we get to these other issues quickly, and so long if this is a genuine attempt to present relevant evidence through a first-hand account, I will allow this request—but, Counselor Trotter, keep in mind that the Court does not look kindly upon grandstanding or unnecessary diversions, especially at a preliminary hearing, and if the Court perceives this, it may look kindly upon any objections raised about this evidence."

Judge Leyland put his glasses back on and turned to some papers in front of him: "Now let's get on. Counselor Winnlow, do you have any questions for Deputy Newberry at this time?"

"No—well yes—yes, Your Honor. Questions…"

Winnlow stood up. "Yes—Deputy Newberry. Yes—okay, you spoke about the footprints at the scene of the crime. Were there any other prints around by the passenger side of the car—besides those you say belonged to Jacob?"

"Yes. But we have not been unable to identify them—they are not all clear—and it is impossible to say exactly when they were made. Also, we would not begin to know where to check against them."

"Yes, I see. So…so these other footprints are not as clear—or identifiable, let's say—as those of Jacob. They can't be checked. I see. You wouldn't know where to begin. I don't think these other footprints were mentioned in the questions from Counselor Trotter—but I might have missed it. Okay. Okay. And other tire prints? Are there are other car tire prints—beside those of the Slagmann truck—close by to where the Slagmann truck was parked?"

"Yes. Ah yes, there are, were, other tire prints. We would expect at least some other traffic, and therefore other prints, in this area."

"When were these other tracks made?"

"We cannot tell with any exact measure when some of these other prints were laid down."

"So—you are saying they could have been made after the murder, or after the boys left Lovers' Lane? Or before. Or while they were still alive. That possible—at all possible?"

Winnlow for the first time went to his notebook. He answered, "Yes," but his tone was dismissive.

Winnlow went on. "And, Deputy Newberry, has the Sheriff's Office investigated these other tire and foot prints?"

"We were unable to derive anything helpful for this case."

"You—you mean you don't know who made the prints, and you don't know when?"

"It is not altogether certain."

"I see. I see. You are not certain. You don't know."

Winnlow turned his back to Newberry. "Sounds like you didn't check."

Newberry gave his fine moustache a quick groom with his thumb and index figure. Winnlow turned to Newberry again. "Now—now Deputy Newberry. You say that evidence that David Slagmann likely died from blows received to the head, while Esther Slough was strangled."

"Yes."

"Does, well, does this seem…well, do you think this is….odd?"

"I don't deal in oddness, just in facts, sir."

"Yes, facts—facts are good. But as someone with experience in these matters, does it seem, maybe, usual—I mean in these two deaths? One victim killed one way, the other a very different way? Especially if, as it seems, they were killed at the same time and, it seems, the same place—since we have no reason or evidence to think otherwise."

"What you are asking is not clear." Newberry let go with a full-blown twitch.

Winnlow attempted to clarify. "Well, I mean, after all, why not murder them in the same way? I mean, if you were the murderer, would you, say, bludgeon someone, and then go put away the weapon, and then strangle the next person, who is right there? Why not use the same weapon? And wouldn't it be difficult, awkward, or whatever, to overcome two persons in this way—in the two ways, I mean?"

Trotter quickly stood up. "Objection. These muddled questions ask the witness to speculate."

Leyland sustained the objection.

Winnlow continued. "Okay…okay. Or, say, say you strangled one person, who was on one side of the car, while the other was there. You finish that person off, and then you have some weapon suddenly, and finish off the other—well, don't you think this seems a little clumsy, or difficult, or something? Don't you think? Did David Slagmann just sit there and watch—this star athlete, a superbly strong young man much used to physical contact? Try to picture the events, either way, as they would have happened, in time, I mean. Don't you think this is a little strange, or an awkward way to…to do things? One of them had to be killed first one way, and then the other—well, what was the other one up to during this time—if indeed they were murdered at the same time or place."

"Objection Your Honor," Trotter stood up. "Is there a question here, or is my colleague just rambling around looking for one?" A snicker or sneer rose from the back of the courtroom.

Leyland seemed unconcerned, and just said, "Sustained. Counselor Winnlow, see if you can come up with a direct question. Soon."

"Thank you, Your Honor," Winnlow continued. "I think I was asking if you, Deputy Newberry, if you might think one of them might run away? Try to run away. Seems, well—what do you think happened?" Winnlow seemed to have everyone confused, maybe even himself. He scratched his knee.

"Well," said Newberry, "we cannot tell with any exactitude—we don't know exactly what happened there. The exact chronology of things."

Winnlow held himself still to give these words space in the courtroom. Then he repeated what Newberry said, slowly: "Yes. Yes! You're right. You are right! We don't know exactly what happened there. Or how. Let alone why. We don't know. I don't, and you don't. How about that!"

Trotter didn't even stand up this time. "Your Honor, please. Objection."

"Sustained."

Despite the convoluted picture Winnlow drew for the court, and despite the objections, it seemed, for the first time, Winnlow almost knew what he was doing. Newberry's gestures had become a little defensive. Winnlow said it one more time, "So, what you are saying, Deputy Newberry, is that we don't know exactly what happened out there that night. How this all happened. And exactly when. And we have to somehow, somehow piece it together in some way. And that is because…well, why Deputy Newberry?"

"Why?"

"Yes, why. Why don't we know exactly what happened?"

Newberry said something it seemed like he didn't want to say: "Because, as far as we know, there was no witness to the crime."

"Oh, yes! That's right. No witness to the crime. Thank you for reminding me. I almost forgot. No witnesses. Not a one."

There were again a few snickers from the courtroom, as well as a few low groans.

Winnlow paced a bit and continued: "But to go back. For one person, a young person at that, to murder two others, one of them his sister, the other a young man, a top athlete, in two different ways, at the same time, in the dark, without one taking off—well, this seems like a remarkable thing to pull off, don't you think?"

"Well, we have to account for the footprints beside the car," Newberry stated.

Winnlow turned quickly around. "I don't have to, Deputy. That's the Prosecutor's job!"

Winnlow was, for a second, in his bumbling way, almost impressive. That he could make Newberry stumble just a bit was something.

Winnlow sat down, put his hand on Jacob's shoulder for a second, and said, "Only one further issue, then, to take up Deputy—Deputy Newberry. About those footprints: Do those footprints in any way indicate that Jacob Slough committed the murder?"

"No, only that he was there, by the driver's side of the car."

"Before, after, or during the time of the crime?"

Newberry hesitated just a little: "We don't know that. There is possible range of time—"

"What kind of a range of time, Deputy? Be exact. Use your expertise."

Newberry did not like this, but he said, flatly, "A matter of, say, six, maybe up to even ten hours, when they might have been made."

"So he might have been up there, maybe a little before the car was there?"

"Well, that seems—"

"Seems what, exactly, Deputy Newberry?"

Newberry added, "Possible."

"Possible. Or, Jacob might have been there well after the crime, seen it, and run away—so shocked by what he had seen, that he didn't go home that night?"

"We don't know that."

"But is it possible?"

"This is not for me to say."

"Or—or he might have come if, say, he heard a call for help, for example?"

"We don't know that."

"Ah, you are right again, Deputy Newberry, thank you—we don't know that."

Winnlow turned and sat down, and in doing so said, "No more questions, Your Honor—at this time."

The courtroom gallery seemed unsettled by Winnlow's way. Doubt, even small doubt, did not sit well. Eastfield had a horrible crime on its hands, and it needed to find its horrible criminal to clean those hands. In the air was the belief that, sitting right there in the courtroom, was what it needed, and its name was Jacob Elijah Slough.

The courtroom took a few moments to settle down from the flicker of uncertainty that Winnlow pulled out of nowhere. Now I almost looked forward to what might come next. I was even a little proud of my concentration in following everything. My anticipation and pride, though, immediately fell: my name called by Trotter. Mom squeezed my hand as I stood up and passed by her. I found my way to the front of the courtroom where Newberry had just sat. I tried not to look out into the gallery. Judge Leyland reminded both counselors that, because of my age, that their questions be "gauged appropriately."

Trotter didn't stand up to begin with. He asked me how long I known Jacob and how far away I lived from him. Despite the judge at one point asking me to speak up, these questions weren't too tough, and I managed, after deep breaths, to get through them by looking at Trotter and nothing else. He worked around to a few questions about what Jacob was like:

"Would you say that Jacob Slough was, well, a strong young man?"

"Yes."

"Very strong?"

"Yes."

"Compared to all the others who are your friends?"

"Yes, I mean stronger than us."

"How do you know this?"

I had to think about this for a second. "He could pick up or break stuff that none of us could." This felt like I was giving the wrong picture, so I blurted out something, anything, in Jacob's defense. "And he is really a great drawer, the best at our school." I immediately felt embarrassed.

"Thank you," Trotter noted, with something of a sarcastic smile. "Nice to know that the accused is an accomplished artist."

He moved on. "Now, would you say that Jacob Slough was aware of what was going on when you did things, or when things were said and done?"

"Well, I think—"

"Sorry. Would he do the things you and your friends would do, when he was with you, that is?"

"Yes—most of the time. Some of the things."

Trotter stood and walked toward me, and he asked about the details of that Saturday night, about what we were up to and who was there. The questions followed the same path that Newberry took when he interviewed me at home: who was there, where we all met, what time it was.

"Now, was there anything with you, with your friends, that night when you went up to Lovers' Lane?"

I had to think. What could that be? My moment of uncertainty was cut short by Trotter making an offering before I could respond, like he thought I was trying to hide something?

"Say—a flashlight?"

Huh, what?

"Yeah—yes. We had a flashlight, I forgot, that Billy brought with him."

"Billy Luckhert?"

"Yes."

"Billy Luckhert. One of your friends. One of Jacob's friends."

There was no answer, since this didn't seem to be a question.

Trotter kept on: "Where did Billy get it?"

"It was his dad's. Billy just kind of wanted to show it to us. You know, something."

I stuttered through this, thinking of Billy out there in the courtroom with his dad, and wondered if this was new information. But it couldn't have been, since Trotter seemed to know all about the flashlight. And for some reason he drilled in on this.

"Could you describe the flashlight?"

"It was silver."

"Made of?"

"Um, some metal, I guess."

"Size?"

"Pretty big."

"Larger than an average flashlight?"

"Yes, bigger."

"Did you get a chance to hold it?"

"Yes, sir."

"What did it feel like?"

"It was heavy."

"Was it old, or new, or broken in any way?"

"New, I think."

"No damage to it?"

"No."

"How do you know that?"

"It was clean and shiny."

"Good, good. Now, what did you do with the flashlight when you took it to Lovers' Lane?"

The questions headed somewhere that I didn't touch on when Newberry talked with me.

"Well, we thought if we found a car at Lovers' Lane, we would shine it into the car for a second before we shouted some stuff out. Then run away. Just to kind of…disturb them for a second or something. For fun."

"Could you describe how this was going to happen? Be as specific as you can."

I tried, but didn't get anything of what this was about. "Billy brought the flashlight. He was going to sneak around to the front of the van while the rest of us were beside it." My voice began to peter out. I could tell Trotter wanted more from me. "He would turn it for a second so we could all see inside—just sort of scare them."

"Scare who?"

"Who was parked there."

"Yes. And—well, what happened?"

"Billy—he went around the front of the car, kind of hiding, then turned it on for a second, we shouted some stuff out and then we ran away to meet at the Old Orchard."

"And what exactly did you see when the light flashed on?"

That moment came back to me. "I—for a second or two, I could see David Slagmann's face—from the side, for just a second. Because we were on the side."

"You sure it was him?"

"Pretty well sure."

"Anyone else—that you saw in the vehicle?"

"And I could see the back of someone's head against the door window."

"Which window?

"The side closest to us."

"The passenger side?"

"Yes."

"You were all standing along the passenger side of the van, some few yards away, with a little bush between you and the van—correct?"

"Yes."

"Where were you, I mean you in particular, standing? I mean, at what part of the car were you beside—front, back, middle?"

"Toward the front."

"And Jacob?"

"He was on, um, my—my right side. The right. More to the front."

"How far away?"

"Maybe—seven, eight yards. Maybe a bit more. Something like that."

"So he would be further toward the front of the van, and he would have a better angle to see right into the van, correct?"

Winnlow stood up. "Objection, Your Honor. That's leading the witness. How can he know what someone else was seeing? And the questioning is pushy with the young witness. I would ask—"

"Sustained," the judge immediately answered.

Winnlow sat down. Trotter continued, just the way he had been going. "So, Jacob was to your right, maybe seven yards or more, more toward the front of the vehicle. His angle would have been different than yours."

"I—yes."

"That was the last time you saw Jacob that night, correct?"

"Yes."

Trotter looked around the court for a few moments, which gave me a few seconds to change my position. So far I probably hadn't moved any part of my body except my lips.

"You said you could see David Slagmann's face."

"Yes."

"And you could tell it was him, and that he was—alive."

"Yes."

"Did you know who that other person in the vehicle was?"

"No."

"Was there anything else you could see or describe about her?"

Winnlow stood up: "Objection. Leading the witness. The prosecution is assuming that the other person in that car at that time was female, when the witness has not indicated that this other person was female."

"Sustained," said Judge Leyland without much conviction.

Trotter immediately continued: "Could you describe anything you noted about this other person in the car with David Slagmann?"

I stumbled. "It was, just…the back someone's head, against the window."

Trotter nodded. "Okay. Leave it at that. And so you all met up at this orchard after you ran away? That correct?"

"Yes."

"All of you who went up there that night?"

"Yes—well, no."

"No? You mean, not everyone who was up by the vehicle showed up? Did Jacob Slough show up?"

"No. Don't think so. Sometimes—"

"Anyone else see him when you met up?"

"No. Don't think so."

"Where was Jacob?"

"I don't know."

"He didn't run away from Lovers' Lane like the rest of your friends?"

"Yes. No. Well, I'm not sure."

"Would you have seen him if he did?"

Trotter did not allow me to answer before he came back with the question in a different way: "Sorry. Was the way back to Eastfield Road along this trail you came up—was this the best, quickest, way to return, to Eastfield Road, where you lived, and where Jacob Slough lived?"

"Probably. Yes."

"And would you have seen Jacob Slough if he went back that way when you ran away from Lovers' Lane."

"Probably. Maybe."

"So, he, maybe for some reason, could have stayed behind when the rest of you left?"

Winnlow interrupted: "Objection, objection Your Honor! The

prosecution is asking the boy to make a conjecture based on knowledge he doesn't have!"

"Sustained," said the judge.

"So," continued Trotter, "Jacob Slough did not seem to join you at the orchard, and everyone else who was with you went you went up to Lovers' Lane did meet up, like you arranged?"

"Yes."

Trotter walked back to his chair and sat down and looked at me for a few seconds. I really hoped that he was done.

"And Billy, Billy Luckhert, your friend who aimed the flashlight in the van—he met up back at the orchard—correct?"

"Yes."

"Did he have the flashlight with him?"

"No."

"He, Billy, didn't have the flashlight with him?" Trotter didn't seem surprised. "Where was it?"

"He said he left it behind."

"Where?"

"At Lovers' Lane."

"Why?"

"He...he said that, something like, that he dropped it because he couldn't turn it off after he shined it in the van."

"So, he just left it at Lovers' Lane, by the vehicle, in front of it, dropped it—and then Jacob didn't show up at the orchard where you were all going to meet, and the rest of you did meet up. You boys have done this little prank before, I understand. That correct?"

"Yes," I admitted.

"And, to repeat, when you did, you said you would meet at the orchard after you ran away. That correct."

"Yes."

"And when you did, on those other couple of times, was Jacob there?"

"I'm not sure."

Suddenly I felt tired and lost. Trotter wasn't.

"Well, just think for second. Try to recall. Did Jacob show up after on those other times?"

"Maybe. I think so. But I'm not sure."

Trotter looked at his notes and seemed to speak more to the judge than to me. "Well, what we do know, is that on the night in question, Jacob

Slough didn't show up at the orchard, and he did not show up at home that night. According to the information from the Sheriff's Office, he was found the following Tuesday, late afternoon. About forty-eight hours after the victims were found. Hiding out in an old abandoned place in Eastfield—on Eastfield Road." He nodded and finished up: "And, according to the report from the Sheriff's Office, Jacob Slough, when discovered in this old house—was found to be in possession of this very same flashlight, and—"

Winnlow stood up and addressed the judge: "Your Honor. There is no question for the witness. If he has some question—"

The judge said straight out: "Counselor Trotter, save your summation. Do you have any further questions for the witness?"

"Apologies, Your Honor. Three quick questions," Trotter said, almost lightly, looking at his notes.

Trotter turned to me and stood a few feet away, and then I knew that he had known the answer to every question he had asked me so far. What was he saving?

"Could you tell the court the nickname you and your friends have for Jacob Slough?"

I had to think for a second because it seemed like a strange question. "Nickname?"

"Yes. What you call him. Not his real name."

I had to think a bit. "Uh, 'Gumboot,' I guess."

"And why do you call him 'Gumboot'?"

"Because he always wears gumboots."

"Gumboots. Another name for rubber boots. And what was Jacob wearing that Saturday night? Can you recall?"

I thought for a second. "A plaid shirt, maybe, I think."

"Sorry—what footwear was Jacob Slough wearing that Saturday night?"

I glanced for second toward Jacob, and then, out of all the faces looking at me, I caught Arnold's eye. Until that moment in my life, I didn't know you could feel so tired and important and sad at the same time. Trotter waited. He knew what I had to say, and I said it:

"Gumboots, I think."

Trotter repeated it loudly: "Gumboots—rubber boots."

"You sure?"

As he got louder, I got softer. "Yes, I think he was wearing gumboots."

Trotter sat down and looked at me: "Thank you."

"Your witness, Mr. Winnlow," the judge said, but then quickly added, turning to me. "You okay, son, to go on? Answer a few more questions? Would you like some water?"

I didn't have the energy to say that I was feeling lousy, and so Winnlow approached me, slowly.

"You know Jacob pretty well, right?"

"Yes."

"Have you ever known him to be violent or anything like that?"

"No."

"Never?"

"No."

"Would you say that he is gentle?"

"Yes."

"Did you ever hear him speak badly or meanly of anyone, maybe even his sister, or a teacher, or his parents—anyone—other kids?"

"No, sir. Never."

"Would Jacob necessarily have to leave that area where you encountered the parked the vehicle—I mean, would he have to leave the same way you all came?"

"No."

"Did you see Jacob go and, say, get the flashlight after it was dropped?"

"No."

"Did Jacob seemed unusual or upset or anything that night?"

"No, sir."

"And Jacob was known for just wandering off on his own, sometimes, for no particular kind of reason?"

"Yes."

"Often?"

"Yes, probably often, I guess."

"What do you mean?"

"Well, sometimes he just kind of wanders away or shows up."

"Did you have any way of knowing who would be parked at the place you were going to that night—Lovers' Lane, I mean?"

"No."

"Thank you. That's all. That's a lot. That's a whole lot."

Winnlow sat down, and I was given time to return to my seat. I felt like I was getting up from a dream in which someone else's words were pulled out—forced out—of my mouth. I sat down between my parents.

Mom took up my hand, and dad put his on my knee for second. I wanted to go home. I wanted to lose interest in whole thing—in everything.

No Further Questions

The rest of the day, punctuated by lunch at a downtown restaurant where I normally pigged-out, went slowly. The afternoon session saw Arnold and then Julian take the stand. Billy, for some reason, was not called. He just sat there, between his mum and dad, holding his breath and looking up and down. Arnold and Julian more or less repeated the same story that I had given about what we did that Saturday, though the details weren't gone over so thoroughly. Arnold seemed to enjoy himself, especially when it came to answering Trotter about what Jacob was like.

"Yes," declared Arnold. "He's strong alright. Real strong."

"And how would you say he acts—when he's with you, I mean?"

"Well, you never know what he's going to do."

"You mean you don't know what he's thinking?"

"He just kind of creeps up on you, and never says much, if anything."

"And on that Saturday night—that was the case?"

"Yes. He just kind of crept up on us that night, too. While we were about to go up The Trail. Me and our gang—The Watchers' Club."

"'The Watchers' Club'?"

"That's what we called ourselves when we did this."

"I see. 'The Watchers' Club.' And Jacob Slough didn't show up at the orchard after you—The Watchers' Club—ran away?"

"No."

"Normally he would have?"

"Yes, he almost always shows up, just a little after the rest of us gather anywhere. He tags behind. Lurks, kind of. He's always lurking somewhere."

"But this time he didn't?"

"No. He didn't."

Winnlow, unlike Trotter, took his time with Arnold, but he did little to counter the tone Arnold developed with Trotter's questioning, except Arnold did acknowledge that, like me, he had never seen Jacob act violent toward anyone or anything.

Julian nervously took the stand and went through the events and relevant information with Trotter. Trotter, at first, it seemed, tried to soften him up by taking a more quiet approach than with Arnold. But then Trotter took a different direction:

"Now, Julian, it has been said that Jacob was a quiet sort—that he never really said anything much about others. That he was gentle."

"Yes."

"He even had rabbits—pet rabbits—that he took care of—right?"

"Yes."

"He took good care of these pet rabbits?"

Julian responded in a way that made it seem he was relieved to be talking about such a thing. "Yes. He took care of the rabbits."

"You say he took care of them. He must have liked them. Did you ever see any the pet rabbits? Say, at school?"

"He brought one of them to school, once, to show the class—for pet day."

"For pet day. And Jacob tended these rabbits at his home—correct?"

"Yes," said Julian, seeming somewhat confused about the questions. We were all confused. Trotter must have known about all this already.

"For whom? For whom did he take care of these pet rabbits of his?" Trotter pressed forward.

"For his dad."

"For his dad. Now, what did his dad do with these rabbits?"

Winnlow interrupted. "Objection, Your Honor. This questioning is irrelevant. It has nothing to do with what did or didn't take place that Saturday night."

Trotter countered strongly. "Your Honor, this directly leads to information which will be fully relevant to Jacob's alleged actions—perhaps his motives, even. In order to determine whether there is cause to go to trial."

Judge Leyland ruled quickly. "I will allow the line of questioning if, Counselor Trotter, it leads to a point—and very soon."

Trotter continued, and Julian slouched. "And so, Julian, what did Jacob's father do with these pet rabbits of Jacob?"

"He—he kept them—for rabbit meat."

"You mean, he bred them, then sold them to someone else who then slaughtered these rabbits for rabbit meat?"

"Yes—no. Mr. Slough—I mean, he, well, did it himself."

"Oh, I see. The rabbits that Jacob took care of…were killed for rabbit meat."

"Yes."

"Where did he—Mr. Slough—do this? Kill them, I mean."

"In their backyard."

"And how did he—how did he do it?"

"No. He—he did it with—"

Winnlow cut him off and objected. "Your Honor, please, with all respect, this is completely irrelevant."

Trotter shot back, "I'm almost there, Your Honor."

Judge Leyland looked up and took off his glasses. "Counselor Trotter, you have about thirty seconds to make your point."

"Thank you."

Winnlow looked very unsettled while Trotter continued with Julian: "So Mr. Slough dispatched these rabbits how?"

Julian looked about as trapped as those doomed bunnies.

"How?" Trotter repeated.

"With his—with his hands. Or he clubbed them with something."

Trotter let this coldly sit in the air for a moment, then turned and repeated it. "Mr. Slough killed these rabbits himself, clubbing them, or with his hands, and the rabbits that Jacob was to take care of—some of them his pets. And Mr. Slough, he sold them?"

"Yes."

"To whom—do you know, Julian?"

Julian slouched. "Yes."

"Who did Mr. Slough sell these rabbits to, that Jacob took care of?"

"To Mr. Slagmann."

"To Mr. Slagmann, the father of the victim David Slagmann? Who has a butcher shop here in Silverford?"

"Yes."

"Mr. Slagmann would come to pick them up at the Slough residence, in his van, the one you came across on that Saturday night parked at Lovers' Lane? That correct?"

"Yes."

"So, Jacob took good care of these rabbits, treated them like pets, then his dad, with his bare hands"—and here Trotter made a kind of brief choking gesture with his hand—"slaughters them for Mr. Slagmann, the father of the David Slagmann, one of the murder victims—"

Winnlow stood up and loudly objected once more. "Your Honor, this is simply too much! Counselor Trotter is constructing something out of thin air, and this line of questioning should be stopped!"

Judge Leyland agreed immediately. "Sustained."

Trotter had already made his way back to his chair.

"No further questions, Your Honor."

Murmurs spread fully through the court, and for the first time Judge Leyland gaveled for quiet, and as he did so, he announced that the hearing would continue tomorrow.

The Long Ride Home

The ride home was long and quiet. Mom and dad each made one comment to me:

Dad: "You did okay, son—told the truth—all you could do."

Mom: "Are you hungry? We could pick something up on the way home. Something nice."

We didn't stop anywhere. I vaguely considered that my parents, and particularly dad, hadn't yet come down on me for what we did that Saturday night, and for then lying about it. Given what was happening to Jacob, I didn't really care one way or the other about eventual consequences—grounded, no TV, extra chores. Whatever. The idea of Jacob's father killing the rabbits suddenly took a cloudy, sickly turn, as if we were all somehow guilty. We all knew about this, and had a few times got a glimpse of what exactly took place. But now, it meant something not so closed, hidden. It was something we were all, somehow, a part of.

We continued along the highway between Silverford and Eastfield and into silver-gray of late afternoon. I still couldn't imagine what might have happened, why Jacob did what he appeared to do. But I didn't believe it, and inside I could hear myself repeat that something needed to be done to help him. Two pictures of Jacob, both in darkness. There he is, over to my right, out beyond Teddy, as we approached the Slagmann's van through the bushes. And there he is, a few days later on that rainy afternoon, in Mrs. Raskolnikov's beaten-up shack, holding the black and white kitten out to me with those sooty hands: "It needs milk," he said. "I drew it," he said. Then a third image rose and moved through me: David Slagmann's white, profiled face as the short, sharp glare of the flashlight struck him. Then I didn't want to see any more.

9
SUSTAINED

While we drove into Silverford the next morning, my parents said that this would probably be the last day of the hearing. I likely wouldn't be called to testify at anymore, but I had to be there just in case. I asked what they thought would happen to Jacob. They said they didn't know. "It will be up to the court to decide if they go to a criminal trial." My mom for some reason then said she was sorry, and it seemed right, maybe like she was saying it for all of us.

The courtroom was packed again, and this time with some new faces, some looking like they were poised to take notes.

The morning started with Trotter recalling Deputy Newberry to the stand. Newberry carried a folder. The judge reminded him he was still under oath.

Trotter began. "Thank you for continuing your testimony from yesterday, Deputy Newberry. And also for bringing together and coordinating a great deal of the information regarding this tragic case."

Newberry nodded.

"Now, yesterday—in your testimony yesterday, you mentioned that, two days after the victims were found at Lovers' Lane, the sheriff and his men discovered Jacob Slough hiding in an abandoned house—an old shack—on Eastfield Road. Is that correct?"

"Yes."

"Now, was the old house searched after he was taken in to custody?"

"That is correct."

"Could you tell the Court the results of the search?"

"The house had little in it: a few random items owned by the person who used to live there some years ago. She died a few years ago. A little broken furniture, an old picture frame or two, a few old papers—a stray cat or two. But," and here Newberry sat up straighter and spoke more deliberately, "we also found a flashlight."

"You found a flashlight. Could you describe that flashlight for the court?"

"Yes. A large, metal flashlight, silver-metallic finish. Quite new. The type used by the police or fire departments because of its rugged construction. We handled the flashlight carefully, tagged it, and took it to forensics for examination."

While Newberry gave his clear, clipped description that sounded more like a commercial, Trotter walked over to the side of courtroom to a side table where he picked a plastic bag with something in it. As he passed the bag to Newberry, Trotter asked, "Is this the flashlight you found with Jacob Slough in the old house?"

Newberry looked at it for a few seconds, and answered, "Yes. The tag numbers correspond."

Newberry passed the bag back to Trotter, who in turn passed it to the court officer. He added, "A forensic expert has examined this flashlight?"

"I have the full report here," Trotter affirmed.

The report was taken by the court officer and passed to Judge Leyland who immediately immersed himself.

"Could you kindly summarize for the Court the findings of this examination?"

"Yes." Newberry shifted and cleared his throat. "Fingerprints were found on the flashlight. Also, the flashlight had some damage done to it— and there was also some blood and other matter on the flashlight."

The courtroom squirmed. My hands went sticky. The flashlight! Billy's stupid dropped flashlight! Newberry waited for the court to settle. Everyone knew where this was going. Once more I thought of Billy sitting there beside his dad.

"Deputy Trotter, could you tell us about the fingerprints?"

"There are fingerprints, mainly nondistinguishable parts of fingerprints, on the flashlight. Many not readily identifiable. But, as the report shows, we can, with certainty, tell which are the most recent and most pervasive fingerprints, since they are embedded into some of the small areas where there is blood on the flashlight itself—not beneath it or covered by it—but right into it."

"What does that mean?"

"It means that, almost certainly, some of the fingerprints were made when the blood on the flashlight was not dry—that is, when there was blood was on it."

Trotter, now almost beside Newberry, turned and looked briefly in the direction of Jacob. "Has it been determined who those fingerprints belong to—the most recent ones, the ones made into the blood on the flashlight?"

"Yes," he said. "To Jacob Slough."

"Without a doubt?"

"Yes, without a doubt."

The courtroom again unsettled itself, and I sank. Judge Leyland looked out at the courtroom as if to silence it. His look worked.

Trotter walked around before asking his next question.

"Now, you also said there is some damage to the flashlight."

"Yes. The glass lens is broken out, and the casing around the lens area is slightly damaged, dented. We did manage to recover the lens in the—"

Trotter, for the moment, wasn't interested in this. He wanted to move quickly to the other areas he mentioned. "And you said there was some 'matter' on the flashlight?"

"Yes. There were some small strands of hair and particles of skin around where the flashlight is damaged, which, along with the blood, were examined."

"And what is the result of this examination?"

"As the report shows, the hair embedded on the flashlight is consistent with the scalp hair of David Slagmann. And so is the blood type—type 'O'."

"That is, the blood type, type 'O', on the flashlight, is the same as David Slagmann's blood type, and the hair as well?"

"Yes."

"And you mentioned that the glass lens was recovered?"

"It was found on the floor of the Slagmann vehicle parked in Lovers' Lane. On the driver's side. We didn't think it meant anything until we recovered the flashlight. Then we saw the fit, the connection."

"So it must have come off in the vehicle?"

"That would be the logical conclusion."

"And finally, Deputy Newberry, does the Coroner's report comment on what might have caused those blows to David Slagmann's head—the blows you described in your earlier testimony?"

"Yes. The injuries are consistent with those wielded by the flashlight, especially given the blood and hair found on the flashlight—as well as the damage to the housing around where the lens broke out."

"In short, Deputy Newberry, the flashlight appears to be the murder weapon?"

For a second it looked like Winnlow was going to stand up, probably to object. But he didn't. Newberry answered the question. "Yes. That would be the conclusion."

"Thank you, Deputy Newberry. No further questions."

Trotter sat down, and from the back the courtroom you could hear a few people quickly leaving. Winnlow rose and walked around, aimlessly, it seemed. The court waited for him to say something. Anything.

Winnlow returned to his seat beside the shrunken Jacob. The judge asked him if he had any questions for Newberry. At last Winnlow began. "Deputy. Deputy Newberry. In your interviews and evidence gathering, is there anything, anything at all, to suggest that Jacob disliked or had acted violently toward his sister—ever?"

"No, none that I gathered."

"Or that he disliked, hated, or even properly knew David Slagmann?"

"No."

"I see. And the fingerprints on the flashlight. There are others, correct—I mean other fingerprints not identifiable?"

"Yes."

"Why?"

"Because they are partial or have been smeared over with some blood and some dirt—mud."

"You suggest that Jacob last held the flashlight."

"Yes."

"And that there must have been a fair amount of blood all over the flashlight, and blood on the hand of whoever held it, right."

"Yes. That would be correct."

"Thank you."

Winnlow looked like he was done as he walked away. Newberry visibly relaxed as he looked around the courtroom. But Winnlow turned, and began again, slowly. "Well . . . this is all interesting. Is it at all possible that the flashlight might have been used by used by someone, bloodied, say, and then picked up, handled later, by Jacob—after the crime took place?"

Newberry, who normally responded quickly, squeezed out a "Yes." He added, "But, given the circumstances, not likely."

"'Not likely,' you say. 'Not likely.' That does not sound like a fact speaking, I'd say."

Winnlow paced around, not looking at Newberry, though Newberry watched him with vague curiosity. In fact, we all did. Winnlow pinched his nose a couple of times before starting again, then gave an odd, extended scratch of his knee: "I see. Possible . . . So, you are saying that—that there is a possibility—that Jacob handled the flashlight after it was used to murder David Slagmann?"

Newberry again took his time. "That is a possibility."

"You mean 'Yes,' I take it. Okay, okay. And do you know how the flashlight got from Lovers' Lane on Saturday night to the old house on Eastfield Road where you found Jacob on Tuesday?"

Newberry blinked quickly a few times, then smiled a little. "Well, you would assume—"

Winnlow, somewhat surprisingly, interrupted. "No, no, no. Not what you would 'assume.' Do you know how the flashlight got to the deserted house on Eastfield Road?"

"I—no."

"Hmm. I see. I see. You don't know. Okay. Were there any signs of blood, type 'O' blood, on Jacob's clothing when you found him?"

"No—it looked like his clothes had been completely soaked with water at some point, likely rain water, and perhaps—"

"None?"

"No, not that we could see."

Winnlow itched again away at one of his knees while pulling out and looking at some crumpled notes from his jacket pocket. Even the judge glanced up and gave him a strange look. All the while he kind of mumbled to himself, "Hmm…hmm…" When he stopped scratching and hmming, he continued: "Jacob, I believe, according to one of the reports, has had a physical examination to see if there were any signs of recent bruising or cuts or marks—something might suggest a sign of struggle?"

"Yes."

"Were any such recent signs noticeable—you know, fresh cuts, scrapes, scratches, or bruising, or anything—on Jacob? Anything?"

"Nothing we could see. A couple of older bruises."

"That would mean 'No,' I take it. And, like you said, there didn't seem to be blood on his clothes."

Newberry shifted in his seat. There was no question to answer.

"Would you—now, would you find all of this surprising for an individual who went through what Jacob allegedly went through?"

"No, not necessarily. There may have been—"

Newberry stopped himself, and it looked as if Trotter was about to stand up to object. Winnlow passed a glance over at Trotter before returning his attention to Newberry: "There may have been what, Deputy Newberry?"

Newberry, for the first time, looked a little flustered. "Could you repeat the question?"

"Certainly, Deputy. Would you have expected to find visible signs, of struggle or something, or blood, given the allegations leveled at Jacob and the nature of the alleged violent assault of the two persons?"

Trotter stood up. "Objection, Your Honor. Deputy Newberry is being asked to draw particular conclusions from non-evidence."

Judge Leyland responded: "Sustained."

"Deputy Trotter—excuse me, I mean Deputy Newberry. You mentioned yesterday that it appears Esther Slough was strangled."

"Yes."

"Choked?"

"Yes."

"Did you find any blood, say, any type 'O' blood, on her neck? Even just a speck?"

"No."

"And if someone with blood on their hands strangled someone else, would you expect to find some blood on the neck of the strangled person?"

Newberry thought for a moment before he answered. "You might."

"You mean 'yes'?"

"I would say—inconclusive."

"'Inconclusive.' Thank you."

Winnlow returned to his seat beside Jacob. It was hard to tell if Newberry was dismissed. After sitting, Winnlow switched his attention to sorting out the mess of papers in front of him. The judge cleared his throat loudly.

Winnlow at last looked up. "Oh, sorry. No further questions, Your Honor."

We were given short break, a recess. People milled around outside the courtroom, passing nervous greetings and nods. Cigarettes lit. Low conversations. A few people looked my way. Mr. Bryer caught my eye and gave me a smiling nod, as if I had done something he approved of. I turned away. My parents managed some small talk, mainly about our new kitten. After about fifteen minutes, a buzzer went off, and we all returned to the courtroom.

In this new session, a few other witnesses came forward, most of them "experts." Winnlow only had one, and he—and old guy with bad hearing—looked pretty shabby. All were asked about what Jacob. The answers from these experts were full of talk about intelligence and personality and the like. Winnlow painfully tried to work around to the idea that Jacob was "not much more than a boy," that he was mentally handicapped, that he had something called "diminished capacity," and that it wasn't appropriate for him to be tried criminally in adult court. Trotter in his turn admitted that while Jacob may have been a "slow learner," he, like any normal person, could grasp what events meant. Under cross-examination, Trotter got Winnlow's lone expert to admit just one thing: that Jacob was aware of what is going on. After closing in on Winnlow's witness, Trotter ended forcefully: "There is nothing—nothing, then, you say—nothing to suggest that Jacob Slough is unaware of what he is doing or the consequences of what he is doing or of his actions?"

The witness could only nod.

"Is that a 'yes' or a 'no'?" Trotter asked. "For the record."

"Pardon?"

Trotter got closer to him and raised is voice: "Is there anything to suggest that Jacob Slough does not know what he is doing or the consequences of what he is doing?"

"Well, no."

"Thank you very much."

With neither side having any further witnesses to call, Judge Leyland said that closing arguments would take place after lunch, and that shortly thereafter he would make his decision about whether or not the case should go to trial.

I whispered to dad as everyone began to stand up, "And that will be all?"

He nodded. "I think so."

"Jacob doesn't have to answer questions?"

"No."

"But wouldn't it help if he just went up and said what happened? That he didn't do it?"

Dad eventually said, "He might say the wrong thing or get tricked into saying something he didn't mean to say. Or maybe they don't do this at a hearing. Not sure."

Dad could tell I didn't quite get it. He added a little more. "They can't talk to him if he doesn't want to talk. That's his right. They have to prove Jacob is guilty, and his lawyer doesn't have to prove anything, in a way." I still didn't see the picture, but I let it go. But it did not seem fair. Jacob just sitting there. He knew what he did, and nobody else.

The morning ended, and I somehow managed to eat most of a club sandwich and fries at small diner not too far from the courthouse. My parents, sitting across from me, watched quietly. Dad said what we needed to hear: "It will be good when all of this is behind us."

I could hardly imagine that ever happening.

CLOSINGS

Counselor Trotter introduced his summation by saying he would quickly get to the point. He didn't. Instead, he talked about what a peaceful, developing community Eastfield was, where children could play safely in their backyards and in the fields and along the roads, where, he said, "there is room to grow and prosper in safety." He made it sound like he lived there himself, but, with his notes before him, he then moved to the facts in a harder manner:

"Your Honor, what we have, based on the evidence and circumstances as presented, as well as the severity of the crime, is more than enough evidence to warrant a full, criminal trial in adult court—and we know the law permits the People to try someone of Jacob Slough's age in adult court. I would cite, for example, the People versus Phipps and the People versus Ingram. Both felony cases."

Leyland took a few notes. Trotter pushed forward. "But to return to the present case. So what do we know? We know that this gang—this so-called 'Watchers' Club'—with the accused, was there, at the area known as Lovers' Lane, that Saturday night in question. And we know that they saw the Slagmann vehicle parked at Lovers' Lane, and we know that they were there before—likely not too long before—the murders took place. We know, on the night in question, that the flashlight was taken to the scene of the crime by this group—and that it was left there by one of them. We know the evidence and circumstances suggest strongly that accused was positioned to see inside the vehicle when the flashlight went on. We know that the accused did not leave the scene at Lovers' Lane with the others, and we know he did not meet up at the orchard with the others later. We know that he did not show up at home that night. We know that the accused was found in a deserted house, hiding out, more than two days later. We know that he was found with the flashlight, which, as a forensic examination of the flashlight shows, is unquestionably the murder weapon."

The courtroom was quieted by these bare truths, and those truths continued. "We also know that the blood on the flashlight matches the type of one of the murder victims, David Slagmann. We know that hair fragments found on the damaged flashlight match David Slagmann's hair around the scalp and head area where he received lethal blows. We know fingerprints of the accused are on that same damaged flashlight, and that he had contact with—had his hand on—the flashlight before the blood dried. We know that the broken lens of that flashlight was found in the parked vehicle, suggesting that is where is broke. We know, too, how strong this young man is. We know his footprints, his distinctive boot prints, were found beside the passenger door. That he was wearing those same boots when he was found, and we know that he was wearing them that night. That the gang recognized the Slagmann vehicle that night parked at Lovers' Lane, and we know that Mr. Slagmann, the butcher, is the purchaser of the slaughtered rabbits that Jacob Slough took care of as pets. In short, the People know a great deal—a great deal, indeed, Your Honor—and we are bound to know more with a continuing criminal investigation and trial."

After a few deeper breaths, Trotter's calculated speech took a more emotional turn: "Now, Your Honor, this double murder, carried out as it was, of two young persons, parking at Lovers' Lane on a Saturday night after a high school basketball game, is both brutal and unprecedented in Eastfield, and the community has, since the murder, been living with some fear. One person bludgeoned to death by large, heavy flashlight, and the other choked to death. Two promising young people of this small community. It is important to pursue this case in order to seek out and settle the truth of the matter, so that the community can restore feelings of safety and confidence. Your Honor, the People would ask that the Court move quickly as possible to a criminal trial of the accused, Jacob Slough, for, as the Court knows, to move to a full trial from a preliminary hearing, it is only necessary that the People's case show that innocence is doubted. And this, Your Honor, I hope, has been shown in abundance. The abundance in what we know—the facts. Thank you."

Trotter sat down and straightened his chair. His partner gave him a very visible nod and showy handshake. They were confident, and the hum from the courtroom underlined that confidence. Jacob would be tried in criminal court. Nothing could stop it, it seemed.

Winnlow took his turn. He stood up, clutching, as usual, a few pieces of paper: "Your Honor. The People's advocate, Counselor Trotter, has attempted to point out what we know." When Winnlow said this, all the court stuff I'd seen on TV came back to me, and I was sure Winnlow was going to come out with some tricky or powerful statement that dismissed all that "we know." Instead, Winnlow meekly offered the opposite: "We won't dispute those particular things."

He moved toward the judge: "So, so perhaps then, I should speak to, well, those terms, or on those terms. What I mean to say—well, I will speak to what…to…to what we don't know."

This hardly set the world on fire. Winnlow pressed on after he stopped to make his almost anticipated knee-scratch: "And the truth, a fact, is this: no one has come forward to explain or testify as to what exactly—to exactly what happened that night—or why. That's—that's the big picture. No one has testified to tell us what exactly happened. No one has said they knew where Jacob went after the boys shouted out those things and ran away. We've not got any reason why Jacob, who has been described as the gentle brother to Esther, might commit such a crime. No one has told us exactly when Jacob put his prints on the flashlight, though it has been admitted that it could have been well after the crime was committed. Say this: say Jacob did go by the vehicle later, after the two had been murdered, and he found the two bodies. Might he not have been traumatized, panicked, by what he saw—his dear sister dead—and run away having picked up the alleged murder weapon at the scene?"

The courtroom had no response—no applause, no nodding to affirm, no nothing.

Winnlow continued: "And—well, there are other tire tracts and footprints that cannot be identified. When they were made, who they were made by. We simply just don't know about these things. And there is also something—something about the nature of the crime that doesn't add up, something that we don't know—that, allegedly, why one boy such as Jacob would, first, strangle his sister, then bludgeon an older boy with a flashlight. Are we supposed to imagine this older, athletic boy standing by? Or if the older boy was bludgeoned first, do we imagine the girl just staying there in the car while this took place? Because that's where she was found: sitting there slumped in the passenger seat. No blood stains on her. Just doesn't make much sense. Try to imagine it. Again, we don't know what happened there that night, but it doesn't sound at all like Jacob could have, would have, attacked these two young people. Plain does not add up. I mean, there's a lot we don't know, Your Honor. A whole lot. We're talking a whole bout of doubts."

Winnlow stopped and gazed around the court. He slowed down, appealing, it seemed, for sympathy: "We get why the people of Eastfield would be shaken by such a crime, but the Court should not take the easy way out, and just set upon the first stone that gets kicked up from the rough—just in order to satisfy this uncertainty. That is not how truth or justice or fairness or—or how it works. And I would ask that at this point the Court take into account the relative youth and mental disposition of this boy in making its recommendation. That's all."

Winnlow placed himself in front of the judge to offer his final words of the preliminary hearing. He found a scrap of paper in his jacket pocket, which looked about the size of a grocery store receipt. He looked at it and crammed it back into his pocket: "Jacob Slough, young Jacob, found himself in the wrong place and at the wrong time—that's all—and I would ask that the Court at least put him in the right place in a timely fashion. Thank you."

Judge Leyland quickly thanked the two lawyers, and said that after a recess he would make his decision. We all rose and he left. *A bout of doubts*, I thought. Was that enough?

WAITING ROOM

Once more we found ourselves milling around outside the courtroom. Billy sat on a bench between his parents, a little away from the main crowd.

He looked pretty wrecked, something like he was that Saturday night at the Old Orchard when he went all quiet and nervously weird. I imagined his efforts to hold back all those hiccups over the last few days. And I could only guess that all of this must be tough for him, knowing that the flashlight he brought and then dropped was what killed David Slagmann. The flashlight could end up being used to help put Jacob away. That stupid flashlight! What if he hadn't brought it? What if he hadn't dropped it? Billy must have thought about this as well. Geezus—poor Billy! And then, what if we had not carried on with The Watchers' Club in the first place?

While I darkly mulled over this, Arnold strolled over, leaving his parents behind with their cigarettes. He was wearing a nice jacket and pants, and as usual his hair was combed back perfectly. He greeted my parents in his well-rehearsed politeness, and they nodded back.

"Gum?" he immediately offered, pulling out a couple of sticks.

We said "no thanks" while he helped himself to a stick. When he wanted, Arnold was the master of manners.

Arnold began speaking to me, but, like Arnold, I was aware that my parents were vaguely listening in, even though they turned around to give us a feeling of some privacy.

"Doesn't look good, does it?" Arnold noted, though he didn't seem all that sympathetic.

"Suppose not," I said.

"Did you feel nervous when you had to talk in front of the court, and answer all the questions?"

"Yeah, for sure."

"Me, too. Winnlow—not the sharpest tool in the shed. I had it all planned what I was going to say."

"Yeah."

"I don't like that Newberry guy, do you?" Funny thing was, Arnold was a little like him in his precise, cocksure, controlled way.

Arnold chewed away looking around at everyone there. He clearly liked the whole scene. He noted, "They didn't ask Billy to go up. Wonder why?"

"Don't know."

"Guess they got what they needed from you—and from me and Julian, too."

"Yeah, maybe." Arnold, as usual, was a bundle of warmth.

His conclusion: "Well, poor Gumboot, I guess."

The conversation was awkward, mainly because I could tell he wanted to say more about Jacob or the hearing, but we were more or less surrounded. And I wasn't exactly full of words at the moment. All the while Arnold folded the gum foil into a perfect, tiny triangle.

"Well, see ya then," he said, "at school."

"Yeah, see ya."

Arnold returned to his parents who were putting out their cigarettes. His mom gave his collar a little straightening-out before they moved.

"We best be getting in, son," said dad. Mom put her hand on my shoulder, and we turned and re-entered the Silverford City courtroom.

RULING

Judge Leyland glanced at his notes and then, taking off his glasses, looked up into the courtroom. For most of the hearing he was quiet and unintrusive, even when he was impatient. Now he looked a bigger. Maybe he combed his hair more carefully for this closing-up. Maybe he put on a clean gown. He began quietly and slowly:

"It is the duty of this Court to decide whether evidence presented at this preliminary hearing warrants moving to a full criminal trial of the accused, Jacob Elijah Slough, charged with two counts of second degree murder. To do so, the Court must be convinced that there is sufficient reason—probable cause—to doubt the innocence of the accused. This is not a criminal trial where all evidence must be in place in order to go beyond reasonable doubt. Presumption of innocence is where the trial begins."

Leyland, put on his glasses, again looked down at his notes: "Over a short period of time, we have heard both testimony and evidence that, first of all, puts the accused at the scene of the crime and in a time frame before the crime took place. As well, we have the footprints of the accused beside the opened vehicle door in which the murder victims were found. We also have the murder weapon with the fingerprints of the accused on it, and it was recovered in the possession of the accused. Expert testimony also points to the accused as being competent to stand trial." Leyland made it sound simple and clear. That was that.

"But," he continued, "nothing presented makes a convincing case for the motivation of this crime, or that it was premeditated. Nothing presented indicates the accused is a hostile or violent person, or that he was involved in any kind of struggle. And it is not clear why the accused went missing or was hiding out when he was found. Finally, as far as we know, there are no witnesses to the crime."

These last words offered some hope. My emotions bounced up. The courtroom's full silence was cut short. Leyland cleared his throat: "Nevertheless, it is the opinion of the Court that there is sufficient cause to doubt the innocence of the accused, and the Court therefore orders that the accused stand trial in an adult court for the crimes for which he has been accused, though the exact charges will be set forth by the prosecutor in a brief arraignment for trial."

The feeling circulating in the courtroom was not hard to read, and it tended toward relief.

Judge Leyland added a few other things about dates, but some people toward the back of the courtroom began to leave. Leyland pounded his gavel once, stood up, and left the courtroom. Jacob's parents reached over to touch their son, and he briefly looked at them with his dark eyes that always said so little. Mr. Slagmann, on the other side of the courtroom, was shaking hands with Trotter and his assistant, while Mrs. Slagmann, expressionless, looked toward the Sloughs. A deputy came over to Jacob and began to take him away. For a moment it seemed like Mrs. Slough would not let go of her son's hand. Winnlow organized his papers at the table. When Mrs. Slough's finally let go of Jacob's hand, it stayed out, reaching toward her son. "My Jacob," she cried, "my Jacob" And he was taken through the side door.

Dad by this time had turned away and wanted to leave. Mom was frozen to the spot. Her eyes teared, seeing the son and the mother separated. At last she turned, and we left the courtroom to the few who stayed behind.

On the way home, mom said to dad, "We should have stayed there with them, just for a while. They were just left there, on their own." Dad, driving, it seemed, more slowly than usual through the late afternoon, said nothing.

10
BUTTERED PAWS

Jacob's trial was set for late spring.

Winter brought a couple of days of snow, but the rains that followed quickly turned it into slush, and then it was gone. I managed to finish *The Adventures of Tom Sawyer*, and I admit it was pretty good, though there were moments when, like Tom, I felt like I too was lost in the caves, only I didn't have Becky with me.

Around Christmas I heard that the Sloughs had put up their property for sale to help pay for the legal costs. When it sold, in January, I overheard my parents say that it went for much too little. "The developer took advantage of them," dad said. When mom asked dad if he knew where the Sloughs were going to go, he said that they now had a trailer some ways out of town.

Julian had been on a high ever since the Dodgers won the World Series. "The start of a dynasty," he said more than once, flashing his ever-growing collection of Dodger baseball cards. "Who's ever going to beat them?" I let him bask.

Except at school, we saw little of Teddy over the winter. He spent more and more of his spare time working away with older brothers fixing up some jalopies for the stockcar racing season that opened every summer at the old Grandview Track just outside of Silverford. He told us he would be racing his own car as soon as he got his permit. We believed him, though he would probably be a maniac out there on the racetrack. We asked him why he wasn't at the trial. He said that after interviewing him, they left him alone. Simple as that. "I kept telling them that I didn't know or remember anything. I drove them nuts, man. They even kind of threatened me, but I just shrugged. Then they quit asking." That Teddy had some guts.

Billy seemed to stay home more than ever since that Saturday night.

At school he was hardly his regular goofy, nervous self. He quietly turned inward on us. Our gang, then, was more or less carved down to the three of us—me, Julian, Arnold—but we no longer referred to ourselves as any kind of club no matter how keen our purposes.

Our kitten, Gumboot, grew quickly, almost like he had some catching up to do. We waited a couple of weeks before we let him venture outside, just so that he was certain of his new home. When at last mom thought he was ready to be let out, she massaged some butter on his tiny feet. "Rub butter on a cat's paws," she said. "It will always come back." She might have been right, for, though Gumboot always wanted to go outside, especially at night and even in the rain, he always returned. No one ever mentioned it, but, except for my brother, we all avoided saying the name we gave him. When we called him to us, we said, "Here puss puss. Here kitty kitty kitty. Psss psss psss."

MONKEY BRAINS

On a Sunday afternoon a few weeks before the trial was to begin, we hung out in Julian's garage, which was slowly becoming more like a real room. Over the winter, Julian's dad put in more insulation as well as some drywall, and he found a big, old radio that we could use. We still hoped that the room might eventually get equipped with a TV. Meanwhile, we listened to radio stations that played music that the regular stations didn't air. Music had suddenly become a bigger part of our interests.

On that Sunday afternoon, while we attempted to muster sophisticated comments on each tune that we heard—"I hate this song," "Haven't heard this one before," "This is cool," "This is sissy music"—our energies were poured into trying to make some homemade darts. The cheap ones that came with the dartboard were broken by the tough workouts we put them through, like winging them as hard as we could into plywood, trees, or anything that might possibly take a dart. We figured we could make better ones that could handle the punishment. "To make heavy-duty, all-purpose, armor-piercing models," Arnold dubbed our manufacturing mission.

We found some thin stainless-steel nails, a couple of feathers from a discarded birthday hat, some nylon fishing line for binding things, and dried balsam wood rummaged from a model airplane kit that never made it off the ground. A lone x-Acto knife and a pair of needle-nose pliers were the tools of choice, and the only squabbles between us while we worked away took the form of, "Aren't you finished with it yet?" So far, we hadn't come up with anything that might work. We assembled the various pieces by wrapping them with thread and applying loads of model glue that eventually would harden into something like plastic.

While we beavered away, Julian popped out with one of his better ideas: "Hey, you know, I bet we could make a kind of really small dart, so that it could go in a pea-shooter, or a straw, and turn it into a blow gun. Maybe use a pin or needle instead of a nail, or something."

Not bad. We nodded our support. Blow guns are good, we agreed. Arnold, armed with his *National Geographic* knowledge, let us know that down in the Amazon, natives used long blow guns to shoot monkeys out of the trees.

"Really?" questioned Julian.

"Really," said Arnold. "They dip their darts in poison that they get from the back of some frog or toad—it's super deadly. The monkeys fall right out of the trees once the dart hits them. Paralyses them."

We let this stew until Julian asked the obvious question: "What they want the monkeys for? Pets?"

Good question. Arnold, of course, had a good answer: "Pets? Ha, no. They want them for soup—monkey brain soup. Their favorite food. Monkey brains."

We didn't doubt it.

Julian came up with one of his typical cracked ad-ons, "Not monkey burgers?"

I immediately tried to trump Julian's stupid comment: "No. They like brain food. You could use some, Einstein."

Arnold almost appreciated my insult, but followed it with a twisted association: "And speaking of monkey brains, wonder what old Gumboot Slough is doing? I mean, right now, at this very moment? Maybe he's become The Bunny Man of Alcatraz."

The mention of Jacob stopped us. The trial was coming up, and one or all of us might have to testify like we did at the hearing. I, at least, had tried to erase the whole thing from my mind. Was Jacob breaking rocks like the chain-gang guys did in the movies? Wearing a striped convict suit? Sharing a cell with anyone? How did he pass his time? Did he have to go to some kind of school? Did he get visitors? Try to escape?

Julian, though intent on the dart he was working on, allowed a rambling remembrance to quietly drift out of his mouth, mixing in with the sickly-sweet fumes of the model glue that the filled the room.

The memory would change how everything would turn it out.

Julian rambled: "Remember that really rainy day. Remember, when we went over to old lady Raskolnikov's wrecked-up place, and you saw Jacob through the window, holding that kitten, now your little kitten, and you thought you saw a ghost or something. When we thought Jacob was one of the dead persons who had been found, and you just took off like a madman and ran all the way back to your place?" He stopped for a few seconds. "And my baseball mitt got really wet."

I remembered. It was not something Julian and I had ended up sharing with anyone, though at the time we meant to. Arnold had immediate interest.

I gave him the details about Jacob holding out the kitten in his sooty hands, and him saying that it needed milk. I admitted I thought I was seeing a ghost or something, since at that point I thought that Jacob was dead. Julian once more added how his precious baseball mitt got soaked.

Arnold was more than surprised. "Gumboot said what?"

"He said, 'It needed milk.' He meant the little kitten he was holding out."

Arnold was a little annoyed that we hadn't told him this. But it quickly turned to curiosity. "That all he said?"

"Yeah," I answered. Then I remembered. "Well, no."

"'No', what?" Arnold. "What else he say?"

"Well, he also said, 'I drew it,' or something.

"He said, 'I drew it'? Drew what?"

"Don't know. But it seemed—"

Julian, interrupting so that, as usual, he didn't feel completely left out, added, "You know, Gumboot—always drawing stuff."

Arnold quickly pushed this aside: "Yes, we know that, Brainiac."

Julian returned to whatever he was fiddling with.

Arnold continued, probing, "Gumboot said first, the kitten needed milk, then—did he say, 'I drew it' right away after that?"

Geez, what was with Arnold? He was kind of reminding me of Newberry and Trotter. "He said it needed milk. Then he said, 'I drew it'."

Arnold went quiet for a moment before he offered, "That could mean about anything." He thought a bit more. "And his hands—what? Had soot on them?"

"Yeah."

Julian piped up again. "Maybe he just came down the chimney. Like Santa. Ho ho ho."

We ignored Julian.

Arnold let this all brew, then said, "You know, we should check it out."

"What do you mean?" I asked.

"Let's go over to the old house. Look around—on the inside. No one will see us. We'll cut through The Trail, 'round the back way. Investigate. I've never been in there." Julian and I hadn't either, and Arnold knew that.

Arnold could tell I was hesitant. He wasn't worried about Julian, since he would do whatever it was Arnold and I agreed to.

Arnold kept up the pressure: "Remember, the Deputy Newberry guy said at the hearing that they looked around the place and didn't find much—what, some wrecked up furniture, or something? No big deal. Make it a mission. For something."

Danny Caine, the older kid who used to live across the road from my house, and who I shadowed one hot summer six years ago, was the only person I knew who had been in the old place. And he went in when Mrs. Raskolnikov, who we all imagined was a witch, was alive. He even talked with her, and he said she could tell the future—and she did. She had these strange old cards, and she gave him one: Judgement. I then thought about what happened six years ago, and how no one ever mentioned it. The rising yellow flame . . .

Arnold made up all our minds: "Let's go."

In truth, there wasn't much risk. We didn't plan to do any damage—not that anyone would have cared, since it was only a matter of time before the place would be torn down, or just fall down on its own.

"Okay," I agreed. "But my parents would go ape they knew I did this."

Julian was still trying to be funny: "Instead of going ape, maybe they could go monkey brain. Ha!"

We both looked at Julian. His comment didn't even make sense. Arnold added the bottom line: "What they don't know won't hurt 'em."

That was that.

We were off, to find—what? Something, anything, Arnold seemed to hint. What I did begin to get from bits of conversation with Arnold over the last while is that he thought that the Sheriff, Newberry, and Trotter weren't as smart as they thought they were. More interesting, though, Arnold gave the feeling that, despite his low regard for Jacob, he thought something was wrong with how things had gone and how they looked like they were going. Something missing. He shared what I, too, somehow thought. But there was nothing to go on. Nothing at all.

And so we were off, leaving behind our half-made darts, our monkey-brained thoughts, and, unfortunately, the cap off the glue.

That Darn Cat

It didn't take long to get to the back of Mrs. Raskolnikov's old place. Here we were fairly hidden from Eastfield Road. Although she had been dead for a number of years, no one had done anything with the property. It had more or less grown wild; in truth, it was never a tidy property to begin with, even when she ran it something like a small farm. She had done something with furs, repairing or cleaning them. Dad said that there was some problem about who exactly owned the property now that she was dead, and that it had been difficult to find any next of kin.

We stood beside the window where I had seen Jacob holding out the kitten.

"We could go in though here," Julian said, looking at the window. "There's hardly any glass."

"Why bother?" said Arnold. Arnold gave the back door a little shove and, though jammed a bit, it opened easily.

"Why'd you think it's not locked?" Julian asked, suddenly suspicious.

Arnold replied, "Well, it's not exactly Fort Knox, is it?"

We entered. It took a minute or so for our eyes to adjust to the light, though there were enough windows to move around easily. We all noted a lingering smell. "Pussy piss," noted Arnold. "And rot."

The back door took us right into what must have been the kitchen area. Except for a broken stool in one of the corners, there was no furniture. The wooden, creaky floors were dusty and rough. Arnold immediately starting looking through the cupboards, and Julian joined him. I tried the water faucet over the brown, rusted sink—nothing. The place was creepy but cool.

"Keep away from the windows," I said. "Just in case."

"Good idea, Dick Tracy," Arnold replied.

The cupboards revealed nothing except what might have been an old sugar bowl and a few broken plates.

We moved through a short hallway to the front room framed by ragged, brown curtains, with some of them heaped on the floor like they covered something. Arnold went over and moved them with his foot. Nothing. A small upside-down table with leg missing. A couple of bashed-up picture frames on the floor.

"We don't need to be here long, right," said Julian, still a bit nervous.

"Keep your eyes open and your gobber shut," Arnold stated.

We entered a small room off the larger room. Not much here. Not even a closet. Arnold immediately turned to search elsewhere in the house, with Julian close behind. I walked around a bit noticed a little crunching under my feet. I bent down and picked up a little of the grainy stuff that covered the floor. Bread crumbs? Yes—Danny Caine had told me that Mrs. Raskolnikov had a room full of breadcrumbs. What they were for, he never said, but at the time I imagined the old wizened, aproned lady might have really been a witch, so of course I figured the crumbs might have had something to do with cooking children. I smirked a little to myself about how dumb I must have been to even imagine this.

I turned with the mystery tucked away. Arnold and Julian were just coming out of main floor's bathroom, or at least what seemed to be a bathroom. I quickly looked in. No toilet, only an old, filthy bathtub with a broken mirror in it.

"Nothing," said Arnold. "Nothing to tell us anything." He looked around. "Let's try upstairs," he said, leading the way. "Maybe where Gumboot slept when he was hiding out."

The thought was a little spooky—Jacob being in this house on his own, with the murdering, broken flashlight and all the dust and the grime and the dark. And the kitten that wanted milk, the kitten that was now our pet. Gumboot, Gumboot.

The narrow stairs groaned as we went up slowly.

At the top of the stairs, we discovered two rooms, one on either side of the landing. Julian and Arnold took the room to the left. I took the one to the right.

A small, high window let in some light that filled the center of the room. A small, dust-covered table with nothing on it stood almost exactly where the light shone down. A battered, colorless rug covered some of the floor. Like downstairs, the walls were musty yellow with some boards showing through broken plaster. One crooked picture frame hung on the wall, but there was nothing in it.

There was also a small closet, which I opened. It had a high shelf, and a single wooden clothes hanger was on the floor among what I thought were some small pieces of coal. I picked one up, but immediately could tell it was a short stick of charcoal, like what we sometimes used at school for sketching. I dropped it and wiped my hand on my pants. Then I noticed the corner of a piece of paper just hanging over the edge of the shelf. I managed to reach up and pull down a small, uneven stack of wrinkled papers, which were yellowed and curled.

The top sheet. Huh? Drawn onto it was a sketch of a group of flowers. I couldn't tell if it was art or anything, but it looked pretty good, even though it was just in black and white and smudged a bit. There were initials in the bottom corner: "A. R." It came to me in a bit: *Anna Raskolnikov,* I thought. The Witch of Eastfield. Anna was her first name—so Danny Caine had told me back then. "A name you could spell forward and backward," he had said, as if that meant something.

I started going through the pieces of paper as I moved slowly to the table, putting the top picture on the bottom. All done in charcoal…little pictures of flowers, all signed "A. R." They seemed calm, somehow, in their soft, powdered details. I was mesmerized with thinking that this is what that old witch lady did: drawings no one would see. I had gone through a couple of them when a yell came from the landing, followed by "Geezus!" My heart leapt into my mouth.

I dropped the sketches and ran to the landing. Julian was just standing there, with Arnold coming up behind him.

"What is it? What?" I said, looking around.

"Cripes!" Julian said, still shaking a bit. "I came out of the room and then this stupid cat, out of nowhere, jumped right in front of me from that window sill! It scared the Sam Hill crap right out of me!"

"Scared of a little cat?" mocked Arnold. "A fraidy cat."

"Hey, you would have freaked, too!" Julian was a little embarrassed.

I looked down the stairs, and there was indeed a cat, flicking it tail. It was Gumboot, my cat! I said so.

"Yeah, it is," said Julian. "Your stupid cat!"

"Must have followed us," I said. The cat trotted up the stairs and brushed up against my leg. I gave it a little scratch behind one of its ears.

Arnold didn't care. "Anything in that room?" Arnold asked me, nodding toward where I came from.

"Oh, yeah. A bunch of old charcoal flower drawings," I said. "The old lady who used to live here must have drawn them. She signed them. Before she died."

"What, you think she signed them after she died?" said Arnold. I got his sarcasm. But his interest was roused.

We headed to the room with Arnold purposefully leading the way.

The sketches were scattered on the floor where I dropped them, and where the light coming through the window hit them.

The cat rushed over and stood on them. Arnold shushed the cat aside picked up a couple and looked at them. "Like greeting cards," he noted.

We all picked up a couple.

Then Julian stuttered, "Hey, this is—is—I don't—"

Now what?

"They're flower drawings," I said, wondering why he was confused. Julian was so stupid sometimes.

"I mean—who could have drawn this?" Julian said. "I don't get it. Not the old lady."

Arnold and I walked over to look at the drawing Julian held in his hand.

Arnold had the quick answer, and then it seemed obvious. "Gumboot," he said. "Must have been Gumboot who drew this."

It was charcoal sketch of my cat when it was a just a tiny kitten, like the first time I saw him. Those four little perfect black paws. The same cat that just scared the begeezus out of Julian. The same cat exploring the corners of the room at this very moment. The picture was smudged a bit, but it was clear enough. Jacob must have sketched it while he was hiding out for those few days in the house!

We picked up more papers from the floor, but they all seemed to be the old lady's drawings.

Then Arnold, holding the sketch of the kitten, said to me, "Turn the sketches over. He drew on the other side—on the other side of the paper that the old lady drew on." He looked at Julian. "One piece of paper. Two sketches. Check them all."

Arnold was right. On the backside of most of the papers were other drawings of the kitten—sitting, sleeping, stretching, licking itself. Gumboot drawing Gumboot, I thought. We turned over each one on our own until Julian let out a strange murmur, "Geeze, what's—what the—this?"

Arnold almost snatched the paper out of Julian's hands and put it on the table under the light from the window. Heads together, we gazed.

"What—like, what does it mean?" wondered Julian.

The importance of what we had before us did not, at first, for those moments, dawn on us.

At last Arnold, having calculated, broke our collective silence: "It means," he said, then stopped and straightened up. "It means everything is changed."

And he was right.

And through my head raced the idea that we might have done something...something maybe, somehow, when nothing else—when no one else—might or could.

We gazed down at the drawing once more. Julian spoke, but with little certainty: "We'll show them, right?"

Gumboot, at our feet, meowed. We looked down at the cat, the cat looked up at us, and then we looked back to the drawing.

Arnold replied with slow but absolute certainty: "Oh, we'll show them, all right."

11
TRIAL

The first morning of trial returned anxious feelings, but was now crossed through with anticipation. Trotter had contacted my parents and told them that he would be calling me to the stand, and he had a talk with me about what I would be asked, given what had now turned up in the old house.

We had a new judge for the trial: a big Italian-looking guy named Judge G. R. Fabbro. The jury was made up of unfamiliar faces—who were these people, three women and nine men? They looked serious and even a little nervous, sitting there off to the side. From the start, the lawyers seemed to talk to them most the time, not to the judge or the rest of the courtroom. It was like we were watching a play about a play.

The trial moved slowly, with all kinds of legal double-talk to work things out. Jacob, sitting there, looking down at his hands, appeared almost the same as he did back in October, only maybe a little thinner and more hunched. He was wearing a shirt and tie; his jacket did anything but fit.

Trotter went through the same pattern as at the hearing, only more slowly, it seemed, and with more details and emotion. His opening remarks made Jacob sound like a ruthless, determined killer. Winnlow was not assured in his opening, but he said he would provide evidence to show that Jacob's actions that night did not add up to murder at all. Spectators in the court fidgeted when he said this. The jury tried to remain unmoved.

A murmur came from Mr. Bryer, who was just behind us. He obviously hoped the worst for Jacob. The word spread around the last few months by those like Bryer was that Jacob was no doubt guilty.

Deputy Newberry was once more brought forward by Trotter to present all the details and facts about time, place, fingerprints, footprints, tire prints, and cause of death. Despite a twitch here and there, he was as precise as his fine moustache. The murder weapon, the flashlight, was presented as an exhibit, along with forensic reports and information from the coroner's office. Winnlow did little to counter or question Newberry's account of events. He did, however, manage to get out of Newberry that there was some serious tearing of the front of Esther's blouse when she was found, something not pursued in Trotter's questioning of Newberry.

As in the preliminary trial, Winnlow questioned Newberry about how it would have been odd or difficult for Jacob to deal with both victims and the same time without some visible signs of struggle. Trotter objected to the issue being raised since it was not Newberry's job to speculate, but the judge allowed it. Newberry, then, could only admit that how the murders exactly took place was difficult to determine with perfect certainty. Winnlow finally asked Newberry if he or any of the investigators had come up with a motive, and, though all expected Newberry to have some answer, he responded, "Motives for crimes are not part of my job."

I knew it was coming. I was called next. I took a big breath, took the stand. Judge Fabbro coached me to relax. "Take your time, son. This is not a race."

Trotter once more took me through the evening and the details I knew, taking the story right to the moment we noticed that Jacob did not show up after the rest of us left Lovers' Lane. He went slowly, and repeated most of my answers for the jury. Compared to the hearing, he acted like we were friendly and all. I couldn't help feeling I was doing little good for Jacob's cause, especially because Trotter thanked me in excess.

Winnlow in his cross examination asked me about what Jacob was like, if I had ever known him to be violent or mean. I said that I hadn't. When it seemed Winnlow was just about to dismiss me, he asked the judge if could recall me later in the trial as his own witness regarding other, newer evidence, just filed, that needed analysis. Judge Fabbro granted the request, though Trotter objected that this would be highly irregular. Trotter's assistant immediately began whispering to him.

Arnold and Julian also testified over the next two days, and they too went over all the details placing us at the scene of the crime with Jacob and the flashlight. Winnlow requested the option to recall them as well. Up until that time, Jacob's fate seemed pretty well set, and it didn't seem like a good fate.

Trotter moved quickly and confidently with his witnesses. Everything, it seemed, fell together perfectly, piece by piece.

Day four. Winnlow began to bring his witnesses forward in defense of Jacob. To the surprise of most, he called Billy to the stand. He had been completely left out of the preliminary hearing. I looked over to Arnold, who raised his eyebrows back at me.

Billy scurried to the stand and gripped the arms of the chair.

After stating his name and confirming that he was part of The Watchers' Club that Saturday night, as well as agreeing with the account of the evening that Julian, Arnold, and I made in our earlier testimonies, Winnlow moved closer to Billy.

"Now, Billy," he said. "Now Billy. When you got to Lovers' Lane that night, you were given the flashlight to go around to the front of the parked vehicle, to shine the light into the front seat area before the rest of the boys were going to shout foolish things out and run away. The others would have been along the side, the passenger side of the vehicle, with Jacob furthest to the front, closest to you. Is this correct?"

"Yes," Billy gulped.

"Now, just relax Billy, and please tell us exactly what you saw when you turned on the flashlight and shined it into the vehicle."

Billy looked small up there on the stand. His hiccups started, and the judge signaled to the court officer to give him a glass of water. This was going to be painful.

"What did you see, Billy, when you turned on the flashlight and looked in the vehicle?"

The court quieted. Winnlow itched his knee and glanced at the jury.

"I saw David Slagmann in the van," Billy said.

"And?"

"And—and Esther Slough."

"You recognized her?"

"Yes."

This stopped me cold. What? Billy all along knew it was Esther Slough in the van? Why'd he keep quiet about it? Is that why he had been acting so weird later than night? Did he think we saw what he saw? What Jacob saw? He must have!

"And Billy, what did you see going on—inside the vehicle? Exactly what?"

Winnlow tried not to lean forward, but it seemed he wanted Billy to focus on him and nothing else.

Billy bit his lip.

"I saw—I saw that David Slagmann had his hands…" His voice petered out.

"Yes? You saw what, Billy? His hands?"

Along with Winnlow, the whole courtroom seemed to edge closer to Billy.

Billy then went quickly, as if he was letting out his breath, letting out his breath after all this time: "I saw that David Slagmann had his hands—on the neck of Esther Slough."

The courtroom fell dead silent. Not a breath.

Winnlow looked around, then to the jury, then back to Billy. "David Slagmann, you say, had his hands on the neck of Esther Slough. What—like he was holding her—hugging her?"

"No. No. More like he—like grabbing her."

The courtroom at once seemed to let out its collective breath, though it was more like a gasp. Judge Fabbro asked for order. Billy drank more water while everyone settled down. Yes, this is why he acted so strange when we met up at the Old Orchard. He had been keeping this inside all along. Winnlow or someone must have got this it out of him in an interview. I looked over at Mr. Slagmann, his face flaming. He looked like he was about to leap up. His wife just sat, seemingly unmoved and unmoving. Trotter and his assistant frantically whispered to each other.

Winnlow waited for silence, and it took a while. "You said, Billy, that David Slagmann had his hands on Ether's neck. Like he was choking her?"

Trotter shot up. "Objection, Your Honor! The witness said nothing like 'choking.' The Defense is putting words in the mouth of the witness! I wish this struck from the record!"

"Sustained," the judge ordered in the direction of the court stenographer. He instructed the jury to disregard the wording of the question—but now it was out there.

Winnlow tried again. "He, David Slagmann, had his hands on or around her neck, you say?"

"Yes."

"Could you show us, act out, how this looked, with your own arms? I mean how you could see his arms and hands?"

Trotter once more objected: "Your Honor, it is entirely inappropriate for the witness, this youngster, to enact whatever it is the Defense is after or wrongly implying."

Winnlow made a decent response. "Your Honor, we are trying to get an exact indication of what Billy saw, and this is the best way to do it. Better than words. A picture is worth—"

The judge cut Winnlow off. "I will allow it. Continue. But we don't want a show of this."

Winnlow asked again: "Now Billy, could you show us how this looked, using your own arms? What did it look like? Briefly."

Billy looked awkward and disconnected as he put his arms out straight in front of himself, his palms almost down, and the ends of this thumbs touching. He held this for just a moment. More gasps from the court. Winnlow let this image sink in for a while before he continued.

Winnlow nodded. "Thank you, Billy. I would like it entered into the record that the witness held out his hands in at—in a choking position."

Trotter, all the while whispering much to his assistant, ignored this— or missed it.

Winnlow: "Billy, did this look violent? I mean the way he 'grabbed' her around the neck?"

Trotter, paying attention once more, objected, and now seemed mad. "The witness being 'violent' is not a matter of observing factually. It is a judgment, and should not be admitted as testimony."

"Sustained. Counsellor Winnlow: do not put key or colored words into the mouths of your witness."

Winnlow continued. "Yes, Your Honor. So Billy, how was she positioned. I mean, how was Esther Slough seated in the vehicle?"

"She was—her head was up against the window."

"Sitting straight up, or over?"

"Slouched, kind of, I guess."

"And how did she look? Her face, from what you could see? Think."

"Her head was like bent over a bit, and her mouth—her mouth looked open."

The court began to reflect something between disbelief and uneasiness with where this was going, and Fabbro ordered quiet. Winnlow went on.

"With the light of that strong flashlight. So her mouth looked open. And her face? Her face? What did it look like?"

Billy only repeated himself: "It looked like—her mouth was open."

"She was moving around? Moving at all?"

"No, I don't think so."

"She was not moving?"

"No, sir."

"And the position of her head? You said it was—what ?"

"Her head was kind of bent."

"Her mouth was open and her head was slouched over?"

"Her head against the side window."

"And then?"

Billy took a short breath. "David Slagmann turned toward me—I mean, toward the light when it flashed on. Then I dropped the flashlight—the switch was kind of stuck, stiff, so I just dropped it. I ran away."

"You ran away to meet the others at the orchard?"

"Yes."

"And did you tell the others what you saw?"

"No."

"No one?"

"No."

"Why, Billy?"

Billy looked at his feet. "Because it was too—I dunno. It scared me. And I didn't know what it meant—what I seen—what I saw. And maybe they saw what I saw, I guess. And then there was the flashlight I left behind, too. I knew I would be in real big trouble, with my dad. It was his flashlight. It was all...I don't know—"

All this seemed to have been stuck deeply in poor Billy, and now it was coming out. It had been waiting.

"That's okay, that's okay. I see. I understand. That's fine. And so you kept this to yourself, until just recently? Is that correct?"

Billy nodded, "Yes."

"And no one forced you to say this?"

"No," Billy said, looking defeated yet relieved.

Here Winnlow stopped, walked around, like he wasn't sure if he was finished. "Thank you, Billy. Thank you very much."

On his way back to his chair, Winnlow turned Billy over to Trotter, who could hardly wait for cross-examination: "Your witness."

Trotter moved in: "Billy, how far from the front of the vehicle were you, when you turned on the flashlight? The flashlight that you brought, that belonged to your father. How far?"

Billy looked like he was thinking, but, knowing Billy, it was look went deeper. Why did Trotter have to repeat that Billy brought the flashlight? We all knew that.

Trotter repeated the question, "How far, Billy? Think."

"Maybe ten yards. Maybe…about that."

"Maybe ten yards. And you could see that Esther Slough's mouth was open, but you couldn't see her full face, right?—how exactly—exactly—it looked?"

"No, not exactly, I guess."

"Humph. You 'guess.' Was her mouth open to speak? Was she talking to David?"

"I don't know."

"You don't know if her mouth was open to speak. She could have been saying something. Billy, how long did you turn the flashlight on for? Or, how long did you have it pointed directly into the cab of the vehicle? A quarter of a second, half a second, a second or two?"

"I'm not—not sure."

"You're 'not sure'?"

"No."

"Was it for a long time or short time?"

"A short time—maybe a second or two, I guess."

"Maybe a second or two? Maybe less? You 'guess'."

"Maybe."

"Okay. Let's go back a bit, just to make sure. Was the light aimed into the vehicle for the whole of the time the flashlight was turned on?"

"No."

"Why?"

"Because it took me a bit to, like, aim the light into where they were. Into the truck. The switch was stuck a bit, too."

"The flashlight was turned on, then, for a second or two, but you say it took you a second or two to aim the light right into the vehicle." Trotter must have felt like he was on to something. He added, "Sounds like the flashlight lit the inside of the vehicle for a very, very short time. Not much time to see much."

Winnlow objected. "Leading the witness, Your Honor. There's no question here."

"Your Honor, I am only trying to establish duration of observation. This is important."

Judge Fabbro directed Trotter to pose clear questions, and to slow down. Billy looked more and more uncertain.

"So, you said that the flashlight was turned on for a second or two, but it took you a second or two to aim into the vehicle? Yes, it must have been a very quick look. A split second. Would you say that is correct?"

Billy mumbled, "Uh, yes."

"And for that split second, you saw her mouth was open, and you couldn't tell if she was just speaking or what she was doing?"

"Yes." Billy seemed to have given up.

Trotter hadn't. He kept up his pace: "So you didn't tell the others what you saw—not at the orchard or even after?"

"No."

"Because—?"

"Because it kind of scared me."

"Because—?"

"Because I didn't like what I saw."

"Because—?"

Winnlow stood up and objected. "Your Honor. The prosecution is badgering, bullying, the young witness. He already said that he was scared because of what he saw!"

Trotter countered, "Your Honor, I'm just trying to find out what went on. This testimony is wildly vague and uncertain—and crucial."

The judge ruled. "Continue. But, Counselor Trotter: once more, slow it down, and phrase specific, clear questions for the boy."

"Sorry and thank you, Your Honor."

Despite his apology, Trotter's tone and his pace barely changed. In fact, he poured on the pressure. "Now, Billy, you said you didn't 'like' what you saw, which was, you said, David's hands placed on Esther's neck. Why didn't you 'like' what you saw with that very, very quick glance, Billy? It wasn't because what you were seeing made you afraid, right?"

Billy didn't answer. Trotter asked again: "Why didn't you like what you saw, Billy?"

"Because—because I didn't know what was going on. And I didn't want to mess what I was supposed to do. It was all—"

"Okay," Trotter interrupted, "so from what you think you saw in that little bit of time, you were not sure what you saw? You couldn't tell what it meant—what exactly was going on, then? Is that correct, Billy?"

Billy had nowhere to turn except to one word: "Yes."

"So, just so we are clear, you couldn't exactly tell exactly what was going on in that vehicle, or what it meant?" Trotter looked at the jury when he asked this.

"Y-yes," Billy almost whimpered.

Winnlow stood up and objected: Your Honor, this is—"

Trotter cut him off and turned away. "No further questions."

What Billy had seen—or thought he saw—became a blur under the weight of Trotter's questioning. That he was responsible for bringing the flashlight, and now, it seemed, for failing to retain some hope for Jacob's cause, made him shrink as he took his seat between his parents. Poor Billy. Poor Jacob.

Jacob's Last Stand

Arnold's tune had changed ever since we discovered the sketches. He now saw himself as a central player in this drama of guilt and innocence, and Winnlow must have felt that Arnold, better than me, could better play the part in Jacob's last stand.

Arnold almost marched to the front of the courtroom before sitting, poised. "Now, Arnold," Winnlow began, "just, not that many days ago, really, you and a couple of your friends were exploring around your neighborhood. Nothing serious. I'm talking about you and your friends going to check out the old deserted house along Eastfield Road, where, back in October, Jacob Slough was found by the sheriff and his men—the old Raskolnikov place. Could you tell us what happened, and what you found?"

Arnold was swimming with confidence and anticipation. He wore a nice jacket and tie. None of us had a jacket and tie. He sat straight and bold and began by saying he was with Julian and me: "Yes, we went over to the old place, just to look around. We weren't going to break anything, or take anything, but we just wanted to explore the old place. It was empty."

"I see. Just boys being boys. And can you tell the Court what you found?"

"Not much downstairs, broken stuff and the like, but upstairs, in one the rooms up there, on a high shelf in closet, we found some sketches on old pieces of paper, done in charcoal."

I had to admit I admired Arnold's certainty. His confidence seemed to challenge Deputy Newberry's. He even looked Newberry's way a few times. I could see why he was best to deliver the information.

"What were they sketches of, Arnold. Could you tell us?"

"Of flowers."

"And do you know who did them?"

"There was an 'A. R.' on each one. I figured that it must stand for 'Anna Raskolnikov,' the old lady who used to live there years ago—I mean in the old house we were in. She must have made the charcoal sticks herself. Just left them behind, when she died. Some years ago." Arnold's assuredness was almost too much. He didn't need questions.

"And, Arnold, you went through the sketches? You looked at them all?"

"Yeah—yes, we looked at them all. For no reason, really. They were just there. Maybe about twenty or so of them."

Off to the side, Deputy Newberry thumbed through his notes like a madman. He may have missed something when he claimed to have searched the old place thoroughly—and he knew it! Maybe the piece to complete the puzzle—or make it more of a puzzle. Newberry said at the preliminary hearing and earlier in the trial that some old papers were found in the search of the shack, but nothing was made of them. They just left them there. I began to feel proud and excited. I too wanted to give Newberry a you're-not-so-smart look. But it wasn't over. Trotter whispered nonstop to his assistant.

Winnlow continued. "Arnold, could you tell the Court what you found. Having to do with the sketches, I mean."

"Yes," said Arnold. "On the other side of most of the papers were other drawings. In charcoal, too."

"Drawings. Of what?"

"Most of them were drawings of a tiny kitten—drawn well, too. We even definitely knew the kitten in the drawings, so they must have been drawn not that long before we found them."

"You knew the kitten? This specific kitten?"

"Yes. For sure. Well, now it's a little cat. My friend's cat. He's right there." Arnold pointed at me. The judge asked the court reporter to enter my name in the record.

Arnold continued. "The markings on its feet, like boots."

"Distinct markings?"

"Yes, distinct. The drawings must have been drawn way after Mrs.

Raskolnikov died, since that cat was not born then. Probably born last—maybe September."

Arnold continued to vaguely wave his detective skills in the direction of Newberry, who now wore more than just a hint of a scowl between twitches. That Arnold!

Trotter objected. "Your Honor, the witness is just left to draw evidentiary conclusions—about drawing, about the drawing, I mean. And dates. He's no expert in these matters. And the identity of a cat. Really! He is only on the stand to answer questions, not to come up with stories about pets!"

Judge Fabbro thought for a second. Winnlow looked like he was also ready to respond.

Fabbro spoke: "Overruled. The Court will allow it, given the first-hand knowledge of the witness. But we hope some point will result from this testimony. And, I hope, some other—other, more clinical and expert conclusions about these drawings later."

"We will, Your Honor." Winnlow continued his address to Arnold. "And who do you believe did those drawings—the ones on the other side of the paper?"

Trotter once more attempted to head this off. "Objection. Again, the witness is being asked to draw conclusions far beyond his expertise."

"Your Honor," said Winnlow. "The witness has special knowledge that is crucial."

The judge answered. "Overruled. It does not appear that the question is leading to wild surmise or speculation on the part of the witness. Continue."

Winnlow went on. "So, who do you believe did those drawings on the other side of the paper?"

Arnold was waiting to answer this particular question, and his words carried a little self-importance. "Jacob Slough. Had to be. He was the best drawer at our school. And since he was at the old house for a couple of days, and there were some charcoal crayons on the floor of the room where the drawings were, and there were always a few cats around the place, including the kitten he sketched—well, it just had to be Jacob who drew them. I have seen his other drawings at school, and they are done in just the same way."

Again, Arnold was almost too confident, but Winnlow just let him go on.

Trotter had to do something, so he objected again, saying strongly, "Your Honor, we are hearing the testimony of merely a boy here, and the Defense, well, they're using him almost like he's some kind of forensic consultant in this highly complex and serious case with potential serious evidence. This witness is inferring and speculating. He is not an art expert. I would ask that he be refrained from answering questions, or being asked questions, that draw conclusions of an investigatory manner from his boyish adventures with his delinquent pals, who, it should be noted, clearly trespassed onto this property. Moreover, this is unrelated and diversionary information and evidence that the Prosecutor's office has not had adequate time to review. I move that this last response and the evidence it invokes be entirely stricken."

Despite the powerful eloquence of the objection, Judge Fabbro ruled quickly, but carefully. "The testimony is ruled relevant, though I would ask the jury to keep in mind that these are the witness' observations. No one else's. Objection overruled."

Fabbro turned to Winnlow: "But once more, the Court would also hope that you, Counsellor Winnlow, will render more documented or alternative verification of this information about the sketches, not to mention their relevance. New evidence is permitted, but, given this kind of evidence and its importance, it must be supported by some second-party, arm's-length, expert verification."

Winnlow answered, "Thank you. It can be—is partly done already—and will be shown to be supported by experts, Your Honor. And this evidence, and how it came about, is absolutely relevant—crucial, even. I believe it is valuable to hear first-hand evidence first. Veracity."

The judge squinted. "Proceed."

Arnold was more than ready to continue answering Winnlow. "But, Arnold, they weren't all drawings of this specific kitten, were they?"

"No."

"Could you describe to the Court what you also saw drawn on the back of one of the sketches?"

While Arnold started his answer, Winnlow moved toward the side of the courtroom where he picked up a piece of paper sealed in plastic. A tag was attached to it.

"Yes. It's a drawing of David Slagmann, with—" and here Winnlow handed the sealed paper to Arnold. "It's a—"

Trotter again objected. Did he know where this was going? "Your

Honor, Your Honor. Objection! The witness is interpreting some drawing. Again, this constitutes new evidence, and the Court does not necessarily have to accept it."

Fabbro's impatience showed. "Again, the Court can accept new evidence—so long as the new evidence appears important, appropriately documented, and relevant. I have assurance from the Defense that this is the case. Overruled. Ample time will be given for you to examine it."

The people in the courtroom were somewhat confused by this exchange, but the drawing clearly now became the center of everyone's interest.

"Arnold, can you tell the court what you have?"

"This is one of the drawings we found in the house."

"And what is on the drawing? What does it portray? Describe it plainly, please. Best you can."

Arnold slowed down and said it clear as a bell: "It's a drawing of David Slagmann—with his arms outstretched. His hands are around the neck of Esther Slough—looks like he is chocking her."

The courtroom fell quiet for second, as if trying to figure out what this meant, and then a few persons seemed to murmur no...no. Zoran Slagmann suddenly stood up, "That Slough boy is an imbecile! An idiot boy—what can he know? My David is gone! That boy killed him!"

Trotter also bolted up and tried to speak over the hubbub: "Your Honor, objection! It is hardly appropriate that a young boy—"

Fabbro cut him off and worked his gavel to call for order. Two court officers restrained Mr. Slagmann, while he kept yelling, "The boy is an—an imbecile! My David is gone, killed by that idiot of a boy!"

During the outburst Arnold caught my attention and slightly raised one of his eyebrows. I nodded once in return.

The judge continued to call for order, and when Mr. Slagmann at last settled in his seat, he was strongly warned about removal from the courtroom if he didn't contain himself. The judge also allowed the court to settle down before permitting Winnlow to continue, and telling Trotter to hold his objection until Arnold finished with the question.

"Is this the drawing you are referring to?" Winnlow asked.

"Yes, this is it." Arnold turned it over to make sure. "And on the other side there's a drawing by the old lady—'A.R.' See?"

Arnold handed it back to Winnlow, noting it as an exhibit. The courtroom remained unsettled.

"Your Honor," Winnlow added, "we can also prove that Jacob's fingerprints are all over these sketches. They're his, no doubt whatsoever, as we will see."

Winnlow just stood there, as if wondering if there was anything else he should do. The judge finally asked, "Anything else?"

"No further questions, Your Honor."

"Your witness, Counselor Trotter," noted the judge.

Trotter exchanged some whispers with his assistant. They had their way with Billy, but Arnold, looking straight out at the courtroom, presented a different challenge. Arnold straightened his tie.

Trotter sat back in his chair, took a long look at Arnold, sitting taller than his years, and said, "No questions, Your Honor. But we ask that he might be recalled after we have an opportunity to forensically fully examine this new evidence."

Over the next two days, other witness, some of them experts in this or that, came and went, confirming things like that fact that Jacob did do the drawings, that his fingerprints were on them, and they even confirmed that the drawn kitten was our cat, Gumboot, when it was younger. Some of the details were so small that their purpose got lost every now and then—or at least for me. I, too, said my piece when called to the stand, and under questioning I confirmed more or less everything Arnold said about finding the drawings, though without the drama of the revelation that went along with Arnold's testimony. But I did add something new when asked about the particular cat, or kitten: I told about the rainy day before Jacob was arrested, that I saw him holding out the little kitten at the old house, and how it scared me and how we ran away. I added that I heard Jacob say, "It needs milk."

"Is that all he said?" asked Winnlow.

He also said, 'I drew it'." Winnlow thanked me.

Trotter did not ask me any questions, and later, strangely enough, neither did my parents.

FACTS

The final day of the trial brought concluding remarks from the lawyers, but not before the judge asked Trotter if he wanted to question the new evidence. He didn't.

Trotter played most of the same hand he did in his summary at the preliminary hearing, going painfully over all "the facts" for the jury, who listened carefully to him. In the end, with enough conviction to put fear into the heart of anyone who might not agree, Trotter stated, "The evidence shows, the facts show, without any doubt, that Jacob Slough brutally assaulted and murdered David Slagmann and Esther Slough. Jacob Slough saw what was going on in the vehicle that night, with his sister, Esther, amorously engaged with David Slagmann—and Jacob Slough stayed behind because it clearly somehow roused some furious passion in a way that ended in a brutal double murder the likes of which Eastfield has never before seen—and, we hope, will never see again."

Trotter went on to say that Jacob was not as "backward" as we all thought: "Murderers are, in my experience, seldom what they seem to be. The drawing done by Jacob Slough," he said, "is little more than crafty diversion—a work of pure imagination, not of fact. And facts, ladies and gentlemen—facts!—determine guilt and innocence, not little charcoal sketches done by someone desperate to hide guilt. Footprints, fingerprints, a flashlight, blood. Facts. Time and place. Facts. Two murdered young students, and we have the fact of another person who was there, and we have the fact of that person with the murder weapon who was clearly hiding out. And," he said, turning to pause and look at Jacob, "we know who that person is."

Trotter moved around, nodding as if to reassure everyone of the truth. "Ladies and gentlemen of the jury, use the common sense of evidence staring you right in the face. The facts go beyond any kind of reasonable doubt for a guilty verdict. Far, far beyond. Find Jacob Slough guilty, and once more return this wonderful, peaceful community of Eastfield to the safety and security it once enjoyed and should continue to enjoy. Thank you."

Trotter sat down with much confidence and authority. His assistant shook his hand like they had already won. Was this an act for the jury, or were they just that confident?

When Winnlow got his chance to make a closing argument for Jacob's innocence, he too began with his own facts: that Jacob Slough had no record of being violent or hateful, and that, as he said very slowly, "we have two—two—unrelated accounts, portrayals, as it were, of David Slagmann with his hands around the neck of Esther Slough."

Winnlow briefly and oddly put his hands out in front of himself in a choking position. "Given Billy Luckhert's testimony of what he saw when he held the flashlight, and given what Jacob drew while, in fear and confusion. Given these two accounts, there can be little doubt that David Slagmann, at the time the boys snuck up on him, had his hands around the neck of Esther Slough and was choking her—had choked her—to death. We know Esther Slough died from strangulation. That her buttons from the front of her blouse were torn points to that fact that David Slagmann was or had been forcing himself upon poor, defenseless Esther Slough. She resisted—she tried. David Slagmann lost his temper, not getting what he wanted. Who was she, this nothing girl, to deny him? This is not a new story. No, no, not at all. But it is a sad, tragic story."

Zoran Slagmann couldn't hold himself back. He didn't stand up, but he shouted, "The family are pigs! Stupid, backward pigs! Now my son is made into a—" Here he stopped. Two court officers were on him, their hands firmly on his shoulders. Judge Fabbro asked them to remove Mr. Slagmann. On the way he spat out, "Stupid pigs!" Mrs. Slagmann sat, unmoved.

Winnlow took a breath. The judge asked for order. Winnlow meanwhile looked at his notes, put them down, and paced. A change seemed to have come over the court. "So, what happened that night after the rest of kids ran off to the orchard? There are large—very large—doubts about the Prosecutor's crafted version of events."

Winnlow again moved around until he was ready to continue. "Jacob, closer to the front of the vehicle, would have, like Billy Luckhert, who was stunned by what he saw—Jacob would have had a clearer view, the angle, to see what was going on the vehicle, compared to the rest of the boys. The other boys, being at the side of the vehicle, we know, could, probably at best, only get a glance of the back of someone's head against the passenger window, and of David Slagmann's shocked face. Shocked, yes. Caught!"

Winnlow awkwardly moved around like he was trying to take up the various positions of all involved, but his staging was, more than anything else, confusing. He went on.

"Now, Jacob would have seen David Slagmann's face as well as some of his sister's face—the side, at least. He would have seen those arms reached out, around poor Esther's neck. So would have Billy Luckhert. The other boys would not have seen this. Like I said, and like the witnesses said, they got a glimpse of David's face from the side, and they saw the back of someone's head against the passenger side window."

Having done with his awkward performance, Winnlow walked to the jury but did not really look at any of them. At moments, it was as if his shoes or the air in front of him held more interest. "Okay, so what happened? Everyone ran away after shouting out, thinking they had just had their fun. But Jacob stayed. He stayed. Why? Because of what he saw from that brief but clear snapshot of light! He saw what was taking place in the vehicle: his sister being assaulted, attacked, choked by David Slagmann! So what happened: he picked up the flashlight Billy dropped, which was still on because of a stiff switch, and he went up to the driver's side of the vehicle—alarmed and fearful for his dear sister's life. David Slagmann, himself certainly stunned by what was happening, caught up in some kind of violent, aroused state himself, almost certainly challenged or confronted Jacob, and Jacob, well, he defended himself in coming to the aid of what he saw as his struggling sister."

Winnlow needed another pause. He took a drink of water then rubbed his knee for a few moments before beginning again. "Again, Jacob may not have even known that his sister was already dead, only that when he got his first glimpse it was clear enough to him that she was being attacked. Jacob—coming in help of his sister. And, ladies and gentlemen of the jury, the law states—the law clearly states: individuals can come and use whatever means possible in defense of person or property, in defense, which is what young, brave Jacob Slough did. That is the law."

Winnlow took another break before continuing. He faced the jury: "Now. Ask yourself: Would you have acted any differently if you would have seen one of your family being assaulted so violently? He did what he did, and that is unfortunate. He then realized his sister was dead. What then? He panicked, ran away, traumatized by what he had seen, and by what he had done to try to save his poor, dear sister. Hiding away in that old house, feeling the fear…the confusion about what he had done—and even guilt for what he could not do—that is, save his dear sister. Jacob, a boy of little expression beyond drawing, drew what he saw in that flash of light that changed so many lives. And the Prosecutor suggests that Jacob Slough, this quiet, simple-minded, almost inarticulate boy, craftily fashioned a drawing, one that was more or less lost, and manufactured as a kind of alibi? Nonsense. It is only because of Jacob's friends finding the drawing by pure accident that we have it as evidence! Evidence, we must note, missed in the original search made by the sheriff's office. Sadly, if there is a cold-blooded murderer, it is of course David Slagmann, a young man with promise, but also tainted with weakness. Jacob, with no history of violence, could never have strangled his sister. But he could, and he did, defend her."

Winnlow finally slowed down. "Ladies and gentlemen of the jury. We already have enough victims in this sad and tragic case. We don't have to have another. Jacob Slough must—must be found innocent of these charges. You only need reasonable doubt to acquit. And there are doubts all over this case. Thank you."

FLOOD

The jury brought in the decision two days later. Jacob Slough was found not guilty of second-degree murder and of the lesser charge of manslaughter. Shuffling and murmurs from the courtroom suggested that the ruling was not popular with everyone.

Sitting there while the ruling echoed and continued to ripple, bits and pieces of pictures and moments and causes flooded forward to this moment…to a flashlight brought with the best of intentions, to a stray kitten that needed milk, to an overthrown baseball lost in the bush, to David Slagmann's startled face, to a smoke ring blown into the silent evening, to flowers sketched by a dead hand—and to the mystery of how things move by chance and by fate, which can, in a moment, become the same thing. This washed over me, and I took a breath as if I had been held underwater for much too long.

Before we walked out of the courtroom, mom made a point to pass by the Sloughs, who now had their arms around their son. We said nothing, but mom put her hand across the back of Mrs. Slough. She looked up and smiled at us. Jacob, too, briefly glimpsed at us with those dark eyes of his, and I caught his eye. "You gave it milk?" he asked quietly.

I nodded.

12
The Watchers' Club

That was then. And now?

Arnold, not surprisingly, is a criminal lawyer down the coast, and, apparently, a nasty one at that—or so he tells me in the funny e-mails I get from him every now and then. His Facebook page tells that he lives in a pretty nice house. Julian made it to AA baseball for half a season before calling it quits. Now he has a small roofing company that took advantage of the development that eventually connected Eastfield with Silverford City. I see him around every now and then. He remains a maniac Dodger fan, but since those couple of good seasons and a few sporadic decent ones, the dynasty he promised never quite came. Billy—well, Billy eventually made it through high school in his nervous, uncertain manner, smoking too much dope along the way. He took odd jobs around Silverford, and at some point went into conservation or parks after seasons of tree-planting. Teddy, the big, crazy kid, who somehow managed to avoid having anything to do with the trial, apparently got pretty smashed up racing stock cars somewhere down south, though no one seems to know the details. I still picture him under the streetlight, having a smoke, looking cool and just a little dangerous. That Teddy!

As for Jacob, his family moved even further away from Eastfield after the trial. No one knows exactly where. That we had somehow helped Jacob avoid an almost certain charge of murder was something good, though knowing the larger picture of what we did—as both cause and cure—leveled any fully reassuring thoughts. Most surprising is that the story of The Watchers' Club had been placed further and further aside before suddenly flooding back with so much clarity.

Then, out of the blue, something in the mail came my way: an oversized, stiff brown envelope. Large, black, awkwardly hand-printed letters captured my name and address. No return address. The envelope contained the unexpected: partially glued to some matting, a delicate charcoal drawing of Gumboot, our cat, as a kitten, cupped in large, dark hands, held by arms that come out of shadows. I knew right away that the arms were Jacob's, covered as they were in the plaid shirt he always wore: the shirt he wore that Saturday night and when, a few days later, I saw him in the dark, in Mrs. Raskolnikov's old place, holding out the kitten, whispering to me that it needs milk. I put the picture aside, and, in truth, I didn't know what to think. It was as if, once more, that kitten was being held out by some ghost—one that haunted from the past and now intruded into the present.

I returned to the drawing a few days later. Should it be framed and hung, or just shoved into one of those lower, packed drawers that house the disremembered? Or just thrown away?

I looked again at the drawing. There was something both dreamy and too true about the whole thing…our little booted cat, following us over to the old, Raskolnikov shack that dark afternoon, and then jumping out of nowhere to scare Julian, which caused me to drop the drawings I had found, one of which changed everything by what its reverse side pictured. Something then passed through me unannounced—and I was drawn to look on the other side of the sketch.

I wish I hadn't.

The sketch pulled away easily from its matting. There, on the other side, a drawing of some arms stretched out. And then large hands around someone's neck who's face you couldn't quite see. But whoever it was, she had long, straight hair. The arms…covered, yes, in that too-familiar plaid shirt. The shirt Jacob was wearing that night when he—when he took the moment into his own hands. Scrawled across the bottom of the sketch on an angle was one word: "whore," and below it, "Lev 21:9."

That Saturday night once again returns. The butcher van, the dropped flashlight, shouting stupid things, and running away. Jacob, oddly, also saying something, though he did not shout it. Yes, saying something. I thought he might have said "horror." Teddy, I remember, though he said "horse."

I burned the drawing three days later.

EASTFIELD

Eastfield grew up over the years. It got some of the picket fences, sidewalks, and city water that crank-ass Mr. Bryer wanted, but, last I heard, his pretty little wife left him and his perfect property for some new guy who worked at the community college—a hippie art instructor, I was told. I only hope she left that yapping dog behind.

As for Gumboot, our little white cat with black paws, he died years ago after living a long life. We were never sure where he went when he wanted out for the night, even when it was raining and with the wind blowing down Eastfield Road past the old house of the witch, which still remains.

READERS GUIDE

1. What is the nasty but revealing pun in the title of *The Watchers' Club*, and, if you get it, how does it change how you view what happened?

2. *The Watchers' Club* begins with the narrator releasing his memories through looking at an old photograph and a newspaper clipping. How much of what we know or think about our pasts are locked into such documents? Do they channel our memory, or just help us to recall; or, perhaps, can they even create a memory that may or not be true?

3. The narrator, without asking, implicitly asks for your trust in the telling of the story. How is this done—and do you trust the narrator? Why or why not?

4. How would you account for and describe the difference between how the narrator and Arnold view Jacob?

5. Given the story, are guilt and innocence absolute? In the end, how does the narrator feel guilty?

6. In what way or ways is this a coming-of-age story?

7. At what point in the story to you feel things might go wrong?

8. What do you think of Arnold? What roles does he play? Is he a positive or negative presence?

9. What is the attitude toward the law and police in the story, or is this guided by the views of the boys?

10. What does Mr. Bryer represent in the story?

11. How would you characterize Winnlow's legal skills?

12. The novel hints of another story—a prequel, in effect—via some allusions to something that happened a few years earlier (parts that mention the old witch lady and someone named Daniel Caine). Are there any hints of what kind of story this might be and how it connects to the narrator?

CPSIA information can be obtained
at www.ICGtesting.com
Printed in the USA
JSHW032317220623
43651JS00005B/31

9 781632 935304